THE CHRISTMAS
Admirer

D0956395

THE

CHRISTMAS
Admirer

LAURA V.
HILTON

WHITAKER
HOUSE

Publisher's Note:
This novel is a work of fiction. References to real events, organizations, or places are used in a fictional context. Any resemblances to actual persons, living or dead, are entirely coincidental.

All Scripture quotations are taken from the King James Version of the Holy Bible.

THE CHRISTMAS ADMIRER

Laura V. Hilton
lighthouse-academy.blogspot.com

ISBN: 978-1-62911-894-9
eBook ISBN: 978-1-62911-895-6
Printed in the United States of America
© 2017 by Laura V. Hilton

Whitaker House
1030 Hunt Valley Circle
New Kensington, PA 15068
www.whitakerhouse.com

Library of Congress Cataloging-in-Publication Data (pending)

No part of this book may be reproduced or transmitted in any form or by any means, electronic or mechanical—including photocopying, recording, or by any information storage and retrieval system—without permission in writing from the publisher. Please direct your inquiries to permissionseditor@whitakerhouse.com.

1 2 3 4 5 6 7 8 9 10 11 **ᗑ** 24 23 22 21 20 19 18 17

DEDICATION

To Loundy, my favorite song.
To Michael, my adventurous one.
To Kristin, my darling daughter.
To Jenna, my sunshine.
To Kaeli, my showers of blessing.

And in memory of my parents, Allan and Janice; my uncle Loundy;
and my grandmother Mertie, who talked about their Pennsylvania
Amish heritage.

To God be the glory.

ACKNOWLEDGMENTS

I'd like to offer my heartfelt thanks to the following:

The residents of Jamesport, Missouri, and the surrounding areas, for answering my questions and pointing me in the right directions.

My husband and children, for traveling there with me and helping with my observations.

The amazing team at Whitaker House—Christine, Courtney, and Cathy. You are wonderful.

Tamela, my agent, for believing in me all these years.

My critique group—you know who you are. You are amazing and knew how to ask the right questions when more detail was needed. Also thanks for the encouragement. Candee, thanks for reading large amounts in a short time and offering wise suggestions.

My husband, Steve, for being a tireless proofreader and cheering section.

Jenna, for reading over my shoulder and editing as I wrote; also for naming the horses and the kitten.

GLOSSARY OF AMISH TERMS AND PHRASES

ach: oh

aent/aenti: aunt/auntie

"ain't so?": a phrase commonly used at the end of a sentence to invite agreement

Ausbund: Amish hymnal used in the worship services, containing lyrics only

boppli: baby/babies

bu: boy

buwe: boys

daadi: grandfather

daed: dad

"Danki": "Thank you"

dawdi-haus: a home constructed for the grandparents to live in once they retire

dochter: daughter

dummchen: a silly person

ehemann: husband

Englisch: non-Amish

Englischer: a non-Amish person

frau: wife

Gott: God

großeltern:	grandparents
grossdaedi:	grandfather
grosskinner:	grandchildren
grossmammi:	grandmother
gut:	good
haus:	house
der Herr:	the Lord
"Ich liebe dich":	"I love you"
jah:	yes
kapp:	prayer covering or cap
kinner:	children
koffee:	coffee
kum:	come
maidal:	young woman
mamm:	mom
mammi:	grandmother
morgen:	morning
nacht:	night
nein:	no
onkel:	uncle
rumschpringe:	"running around time"; a period of freedom and experimentation during the late adolescence of Amish youth
schnitz:	dried apples, usually used for pies
ser gut:	very good
sohn:	son
süße:	sweetie/sweetness
verboden:	forbidden
welkum:	welcome
wunderbaar:	wonderful
youngies:	young unmarried individuals in the Amish community

CHAPTER 1

*S*usanna King paused in the kitchen doorway and stared at the single long-stemmed red rose, artfully arranged in a glass vase with clusters of baby's breath and fronds of a green fern-type plant, sitting in the middle of the table.

She'd been the last one to bed the previous nacht. She'd stayed up late reading *A White Christmas in Webster County* and had trailed Daed upstairs over an hour after he'd gone up there.

There'd been nein rose, red or otherwise, on the table last nacht, for sure and for certain.

With trembling fingers, Susanna set the lit lantern on the table, then touched a soft red petal. She pulled the white envelope free from the plastic card holder. "Susanna" was written on it in a neat block print.

Her breaths quickened, and she looked around, hoping for some clue as to who had kum inside the unlocked haus to deliver the flowers.

Nothing. Not even a footprint left on the recently swept and scrubbed floor.

She carefully lifted the flap of the envelope and slid the card out. It was white, with a red rose on the left side. The words "With Love" were printed in gold script in the upper right-hand corner.

In the middle of the card, written in the same block print as on the envelope, was this message:

I have loved thee with an everlasting love. (Jeremiah 31:3)

Always, Your Secret Admirer

If only she could take this card, march outside to Daed's glass-blowing shop, and confront Benaiah Troyer with what she wanted it to be—proof he was her secret admirer.

But he couldn't possibly be. He hadn't arrived at work yet. And she *knew* his handwriting. He'd written her several notes during the too-short time they'd courted last year, and his script didn't resemble this in any way.

Didn't he know how much it hurt to see him almost every day when he came to work for Daed? He'd shattered her heart when he'd broken things off. And she surmised, from the sheen of tears in his eye whenever they interacted, that it hadn't been any easier for him.

But he'd maintained his resolve. Ten months ago, his parents had died, and with them the wedding he and Susanna had planned. He couldn't—*wouldn't*—ask her to step in and raise his younger sisters or take care of his großeltern. He hadn't asked. Didn't he know she would've gladly—*gladly*—volunteered?

She'd opted not to try to convince him, though. He wouldn't have listened, and she wouldn't resort to begging. It was better to let things end with a semblance of dignity.

Dreams should make noise when they died a violent death. A loud scream, a cry of pain, a shattering similar to glass breaking—any of these would've been appropriate. Dreams shouldn't be taken from you silently, without warning.

Susanna blinked, hoping to clear her blurry vision, and slid the card back inside the envelope. She would add it to her collection of cherished treasures from her unknown lover. Even if that person wasn't Benaiah. Someone loved her, but she worried that her acceptance of the gifts might count as cheating on Benaiah. Not that she could return the gifts, even if she wanted to. Her admirer's identity was unknown.

For now, she tucked the card inside the pocket of her apron. She needed to start breakfast.

She mixed dough for cinnamon rolls, then covered the bowl with a towel and set it near the stove to allow the dough rise. The sweets, warm and gooey when fresh from the oven, would be a nice treat for

Daed and Benaiah. Then she sliced several bananas, arranged the pieces atop the pan of oatmeal she'd prepared the nacht before, and slid the oats into the warm oven to bake.

"Gut morgen, Susie." Daed shuffled into the room in his slippers and stopped beside the door.

"Gut morgen, Daed." She set a kettle of water on a burner to heat for koffee.

Daed reached for his old work coat, put shoes on instead, and slapped his hat on his head. Then he opened the door and stepped out into the darkness. "I'll feed the chickens today. You stay warm inside."

"Danki." It would be nice to avoid going outside in the cold today. Especially with all the preparations she had yet to do for Thanksgiving dinner tomorrow.

She grimaced. Last Thanksgiving had been the best one of her life, and now it was the holiday that caused her the greatest pain.

"I've got something to talk to you about when I kum back in." The door closed behind him.

What could that be? And why hadn't he told her about it last nacht? Susanna opened the gas-powered refrigerator and reached for the carton of eggs—store-bought, since it was too cold for the family's hens to lay. Her hand stalled mid-reach. There, front and center on the shelf, was a glass bottle. Starbucks French Vanilla Frappuccino. Her favorite treat, when she had a few extra dollars to spend on herself at the grocery store. She glanced behind her at the door, then scanned the room. Benaiah knew of her fondness for the drink; but then, probably half the people in their community had seen her in the grocery store, gazing longingly at the display of Starbucks bottled drinks when she didn't have the money to purchase one.

She patted the note in her pocket. She would enjoy her treat later, while she reviewed all the notes she'd collected from Mr. Secret Admirer. There had to be some clue.

She shifted the bottle to the side, then grasped the carton of eggs and a glass jar of homemade butter, both of which she set on the counter. After closing the refrigerator door, she reached for a cast-iron skillet. Benaiah liked his eggs fried in bacon grease. If only she could fix him breakfast every morgen after waking up together…. Her face heated, and she hurried to distract herself from the scandalous thought by slamming the skillet down on the stove a little harder than necessary. She returned the butter to the refrigerator and got out a slab of bacon Daed had brought in the nacht before.

Their neighbors to the north, the Zooks, had recently had their whole hog ground into sausage. Daed preferred a variety of meats, so the Kings' cold storage was filled with bacon, sausage, roasts, chops, steaks, and more. It gave Susanna more options to work with for meals. And more opportunities to impress Benaiah with her cooking skills. To show him she was more than capable of planning a varied menu for his family.

She grimaced at the prideful thought. *Forgive me, Lord.*

But it'd be nice to cook for more people than just herself and Daed someday.

She walked to the hutch to retrieve some plates. Atop the stack of dishes sat a gift bag decorated in fall colors. Tufts of orange and yellow tissue paper stuck out the top. On the attached tag, printed in the same block letters, was this message: "'I thank my Gott at every remembrance of you' (Philippians 1:3). Happy Thanksgiving, Susanna."

Her breath lodged in her throat. With a shaky hand, she picked up the bag and reached inside. Her fingers closed around a set of coordinating pot holders, kitchen towels, and washcloths, all decorated with colorful leaves. For her hope chest? Or for immediate use?

Her hope chest. Definitely her hope chest.

Smiling, she held the bag to her heart, then ran upstairs and set it on top of her dresser with her latest card and the hodge-podge of other items. From last January, a stuffed snowman clutching a pine tree, with a box of hot chocolate packets attached. From February, a couple of tiny plush hearts printed with the phases "I love you" and "Be mine," along with a heart-shaped box of chocolates. From March, a candy dish shaped like a maple leaf, filled with maple syrup candies. (The sweets themselves were long gone.) April's theme had been "I'm blue without you," and Susanna had received a navy-blue umbrella, a violet that had bloomed for most of the summer on her bedroom windowsill, and blue fabric for a new dress. She hadn't done anything with the material. It sat in her hope chest, waiting for a wedding that, for now, would never happen. A sad reminder that it was over with Benaiah. The accompanying bag of jelly beans in assorted shades of blue had comforted her as she'd cried herself to sleep nacht after nacht, mourning the loss of her much-hoped-for marriage.

Susanna turned her back on the remaining months' gifts and returned to the kitchen. She arranged three place settings on the table, with plates, mugs, bowls, and eating utensils, expecting Benaiah to join them, as he did almost every day. For lunch, too. Fueling her hopes and dreams. Yet the mumbled excuse he gave was something about his mammi's having enough to do without fixing meals for him.

A headlamp attached to a buggy lit the window for a moment, and Susanna's heart jumped. *Benaiah.*

She glanced at the red rose, still positioned in the center of the table.

Maybe, when he came inside, he'd react to the flower in some way. Then she'd know for sure.

Lord, let it be so.

BENAIAH LED HIS horse, Peppermint Twist, into the vacant barn stall that Susanna's daed, Peter King, allowed him to use during the winter months. When the weather was warmer, Benaiah let the former race-horse roam free in the pasture. But now, with the wind blowing hard, heavy gray clouds overhead, and the scent of snow in the air, he figured the animal would be happier in the barn.

"The north wind doth blow, and we shall have snow," Peter muttered as Benaiah led the horse past him.

Benaiah nodded but couldn't summon a smile at the older man's levity. This would be the first holiday season he spent without his parents. He wasn't sure how to begin to put on a festive mood for Thanksgiving, let alone Christmas. He wasn't even sure he wanted to try, especially with Mammi sick with the flu. Losing his folks and breaking up with Susanna in one fell blow had left him reeling, and he wanted to crawl into a dark hole somewhere and just grieve. But life went on. He had to be the provider. The strong shoulder for the family.

If only he felt capable.

Peter cleared his throat. "Have something to tell both you and Susanna after I finish the chores. Take care of your horse, and then go on up to the haus."

"Okay...." Except he didn't want to be alone with Susanna. Not in his fragile emotional state. Not with the loss still fresh in his heart, even though it'd been eleven months since....

He swallowed the lump in his throat. "Maybe it'd be better if I helped you with the chores, and then we went in together."

Peter's glance was too knowing, but he nodded. "I told Susanna I'd take care of the chickens."

"I'll do it. Just let me finish up with Peppermint." He tugged on the horse's halter.

"Then get the fire started in the shop. I should be finished the milking by that time."

"Will do." Benaiah settled the horse into his stall, gave him a bucket of oats, and filled the trough with water. Then he shut the gate and headed to the other side of the barn, where the chicken coop had been added on. There was one entrance, for the humans, from inside the barn, and one for the fowls on the outside, with a ramp for easy access. Not that they seemed to need it. The stubborn birds would nest in trees, if permitted.

When the chickens were fed and watered, Benaiah walked the short distance from the barn to the shop. Peter had designed and built this place with such foresight, providing easy access for customers and family alike. Benaiah built up the fire in the shop, then headed back to the barn. He met Peter at the entrance. "Ready?"

Peter nodded, then paled as he glanced toward the haus. "Might want to say a prayer or two. She's not going to handle this so well."

Benaiah hitched an eyebrow. That didn't sound gut. But Peter would never do anything to deliberately hurt Susanna.

Never in a thousand years.

Susanna set the platter of fried eggs in the center of the table next to the plate stacked high with toast. As she took the baked oatmeal out of the oven, the kitchen door opened. Daed strode inside, followed by Benaiah.

Daed slapped his hands together. "Downright frigid out there, Susie. I daresay we'll have a foot of snow by Thanksgiving. You have all your shopping done, ain't so?"

Benaiah stopped right behind Daed and lowered his head to gaze at his feet. Seemed he couldn't bear to look at her anymore. What had she done to turn him against her? She still held out hope that he was behind the anonymous gifts. He hadn't supplied any real explanation when he'd broken up with her. He'd simply said, "It's not you, it's me. I just can't bring you into my home without Mamm and Daed...."

As if she needed his mamm to teach her how to run a home? Hadn't she been doing that very thing since she was five, when her own mamm had died?

Though, initially, she'd had Grossmammi by her side to help, teach, and guide. And his grossmammi was still at home.

It'd been a convenient excuse.

She watched for a reaction to the beautiful rose on the table, but Benaiah seemed determined to keep his gaze averted. Had he looked her in the eyes even once since breaking up with her?

Susanna straightened her shoulders, set the pan of baked oatmeal on the table, and turned to get the orange juice out of the refrigerator.

"Susie?" Daed sounded a bit...not irritated, but maybe impatient.

She pivoted once more. "What?"

"I asked if you had finished all your Thanksgiving shopping."

"Ach, nein. Can you take me later?"

"Make your list. I'll have Benaiah take you."

Benaiah's head snapped up and moved slowly from side to side. His eyes widened as he looked at Daed.

There'd been a time when he would've jumped at the chance to escort her to the store. Susanna swallowed. "Nein, I'll wait for you."

Daed stood up straight, having removed his boots, and crossed the room to the sink to scrub his hands and arms. "Benaiah will take you. We're having company, and I have other preparations to make."

"Of course." But who was coming? Last year, Benaiah and his entire family had joined them, along with several of her aents, onkels, and cousins.

She spun around to face Benaiah. "Are you coming this year?"

"You're certainly welkum." Daed moved to stand beside Susanna. "In fact, bring your whole family. I'd like you to meet my future frau."

"Your—who?" Susanna juggled the unopened bottle of orange juice to keep it from crashing to the floor. She scrambled to think of any widows in the area that Daed might have been spending time with. She couldn't think of any. Though he had been whistling more, as of late.

A chair squeaked across the floor as Daed pulled it away from the table. "Have a seat, Susanna. Benaiah."

Benaiah made quick work of shucking his outerwear and washing up. He sat next to Daed. Across from Susanna. "What's going on, Peter?"

"Irene and her kinner will arrive from Iowa sometime this evening. We'll marry in January." The words came out in a rush, as if Daed felt he needed to get them said before they stalled. Daed lowered his head and folded his hands. "Let us pray."

Pray? After Daed had dropped such earth-shattering news? Susanna could barely put together a coherent thought. Her mind flooded with questions. When and how had he met this woman from Iowa? How many kinner? What ages? And where did he suppose they'd all sleep?

Susanna stared at Daed a moment longer. Then she glanced at Benaiah. His gaze was locked on her. Concern filled his eyes. Nein doubt he wondered how she was handling the announcement that her world would soon be ripped apart, stitch by carefully sewn stitch. At least he'd finally made eye contact with her. Even if his expression somewhat mirrored the last one he'd given her when he'd fully looked at her—at his parents' funeral.

"Amen." Daed raised his head and pulled in a deep breath. "Ach, and Benaiah, I'll be putting the business and the farm up for sale. Susanna and I will move to Iowa to live with Irene. She doesn't want to leave her community."

Irene doesn't want to leave? Susanna clenched her fists so tightly, her nails bit into her palms. *What about me?*

The concern in Benaiah's eyes deepened to a look of worry. He slowly turned his head to face Daed. A muscle worked in his jaw, and one of his biceps bunched, as if he were clenching his fist in his lap.

Susanna swallowed the bile that had risen in her throat. "But... but Daed, I don't know anything about Irene. This is the first I've heard of her. And I don't want to move to Iowa. Our family is here." *Benaiah is here.*

"Irene and I have written to each other for a year. I went to Iowa to visit her over the summer, remember?"

"I thought that was for business." She hated the hitch in her voice.

"Jah, business, too. You'll prepare nice meals for her, Susie. She's looking forward to having your help in the kitchen." Daed reached for the oatmeal.

"You're selling the business?" Benaiah's gaze moved from Susanna to Daed. There was a roughness in his voice, as if the news shattered his world, too.

Daed shrugged. "If I can find a buyer. Irene's late ehemann raised corn and beans. She wants me to take over the farm. I won't have time for artsy foolishness for the purpose of cluttering Englischers' homes. If it doesn't sell, you can fulfill the remaining orders, then close it down."

But Daed loved the "artsy foolishness." And Benaiah would be out of a job. How would he support his family now? Would he have to do more farming?

Benaiah frowned. Passed the pan of oatmeal without taking any.

Funny. Susanna's appetite was gone, too.

CHAPTER 2

*B*enaiah swirled cream and sugar into his koffee as Peter ate—silent, now that he'd disrupted everyone's world with his abrupt and unwelkum news. Susanna had gotten up from the table and now busied herself with something at the counter. Her back was to them, and she held herself stiffly, as if struggling not to fall apart.

He would hate to see her uprooted, moved to a different community, and going from being in charge of her home to answering to another woman. On the other hand, he might have a chance to heal if she went away.

"You will join us for Thanksgiving again, ain't so?" Peter lowered his spoon to his bowl.

Benaiah cleared his throat. "Jah, if you're sure you can accommodate us. Might be easier on Mammi. She's recovering from a stubborn bout of the flu and hasn't gotten her strength back. Talked about buying some of those premade pizzas from the grocery store." Grief likely tied into her slow recovery. Will of Gott, or otherwise, she'd taken the loss of her sohn very hard. Plus, she'd gone from being semi-retired to running a haus filled with an active family of young adults, teens, and tweens.

"Could she use help?" Susanna turned to him, hope lighting her face. If only he could read her thoughts. But if she wanted to step in and help Mammi Wren, she could.

He nodded. "She'd be grateful." However, he'd have to stay away from home while Susanna was there, because seeing her in his kitchen would surely keep him from healing.

"But Irene and her kinner will be here for a few days," Peter objected.

Benaiah stirred his koffee some more. He doubted it'd stay down if he drank it. Especially with his stomach still roiling from Peter's news.

Selling the business? How would he support his family now? Probably a gut thing he hadn't taken on a frau. He had planned to ask Susanna to marry him this fall. But that was before everything changed.

"I don't suppose it'd hurt anything, though," Peter conceded. "Just so you don't leave Irene alone to do the work here. You can go help Benaiah's mammi for a couple of hours each day." Peter finished his breakfast. "Aren't you going to eat, Benaiah?"

"Maybe later." He pushed himself to his feet. "I'll get started on the latest orders. Susanna, let me know when you're ready to leave."

"Can't I drive myself?" she asked her daed, ignoring Benaiah's comment. "I'll be careful, I promise."

Of course, she probably wanted spend as little time alone with Benaiah as possible after what he'd done. The way he'd hurt her.

"Nein, I want Benaiah to drive you." Daed stood. "Irene is quite fond of ham. Maybe you could put it on the supper menu to-nacht?"

Susanna nodded.

The last time Benaiah had eaten supper with the Kings, Susanna had served ham, scalloped potatoes, green beans seasoned with onions and bacon, and creamy raisin pie. The meal had been beyond delicious. And despite his current lack of appetite, his stomach rumbled. Hoping to cover the sound, he shoved his chair against the table and strode toward the door.

Selling the business. Their home. Moving to Iowa.

His heart shattered anew.

At least he didn't have to worry about losing his home. Uprooting his family. He could be thankful for that.

Benaiah dared to glance over his shoulder at the vase sitting in the center of the table. How had Susanna reacted when she'd first seen it? Had she smiled? Hoped it was from him? Or did she think the arrangement had kum from the man he'd seen bringing her home from the singing after a wedding the other nacht?

That sight had left a sour taste.

Peter hadn't said anything about the flowers, either. But maybe he suspected Benaiah had left them. He probably knew he'd never released Susanna from his heart. Knew he'd never love another woman the way he loved her. After all, Peter had never married again after his frau had died…at least, not until now. He'd claimed he could never love another the way he had loved his Marie.

Why would Peter want to marry a woman who selfishly insisted on having her own way? Who expected her new ehemann to give up all he knew, owned, and loved, in order to become someone else? Peter King was many things, but a farmer he wasn't.

Benaiah's gaze moved to Susanna. He'd do anything for her. Hadn't he let her go so that she wouldn't be forced to become an instant substitute mamm to his sisters?

He'd made the only loving choice he'd identified, even though it had meant sacrificing his own happiness.

Susanna didn't want to focus on shopping, or any other Thanksgiving preparations. Not this year. Not with strangers coming to spend the holiday with her family. Wherever would they put Irene and her kinner? There were two empty bedrooms in the vacant attached dawdi-haus, and one empty bedroom upstairs, but she still didn't know how many kinner the woman had. Daed hadn't told her anything.

She hadn't even known he'd been corresponding with someone.

It wouldn't be just the two of them anymore. A new mamm. Stepsiblings. She'd have to learn another woman's way of doing things. Would she be expected to call this strange woman "Mamm"? *Ach, nein.*

Susanna blinked away the burning sensation in her eyes, reached for a notepad and pen, and started planning the menu for Irene's visit. Daed said she and her kinner would be staying a few days. Including Thanksgiving. Arriving to-nacht. She swallowed hard, pushing back tears. Her unhappiness didn't matter. It wasn't gut for a man to be alone. Hadn't Preacher David made that very statement in his last message? At the time, she'd hoped Benaiah was listening closely. Not Daed.

She couldn't allow herself to think of this. Not now. She focused on the word "menu" that she'd written at the top of the sheet of paper. Daed had suggested ham for dinner to-nacht. She added it to the list, where she'd already marked down turkey for Thanksgiving. Pork chops could be for another meal.

She paused in the menu planning to put the cinnamon rolls in the oven to bake, then checked the pantry for anything else they might need. When her list was finalized, she removed the cinnamon rolls from the oven, iced them, and set two on a plate to deliver to Daed and Benaiah in the shop.

Heat hit her when she opened the door. Daed fed wood to the fire—it had to be kept at a specific temperature—and Benaiah sat in a chair, shaping softened glass into lilies for an Englisch wedding.

Benaiah looked up at her. "Ready to go? I need just a minute to finish this."

"I'll hitch the horse to the wagon." She set the plate of rolls on a worktable.

"I'll do it." One side of his mouth twitched. "Those look gut, süße."

Sweetie? He didn't look at her. Showed nein sign of having called her by an endearment. Maybe he'd said "Susie," and she'd heard what she'd wanted to. Though his face did seem a little red. But that could be from the hot fire.

"Want to take one to go?"

He nodded. "Danki."

Since he needed to finish the glass lily, Susanna returned to the haus to make sure the kitchen was spotless. She carried the rose upstairs to her bedroom and set the vase on the bedside table. Couldn't

Benaiah have shown a little bit of interest in the flowers? Asked who they were from? Something? Though his shock over Daed's news might've kept him from noticing them.

She wrapped a cinnamon roll in foil, grabbed several paper napkins, and headed back outside. Benaiah stood at the bottom of the porch steps. Peppermint Twist and his buggy waited just behind him.

"May I help you in?" He held out his hand.

And because she couldn't stop herself, she took it.

His gloved fingers closed around hers, sending a surge of warmth and contentment through every cell in her body.

This was where she belonged.

Next to him.

TAKING A BUGGY ride with Susanna close beside him was a painful pleasure for Benaiah. He shifted slightly farther away from her as the horse settled into a trot. Too soon—or maybe not soon enough—they arrived at the Amish Market. Susanna went into the store while he tied the horse to the hitching post. By the time he entered the building, she'd disappeared among the cluttered aisles of shelves. Uncertain whether to search for her or to loiter by the tempting candy display near the checkout, he hesitated. The lure to be near her soon drew him deeper into the store. He found her in an aisle of dry goods, lowering a bulk-size bag of steel-cut oats into her shopping cart. She'd already loaded in a bag each of flour and sugar—not the twenty-five-pound bags Mammi always purchased, but the four-pound size, suitable for a family of two. She hesitated, then added another bag of each.

"Need me to get anything for you?"

She glanced at the list she clutched in one hand. "Do you think she'd prefer grapefruit or oranges?"

He shrugged.

Tears glittered on her eyelashes. "Why is he doing this, Benaiah? Wasn't I enough for him? Why'd he have to go and fall in love?"

"Love happens, sü—Susie." He should know. Hadn't he fallen in love with Susanna when he was twelve, and they'd been paired up for the annual Christmas program at school? Somewhere between working together to memorize their lines, they'd talked, laughed, and gotten to know each other—and he'd given her his heart. She hadn't given it back.

"I don't want to move to Iowa." Her lower lip jutted out in a slightly stubborn pout.

He didn't want her to, either. But he forced a shrug. "Doesn't seem that you have a choice."

She raised her eyebrows. "I have a secret admirer. Maybe if word gets out that I'm moving away, he'll step forward and ask to marry me." She studied his face as she spoke.

He hoped his expression gave nothing away. But he couldn't keep a sigh from escaping his lips. He scratched his head slightly above his ear. "That so?"

"Don't you even care?" She stomped her foot, but it didn't make a sound.

Ach, he cared. Too much.

Her pout became more pronounced.

He wanted to kiss it. Her. "Jah…and I'll miss you."

Too much truthfulness to that.

"I could get a job. Maybe. And move in with friends."

Benaiah hitched an eyebrow. He'd love it if she stayed—if she were his. But seeing her with another man? He grimaced. "Think your daed would let you?"

She turned away and stalked off, leaving him with the cart. He pushed it along after her. "What else do you need?"

"Just some more baking supplies." She whirled to face him. "You don't need to follow me around the store, you know. Nein need to feel obligated to watch me every step of the way. I've made it this long without you. I can survive a simple shopping trip, ain't so?"

Then she slapped her hand over her mouth, her eyes widening. Her outburst was a bit revealing. She'd never lost her temper with him before. The uncharacteristic behavior was probably due to the shock of finding out she would soon be uprooted. She whirled again and ran, straight into a wobbly display shelf.

Canned goods flew every which way as the shelving unit crashed to the ground, with Susanna sprawled on top.

CHAPTER 3

*I*f only Susanna could crawl beneath the pile of canned goods and sink through the floor. Since that wasn't an option, she pushed herself off the metal shelving and sat cross-legged on the tile. She'd take a moment to evaluate her pain level before trying to move.

Then she noticed the crowd gathering around her. The cans scattered like Legos after a child's temper tantrum.

Embarrassment hit before she was ready. Her face burned.

"Susie!" Benaiah crouched beside her. His hand on her back sent waves of heat coursing through her nerve endings. "Are you hurt?"

Such a caring man—and she'd been rude to him. She ignored the aches in her body and her heart as she stood. "I'm fine, just fine. I'm sorry for what I said about not needing your help. It's pretty obvious I do, ain't so?"

To his credit, Benaiah didn't chuckle. He reached for a few cans and picked them up, then stood to his feet. "I'm sure you would've been fine if I hadn't upset you. I'm sorry. Though, to be honest, I'm not sure what I did."

An Englischer righted the display shelves, and the gawkers returned their attention to their own shopping.

"You didn't upset me," Susanna said, once they were alone again. She began stacking cans on a shelf.

"Lying is a sin, you know," Benaiah murmured.

"That wasn't a lie. You didn't upset me, you *hurt* me. But I'm over you now." Okay, that was a lie. And another instance of rudeness.

"Daed upset me. Surely, he knew sooner than this morgen that his *girlfriend* would arrive today. Why didn't he tell me when he found that out? Better yet, why didn't he tell me when he took up correspondence with her? Or got serious with her? Or went to *visit* her? Why now? And don't tell me courting is kept secret. I know it. But I'm his dochter. There should be an exception made."

Silence fell for a long moment.

"You're over me." Benaiah's lips flattened, his eyes darkened, and he turned away. "Gut to know. I'll...I'll wait by the checkout."

Susanna's eyes burned. He'd picked up on the one hurtful thing she'd said. Could this day get any worse? Jah, it had the potential. She closed her eyes for a second, then opened them and finished cleaning up her mess. Then she'd go find Benaiah and apologize. Again. For lashing out and for lying. And for being rude.

Susanna's former schoolmate Gizelle Miller, a longtime employee at the market, approached. She picked up a can that had traveled some distance, and returned it to the shelf. Then she patted Susanna's arm. "Accidents happen. I told the manager, Joel, that this was a bad place for the display. He thinks he knows better. It's only the third time this week it's been bumped or knocked over. I wonder how many more accidents it'll take before he listens."

Susanna managed a little grin. "Glad it wasn't just me." It was still humiliating, though. And then, to have hurt Benaiah the way she had.... If he was her secret admirer, she'd killed it right there. Though, of course, he wasn't. The handwriting wasn't his.

She glanced over her shoulder but didn't see him.

"How are you doing?" Gizelle asked. "I haven't had a chance to talk to you in ages."

"Gut. We're gut." Another lie, but Susanna didn't want to do a massive verbal dump in the middle of the grocery store. She backed up a step, then stopped. She wanted to ask about Gizelle's daed, who'd required multiple surgeries and rehabilitation to recover from a farming accident. "I was glad to see your daed in church last Sunday."

Gizelle smiled. "He's doing so much better. The surgery really helped. I think it also helped when my sister and Josh had a boppli bu.

Now Daed has a gross-sohn following him around, and to someday take fishing with him. And the boppli, Andrew, is so sweet. We all love him to pieces."

Susanna shifted, not wanting to be rude to her friend by dashing off, but needing to get home and see what else had to be done before Daed's girlfriend—that sounded so wrong—arrived. Still, she needed to show at least a smidgen of interest in what Gizelle said. "I can't wait to meet him," she hastened to say.

"Kum by any time. Greta and Josh would love a visit." Gizelle shuffled some cans around as the manager wandered by, glaring.

"See you later." Susanna took that opportunity to escape. She grabbed the few canned goods she needed and made her way toward the checkout. She stopped for a moment at a small refrigerated display to add a couple of soda cans to the cart. One for her and one for Benaiah. She'd offer the beverage alongside her apologies.

Benaiah stood near the checkout counter, talking to Caleb Bontrager. Benaiah's dark gaze caught hers and held it captive for a second before he looked away. Caleb glanced over his shoulder, said something to Benaiah that she didn't catch, then turned to her with a smile. "Gut to see you, Susie. I'm in a bit of a hurry, just stopped in to grab a bite for lunch. Heard you might be job hunting. I have a possible lead for you, but I need to check something first. See you around."

"Danki," Susanna managed, though she frowned. Why had Benaiah taken the liberty of telling Caleb she might be looking for employment? She hadn't talked to Caleb since the last wedding singing, when he'd driven her home out of obvious pity. He'd spoken of lessons learned the hard way, and she hadn't been certain whether he was talking about himself or about her mourning her lost relationship with Benaiah.

"Not a problem." With another grin, Caleb strode off toward the display of premade sandwiches and salads.

Susanna blinked and looked up at Benaiah. "Did you tell Caleb I'm looking for a job?"

One shoulder rose, but Benaiah didn't meet her gaze. "I said you might be."

Susanna sighed. Why couldn't he just say that he wanted her to stay? She would, with nein problem, if he asked. Of course, she still planned to resist moving away with everything in her.

She turned toward the checkout counter. Nobody stood behind it, but a moment later, Gizelle hurried into position.

"Did you find everything you needed?" Gizelle asked, with a perky lilt to her voice that rubbed Susanna the wrong way.

And anyhow, she wondered why that was the standard cashier's inquiry at every grocery store, whether Amish or Englisch. If Susanna hadn't found what she needed, would she be standing in line to pay? Nein, she'd still be shopping, or asking for assistance.

Benaiah stood quietly beside her, taking each filled bag and loading it into the cart.

Moments later, Susanna handed Gizelle the cash Daed had given her. Benaiah took the bags and disappeared out the door.

Susanna caught up with him at the buggy, where he'd loaded the bags into the back. She reached in and riffled through the purchases. Finding the sodas, she turned and held one out to him. "I'm sorry. I didn't mean to be rude."

She wouldn't admit to not being over him, though. She had to protect herself that much. But she also had to fix the relationship enough that she could still kum over to help his mammi and undo the damage, in case Benaiah was indeed her secret admirer. And she had only the buggy ride home to patch things up before he resumed avoiding her.

"It's fairly obvious I wouldn't survive a shopping trip without help, ain't so?"

He didn't crack a smile, nor did he take the offered drink. "Not so obvious. You did fine."

She held the soda higher. "Want it? I got one for myself, too."

After a moment's hesitation, he took it, turned away, and unhitched Peppermint Twist from the post. "Danki."

"Friends?" Susanna hoped her smile was merry and bright. He couldn't be allowed to see her broken heart. At least if they were friends, she'd be one step closer to winning his heart again. Much better than the silent treatment and averted eyes she'd tolerated for the past ten months or so. She climbed into the buggy without waiting for him to help.

Pain filled Benaiah's eyes as he settled next to her. She hadn't meant to hurt him. Only to protect herself. She winced. How could she make this right?

He popped the tab on the soda can, and the contents shot out as if spewed from a geyser.

"I DON'T THINK I can be your friend, Susie." Benaiah wiped the cold, syrupy liquid off his face as best he could with his sleeve. If only he had a damp towel. A more thorough cleaning would have to wait until he got home that nacht. Unless he stopped there for a quick shower and a change of clothes before taking Susanna home.

"I really wish you would try." Her comment was quiet. Too quiet. Meaning tears were close at hand.

He should receive hazard pay for taking her shopping.

"I'm going to stop by my haus, since it's on the way to yours. I need a change of clothes." And a shower, but he wouldn't say that in front of her. Hopefully, the change of subject would work to ward off her crying.

"Ach, gut. I need to talk to your mammi and see if she's willing to make her usual schnitz pies for Thanksgiving. I'll offer to help her out, since you said she's been feeling poorly." Susanna set her unopened can of soda on the buggy floor, bracing it between her feet. "I'm not going to take a chance opening this one. Ugh. I didn't realize they'd been shaken."

"They might've been in the bag I dropped." Probably were. He hadn't opened it to check the contents, since she'd bought only a few canned items.

"You dropped a bag?" Susanna twisted slightly in the seat.

"Accidentally. Trying to carry too much at one time." And in too big a hurry to get away from her. Not that it had done much gut, since she now sat close enough to touch. He longed to wrap his arm around her shoulder, tug her nearer, and hug her against him, the way he used to do when they were courting.

Or, at the very least, entwine his fingers with hers.

He flexed his hand holding the reins, an involuntary movement that prompted Peppermint Twist to pick up the pace.

Susanna lapsed into silence, her hands balled into fists on her lap. She was probably thinking about her daed. And that reminded Benaiah of Peter's expressed desire to sell the business. Putting Benaiah out of a job. Worry washed over him anew. What would he do? Maybe he should've mentioned his own imminent need for employment, instead of Susanna's, to Caleb Bontrager. But nein, he'd put her needs in front of his. The way his heart longed to do for the rest of his life.

Finally, they pulled into Benaiah's drive. He set the buggy brakes and tied the reins to the porch railing. Susanna climbed out and was up the steps before he finished. He hurried to open the door for her.

Nobody was in the kitchen. "Mammi? Daadi?" Benaiah called out. "Susanna is here for a visit."

"Coming." Mammi's voice rose from the basement. "Ach, Ben, you got a letter. It's on the table."

Benaiah picked up the envelope. According to the return address, it was from their landlord. Odd. They rarely got mail from him, as long as Benaiah made the payments on time. Had he remembered to pay this month? He was pretty sure he had, but he would check when he got home for the evening. "Wait here," he told Susanna. "I'll be right back."

Mammi emerged from the basement, carrying several jars of home-canned chicken noodle soup. She set the jars on the counter and engulfed Susanna in a hug. "So glad you brought your girl. It's been ages since she's been here."

Benaiah shook his head. "Not my girl. We broke up, remember?"

"Pure foolishness."

Apparently not. Susanna had said she was over him. She wouldn't be if she'd loved him the way he'd loved her.

The way he still loved her.

"Nein," Susanna whispered as her haus came into view. She stared at the white van parked in the driveway and wrung her hands. "They can't be here already. I have too much to do yet."

"They are, though." Benaiah stated the obvious.

Daed stood by the open hatch, helping the driver unload several suitcases. Then he took out his wallet and handed the driver some money.

A tall, spindly woman stood on the porch, arms crossed over her stomach, as she watched the men. She pursed her lips as the van drove off.

Benaiah pulled the buggy into the spot the van had vacated. He climbed out, then turned to assist Susanna. "I'll carry the groceries in for you."

"Danki." Susanna pressed her hand against her stomach, willing the contents to stay put. Why did they have to arrive so early? Why couldn't Daed have given her more advance warning? As it was, she'd had less than nein time to prepare.

At least the haus was clean. Daed's girlfriend couldn't find fault with it. Not that she could possibly be the type to do so, anyway. She had to be nice, because Daed loved her. At least he liked her enough to want to spend the rest of his life with her.

Irene stepped sideways as Susanna joined her on the porch. Daed trailed her with the suitcases, Benaiah right behind him with groceries. "Irene, I'd like you to meet my dochter, Susanna. Susanna, this is Irene Shepherd. Her kinner are around here somewhere."

Irene stepped forward and kissed Susanna right cheek and then her left, as if they were two parishioners greeting each other on a church Sunday. "So nice to meet you. I've heard gut things. But I expected you to be here when I arrived."

Jah, Susanna had expected the same. And she would've been here, had Daed given her earlier warning.

Daed worked his jaw a moment, but apparently wasn't ready to admit he hadn't told Susanna about Irene's planned visit until that very morgen. And it wasn't Susanna's place to fill her in. Maybe Daed would tell Irene later, in private.

"I'll carry your suitcases upstairs, Irene," Daed said. "There are two empty bedrooms, one for you and the other for your kinner."

"The girls should share Susanna's room. She'll need to get accustomed to sharing, anyway, ain't so?" Irene's steady gaze dared Susanna to argue.

So, her own personal space was about to be invaded? What about her belongings? All the gifts from her secret admirer? The cards and letters? They were all on display. Maybe she could excuse herself for a quick minute and hide it all.

Susanna shot a glance toward Daed, one that was meant to convey her pain and confusion. But if he noticed, he ignored it. That hurt, too.

"Mein haus ist ihr haus, mein liebe. Do as you wish." Daed opened the door and went inside.

My haus is your haus. Susanna inhaled a deep breath and followed Daed inside.

"If I were expecting company, my shopping would've been done before the last minute." Irene's words were served with a smile. And accompanied by a knife in the back.

Mine would've been, too, if Daed had told me. Susanna bit back the words. It wouldn't do to disrespect her elder. But Irene's comment was a slap in the face.

Words did hurt. Susanna sighed, remembering her own unkind words to Benaiah. He hadn't deserved them, either.

Benaiah's glance was sympathetic as he piled the grocery bags on the table. Then he made a hasty retreat, probably to unhitch the horse and hide in the shop for the rest of the day.

If only Susanna could join him.

Instead, she pasted a polite smile on her face and prepared to get to work. That's when she noticed her trembling hands. How would she manage to complete all the baking that needed to be done for tomorrow with this woman standing over her?

Maybe she could talk her into taking a rest, or doing something else that would get her out of the kitchen. "You must be tired after such a long trip. You'll want to rest before Daed shows you around the property."

Besides, Susanna needed to run upstairs and put away her cards and gifts before her room was invaded by kinner of unknown ages. Where were those kinner, anyway? As if in answer to her question, pounding sounded overhead. They must be running races up and down the hallway. Was it too late? Had they already gotten into her things?

"Rest? With so much to do?" Irene made a tsking sound with her tongue. "Maybe Peter and I will take a walk after dinner. Now, how can I help?" Irene walked over to the pantry and opened the door. "Ach, look at this mess. I don't know how you can find anything in here. I'll be glad to help you organize your kitchen, Susanna. It'll help you to be so much more efficient."

Mess? She had similar items arranged on each shelf. Baking ingredients in one area, pasta and sauces in another. Most important, she knew where everything was.

"Let's reorganize before we start baking," Irene said.

"I have things the way I like them. The way my grossmammi always kept them." Susanna tried to keep her voice pleasant, but she wasn't sure she'd succeeded.

Irene glowered, her lips pursed.

Daed wanted to marry this woman? Susanna clenched her fists and forced her smile to stay in place.

He could marry her. But she would talk to Caleb about that job he'd mentioned, and try to figure out who her secret admirer might be.

She would *not* go to Iowa with Daed and his new frau.

CHAPTER 4

$\mathscr{B}$enaiah glanced at the wind-up cuckoo clock hanging on the wall as the little wooden bird made its hourly appearance.

Lunchtime already? He wasn't sure he was ready to face Susanna and Peter—or the soon-to-be new members of their family. A constant reminder of the upcoming heartbreak when Susanna would move to another state.

Although, again, it could be that the old cliché would prove true: "Out of sight, out of mind." Then both of them could move on.

Not just her.

I'm over you. Her hurtful words hurled at him at the grocery store replayed in his mind. If only he could tell her the same.

One of Irene's kinner threw a ball that bounced against the shop window, startling Benaiah. He wasn't used to noisy play during the workday. It was usually perpetual quiet as he, Peter, and Susie went about their chores. But he didn't mind the racket. It reminded him of his brothers and sisters.

How was Susie handling this home invasion by Peter's intended's family? She'd been the only woman in the haus-hold for a long time. Her grossmammi had passed away when Susanna was thirteen, leaving her and Peter alone. And now, with this other woman coming in, her elder and Peter's future frau, she'd be expected to submit without argument.

And all her kinner...Benaiah didn't have an inkling as to how many there really were, what with their running all over the place. It seemed to him there were at least a dozen.

Ach, well. It would be interesting—and telling—to see how Susie reacted. Because if Benaiah brought Susanna home as his frau someday, then she'd have Mammi telling her what to do, and his littlest sisters running around, playing. Nowhere near a dozen, though.

Not that he'd ever take her home as his frau. He sighed. Nothing had changed. He still had sole responsibility for his großeltern and his siblings. And while he didn't mind or begrudge the opportunity to take care of his family, he had always wanted the chance to get married. To have kinner of his own.

His wants no longer mattered.

Funny how nobody seemed to understand his predicament. Mammi still wanted him to marry. Daadi talked about bouncing his future gross-boppli on his knee and taking them fishing. Didn't they see that Benaiah had years of sibling-rearing ahead? Nein woman would take on his ready-made family.

Not even Susanna.

With undiluted clarity, he still remembered the words she'd said the weekend before his parents had died: "Ach, Ben. I can't wait until we're married and can be alone."

At the time, he couldn't wait to be alone with her, either.

Alone. He scoffed. Another stab to his already wounded heart.

The warm memory of Susanna snuggled against him in the darkness of that cold January weekend still tarried. The heat of their lingering kisses. The plans they'd been making for their future. Those remembrances remained in his thoughts after all these months without her.

Jah, it hurt. So did the pained expression on her face every time she looked at him. He didn't know what it meant, exactly. But he was aware she dated other men, and it was the ultimate anguish watching her catch rides home from frolics and weddings with other buwe. Watching her move on.

And Mammi didn't seem to grasp that he and Susie had broken up. She talked as if she expected Susanna to kum visit at any moment. Like she used to do.

Having Susie at the haus to assist Mammi wouldn't help the situation.

Benaiah groaned loudly, glad nobody was around to hear. Peter had wandered off half an hour before, happy and whistling, probably to go whisper sweet nothings into the ear of his future frau.

Couldn't Peter see how unhappy Susie was?

Or did he just assume she would adjust to her new circumstances, as she'd had to do every time something major had been taken from her?

Or…. Benaiah's jaw tightened. Was this a ploy to get him to declare his eternal, undying love for Susanna and ask to marry her, as originally planned?

If it was, it didn't speak well of Peter, thinking Benaiah would abandon his family—even though doing so would allow him to be with the woman of his dreams.

"Hey." A youthful male voice broke into his thoughts.

Benaiah turned from the now-silent cuckoo clock to the doorway, where a towheaded boy with a smudged face and soiled hands stood in a stance of impatience. "Jah?"

"Mamm said to tell you lunch is ready. Didn't you hear the bell?" He spoke with a cocky tone Benaiah didn't care for.

And even though Benaiah wasn't the least bit hungry, he eased to his feet, eager for a chance to see how Susanna was coping.

He laid the glass lily he'd been blowing on the worktable. It would need to be reheated, anyway. Then he strode toward the door, wiping his hands on his pant legs. He could hardly believe Peter's fiancée approved of his eating lunch with the family, since he was just a hired hand.

Or maybe his first impression of Irene as a harsh, unyielding woman was wrong. Maybe the pursed lips and narrow-eyed stare had been her normal expression. And she certainly couldn't help that she had a pointy nose and a narrow chin, which added to her angry bird-like appearance.

Considering her looks, it must've been her personality that had won Peter's heart. As it said in Proverbs 31, *"Favor is deceitful, and beauty is vain: but a woman that feareth the* Lord, *she shall be praised."*

This woman—Irene—must have a wunderbaar relationship with the Lord.

Lord, help me not to judge others based on appearances, Benaiah silently prayed. *I realize she must be a fantastic woman who will make a great step-mamm for Susie. Help me not to begrudge Peter his chance at happiness, despite the disruption it's causing in my own life.*

The bu had disappeared by the time Benaiah closed the shop door behind him and started across the yard.

The haus, usually quiet and peaceful home, seemed almost shell-shocked, quivering in fear of all the activity going on inside. Benaiah walked into the kitchen, his gaze going to Susie. She stood at the counter, her back ramrod straight, as the buwe and men all washed up and sat down at the table that had seemed plenty big for three. Now it was dwarfed, with…he counted four buwe, Peter, and an extra chair for Benaiah, pushed into his regular place.

Susie was the only female in the kitchen. And one of the bu, apparently the oldest one, openly gawked at her. As if he might be interested.

Benaiah scowled. His stomach hurt. His heart ached. He wanted to hug her close and stake his prior claim.

He had nein claim. Prior, current, or future.

"We're eating in shifts. Men and buwe first, then the women," Peter explained as Benaiah washed up. Once he'd seated himself in the empty chair, Peter added, "Irene went upstairs to check out the sleeping arrangements, but I daresay we'll be using the dawdi-haus for the buwe." He bowed his head. "Shall we pray?"

Benaiah dipped his head. "*Lord Gott, danki for this food and the hands that prepared it. Please give Susie strength. Guide us—*"

"Amen," Peter said.

As Susie started to carry the dishes of food to the table, Irene came into the room clutching the yellow gift bag Benaiah had delivered in the wee hours of the morgen. But now it was stuffed to overflowing.

In her other hand, she held the vase holding the rose bud.

SUSANNA SET THE bowl of mashed potatoes on the table near Daed, then turned around to retrieve the dish of homemade applesauce. She stopped mid-step, her gaze going from Irene, down to the bag and the rose, before she looked up again. She froze, her breath lodged in her throat. Waiting.

Irene's lips were pursed. "Peter. Your dochter has been hiding haus-hold items in her room. Candy dishes, towels, pot holders, and more." She held out the rose. "And she took the flower you bought for me."

One of the buwe at the table snickered.

Daed glanced at Benaiah, as if expecting him to answer. But they both remained silent. For one beat. Two. Three.

Would Susanna be justified in speaking in her own defense by explaining that those gifts had been given to her by a secret admirer, and that she wasn't stealing from her father? Or from her future step-mamm?

"Irene, Susanna has a beau," Daed finally said, quietly. "Those gifts were given with intent and a promise."

Susanna didn't know how much of either intent or promise there was behind the gifts, since they'd been given anonymously. But she wordlessly accepted the bag Irene shoved in her direction and tried to ignore the woman's glare.

Irene thumped the vase on the table. "Well, she at least could've left the flowers here for us all to enjoy."

Susanna nodded her agreement. Then she set the gift bag on the counter and carried the applesauce to the table as Irene swished out of the room. After mouthing a silent "Danki" to Daed, she said, "If it's okay, I'll go put these gifts somewhere else."

She didn't glance at Benaiah, but she wondered what he'd made of Daed's announcement that she had a beau. One "with intent and a promise." *Ach, if only it were true.*

"Go ahead." Daed studied his plate. "You might want to get the other things out of your room, too."

Other things…like the stuffed toys. Not to mention the cards and letters. The personal notes needed to be hidden away, for sure. Except that if Irene had been her room long enough to collect this many items, she'd already seen the rest of it—and probably snooped at the notes, too. She must have known there was a secret admirer, and yet she'd decided to wrongfully accuse Susanna, anyway.

Leaving the yellow bag on the counter for now, she grabbed a reusable tote bag from the drawer where she stored such things, and shook it open as she hurried from the room and climbed the stairs.

Her bedroom had been invaded by Irene and her four *dochters* of various ages. The girls all sat along the edge of Susanna's full-sized bed, the youngest clutching the stuffed snowman from last January. The oldest held the collection of cards and notes, openly reading them. Irene was going through Susanna's dresser drawers, removing her personal items of clothing and loading them in a box. A violation of her privacy, for sure.

Anger flared within Susanna, but she struggled to contain it. She stopped in front of the girl reading her personal notes and stared, hands fisted on her hips.

Her cheeks flushing pink, the girl held the notes out to Susanna, keeping her eyes downcast. Susanna forced herself to be gentle as she accepted the stack of correspondence, rather than jerking it away. "*Danki*," she murmured. Hopefully, *nein* hint of her sinful attitude had flooded over into that quiet word.

But who gave Irene and her *dochters* permission to invade her personal space, violate her privacy, remove her belongings?

A heavy sigh escaped. *Daed* had, with his quiet comment from earlier: *Mein haus ist ihr haus, mein liebe. Do as you wish.*

Susanna decided to let the youngest girl hold on to the snowman, but she collected the rest of her gifts, making sure each one was accounted for. Then she slipped out of the bedroom, went downstairs, and returned to the kitchen to collect the yellow gift bag. The menfolk ate quietly.

The best place to put everything? She looked around, mentally suggesting and dismissing various hiding places. Benaiah nodded his head toward the window. Outside? He was probably indicating that the glassblowing shop would be the safest place. He was right. Irene had nein apparent interest in the space, since she'd already deemed glassblowing a frivolous activity, and Daed wouldn't allow her kinner in there to go wild. Not with all those glass lilies being prepared for an Englisch wedding. Profits would suffer if they were destroyed.

At Daed's nod, Susanna hurried outside and across the yard to the glass shop. It was hot in there, belying the chilly winter air outside.

She opened a cabinet, the one where Grossmammi used to hide all the Christmas presents she'd bought or made so her grosskinner wouldn't find them. Only Susanna had known where they were hidden, but she'd never peeked. Not until the year Grossmammi died, and it became her responsibility to get the gifts out and wrap them. She brushed a tear away with the back of her hand, then crouched down and carefully slid the tote and the gift bag to the back of the bottom shelf of the cabinet, shifting things around so her items were hidden behind the box containing the black socks she'd knitted Daed for Christmas.

She closed the cabinet door, straightened, and stood still a moment, her hand on the countertop. Would she be expected to make Christmas gifts for Irene and her eight kinner? Probably so.

Scarves for eight, coming right up. But what to make for Irene? A fuzzy throw to snuggle under with Daed as they read in the evenings? The image that conjured didn't sit well with her. Plus, that was a gift she'd planned to make for herself and Benaiah to snuggle under.

She pushed that thought away, wiped at another tear, and turned. The lily Ben had finished earlier that morgen rested on a small table beside the chair where he usually sat while blowing glass. She walked over and picked it up. Even though it wasn't finished—it needed leaves and a steam—it was beautiful. The Englisch bride would have a keepsake to cherish for always.

Susanna carefully set the flower down and added another log— two logs—to the fire. It didn't seem hot enough to melt glass.

The door opened, and with a gust of wind, Benaiah strode inside.

"Ach, you're done with the meal? I wanted to serve dessert."

He stopped near the counter where she'd hidden the gifts. "Don't worry. Your daed took care of that. The apple pie was ser gut. Irene wasn't in the room to stop him, and she won't find out unless one of her buwe tells her."

"Have you talked with any of them?" Susanna asked.

Benaiah shook his head. "Not a one. We weren't formally introduced, even. Guess your daed figures I don't need to know. He just told them I was his employee. Didn't give them my name." Benaiah's gaze turned solemn as it rested on her. "How are you holding up, Suz?"

She wouldn't be a boppli about this. Benaiah had already listened to her whine on the way to the store and back again. That was enough. Time to act like a grown-up. She squared her shoulders. "If Daed is happy, that's all that matters."

He hesitated, then nodded. "Probably would do you gut to go to my haus for a few days to help Mammi. Not only does she need you, but you'll be glad for the space."

Ben's sweet little sisters sure beat eight nosy, leering, romping kinner.

Susanna gave a slight smile. "At least we're communicating again, because of this."

Benaiah rubbed his chin. "I never wanted to stop."

Funny, because he hadn't as much as looked her in the eye after their breakup.

"It's gut to know you've moved on, Suz."

BENAIAH PUT HIS work apron back on and checked the temperature of the fire, conscious of Susanna lingering by the box of finished glass lilies ready for pickup. Only five more to finish, and he—or Peter—could call the bride-to-be.

"About that," Susanna said quietly. Her voice was almost drowned out by the roar of the fire as Benaiah prodded a log with the iron poker. "I lied to you. I...I'm not over you. It was a matter of pride, and it was unkind. And untrue. I'm sorry."

Benaiah poked at the embers under the logs, sending sparks shooting up. He closed the door of the wood furnace, wondering whether he'd heard her correctly. But, whether she was over him or not, nothing had changed. Well, except for the somewhat mollifying knowledge that she still suffered the loss of their relationship, just as he did.

He didn't have the foggiest idea what to say to her admission of lying and pride, or her apology. He had to acknowledge her comments in some way, but he couldn't begin to think of how—other than to open his arms wide and welcome her soft, womanly body against his chest.

That would solve nothing and would only make things worse.

So, he dipped his head and shuffled his feet. Probably looking like a dummchen. He pulled in a breath. Exhaled. *Lord Gott, some words? I don't know what to say.*

Susanna approached him, coming so close that he could smell her green-apple scent. So close that he could touch her without much effort. Close enough that he could lean forward and kiss her....

He lifted his gaze from the cement floor to her rosy lips. His desire to taste them grew, threatening to overcome him.

She reached out and touched his hand with hers. "Please, Ben. Can't we be friends?"

Friends? The word formed, filled his mind in letters as clear as glass, then shattered and fell, leaving shards of glass pricking his heart. Stabbing into it. Taking up residence.

"I can't, Susie. I just can't."

CHAPTER 5

Susanna trudged back to the haus, dreading dinner more than any meal of her life. Since the men had eaten first, she would be dining with her soon-to-be step-mamm and stepsisters. She wanted to speak to Daed about how Irene had found fault with the way the kitchen was organized. How she'd undone everything Grossmammi had arranged, disrupting the system Susanna had followed all these years. The familiar system that had allowed her and Daed to find everything easily, without having to hunt.

She clenched her fists so tightly, her nails dug into her palms as she recalled Irene moving dishes from one cupboard to another, and then reorganizing the entire pantry, all the while muttering to herself about Susanna's lack of haus-keeping skills. She lacked skills? Really? The floor might not be clean enough to eat off of, but who had picnics on the kitchen floor? And with Daed and Benaiah tracking in and out of there all day, even though they removed their shoes at the door, dirt came inside. Not as much as if they'd been farmers, but still.

The door opened, and Daed stepped outside. He shut the door behind him. Now was her chance. "Daed?"

He stepped to the edge of the porch, all smiles and dimples. He beamed at Susanna as she reached the bottom step. "It's wunderbaar, ain't so? I can't wait to start my life with Irene. We're talking about marrying as soon as Benaiah and I get this wedding order of lilies done. Just a few more pieces to go. In less than a month, we'll be settling into our new home in Iowa. I hope the farm and business sell quickly." He walked down the steps and out to the shop without waiting for a reply, whistling as he went.

And taking with him Susanna's chance to complain. Her shoulders slumped. How could she say anything now, with Daed so clearly in love? He was happier than she'd ever seen him. She couldn't remember ever seeing a bounce in his steps before.

It hurt to think she hadn't been enough to make him happy. But she was only his dochter. Grossmammi had spoken to her about the brother she didn't remember who'd died in Mamm's arms, and how much Daed had mourned that loss. Mamm had suffered miscarriages after that. Selfishly, Susanna had imagined that she had taken the place, filled in the hole, of any lost brothers or sisters. Maybe even had taken the place of Mamm and, later, Grossmammi. She'd tried to keep the haus-hold running smoothly and perfectly so Daed wouldn't miss them.

Even though Daed had never complained, she must've failed. Otherwise, Irene wouldn't have swept into the haus like an unwanted wind and redone everything. *Everything!*

And Susanna thought she could help Ben's mammi Wren? After this cruel awakening to her failures, Benaiah would likely hear complaints from his mammi that she did everything wrong, wrong, wrong. And that would eliminate any chance of her winning him back.

Not that she could. He didn't even want to be friends.

Her appetite settled into a hard ball in her stomach, taking up any room that might've been occupied by food.

The only gut thing about moving to Iowa would be a fresh pick of Amish men. A chance to stop mourning the loss of Benaiah. To stop dreaming of a secret admirer who was too shy to step forward. To stop receiving mercy-rides home from the boyfriends of her cousins and friends.

She opened the door and found the female contingent of her future step-family sitting around the table, heads bowed in silent prayer. She slipped quietly into her place and lowered her head. *Lord Gott, please give me grace. Help me to serve these strangers as You would have me.*

Martha in the Bible had been a devoted hostess, serving others tirelessly. Had she ever resented strangers filling her home when Jesus visited her? Surely, there would have been impossible-to-please people among them.

Lord, help me to serve as Martha would.

Dishes clattered as the food was passed. Someone nudged her arm, and she raised her head, looking around the table with the brightest smile she could muster. "I'm Susanna. It's nice to meet all of you."

Irene scowled. "First of all, Susanna, in my haus, if people are late to meals, they don't eat. Simple as that. You're excused from the table. Second, I have a Susan." She pointed to her oldest dochter, the one who'd been reading Susanna's private notes from her secret admirer. "And I have an Anna." She pointed to the youngest. "You are going to have to go by your middle name so we don't get confused."

"My middle name?" Susanna blinked. She had to sacrifice her name, as well?

"We will call you Rose."

Was Daed okay with this?

Wait a minute. Irene had said "in my haus." This wasn't her haus. It was Daed's. Should Susanna accept this injustice and depart obediently? It wasn't as if she were hungry. Yet she was the one who'd prepared the meal. She felt somewhat inclined to stand her ground.

Disagreeing with Irene would mean risking Daed's happiness. Susanna pictured him as he'd been just a few minutes earlier, looking happier than she could remember him.

"I'm sorry I was late for dinner." Susanna pushed her chair back and stood. "I'll try to be punctual in the future." If only she could flee to Benaiah's haus and help Mammi Wren right now, instead of waiting until Friday. But maybe she wouldn't object to her coming today, after all, to help with her preparations for Thanksgiving. "I'll—"

"I would tell you to start working on the Thanksgiving dinner, but I shudder to think what might happen. You may start washing the men's dishes."

Susanna inhaled deeply. Exhaled. And counted to ten. Twice. "Okay. After the dishes are done, I need to go help someone with her Thanksgiving baking."

Irene frowned. "Instead of doing the baking needed here? I think Peter will have something to say about the irresponsible behavior of his dochter."

"Jah, I suppose he will." Hopefully, he'd say something along the lines of "Go in peace, and Godspeed." Susanna forced her smile back into position as she turned to the girls. "Nice to meet you, Susan and Anna, and…?"

Irene pointed to the second oldest. "Naomi." Her fingertip darted toward the second youngest. "Rebekah."

"Nice to meet you, too, Naomi and Rebekah."

The girls all dipped their heads and stared at their plates. With nein comment.

Message received. Wasn't there a fairy tale about a girl whose daed remarried a woman with several dochters of her own, and the daed's dochter was reduced to a servant? Except—that girl ended up married to a prince.

There was nein prince in Susanna's future.

She marched over to the sink and started on the dishes. She'd no sooner finished all the men's dishes when the girls carried over the dishes from their meal and stacked them beside the sink. So, she washed those, too. Cleaned the counters. Wiped the table.

Where was everybody? Only Irene's whereabouts seemed obvious—she was in the cellar, likely reorganizing, judging by the recurring sound of glass jars clinking together. Why would she go to all that trouble when she was supposed to be here only a few days, and then Daed would be moving to her already-established home in Iowa? Was she trying to drive Susanna away? To establish boundaries ahead of time? Maybe she simply had OCD.

Susanna hurried out of the haus, ran across the driveway to the shop, and burst inside. Daed sat in a chair as he rolled hot orange glass on a long pole, shaping it with a long, flat tool that was shaped like a spatula. Benaiah held another long pole into the fire, the glass turning orange from the heat.

"May I go help Benaiah's mammi with her baking?"

Daed slid the black spatula into its place on the side of his chair. "And neglect our baking? You can't leave Irene to do it all."

But she said she'd shudder to think what my baking would be like. She couldn't say that out loud. Nor could she say that even though Irene had insulted Susanna's cooking, she and her dochters had finished off their meal, even going back for seconds and thirds. Instead, Susanna swallowed. "I think she'd be happier if I wasn't in the way."

Daed frowned. "Nonsense. She's anxious to get to know you. Said what a beautiful name you had. And she already complimented your haus-keeping skills to me."

Really? Because all Susanna had heard were complaints.

"Ach, she's busy rearranging the cellar shelves. And said I needed to start going by Rose."

Benaiah's shoulders jerked. He backed away from the fire, side-stepping the gray tabby cat at his feet, and stared at Susanna. "Rose. Really?" He settled into his chair.

Daed stood up and approached the furnace. "Is that so? Seriously now, Suz, why would she insist on using your middle name?"

"She said that since she has a Susan and an Anna, it would be too confusing to have a Susanna, too."

"Hmm. I'll have a talk with her. Though, she does have a point, ain't so? It *would* be less confusing to call you by your middle name."

Less confusing for them, maybe. Much more confusing for her. But apparently she was a nonissue. "So, can I go?" she asked again.

Daed frowned. "Nein. You know what I expect to see on our Thanksgiving table, and you know where to find all the ingredients to make it."

Well, she *used* to know.

"Besides, Irene will need your help."

"Mammi could use her help, too," Benaiah put in quietly. "She's having some hip problems, on top of her recent illness."

"Hmm." Daed scratched his neck. "Then…maybe see if Irene needs you. If she doesn't, you may go."

"Danki." Susanna shut the door quietly behind her, then trudged back across the driveway. If she was needed for anything, it was dish duty. Not for cooking, considering the way Irene had spoken to her of her kitchen skills. It sure seemed as if Irene were two-faced, saying one thing to Daed and something else quite different to Susanna.

"There you are, Rose." Irene greeted her in the kitchen. "I've been searching for you. I found a cot in the cellar. Would you rather sleep down there or up in the attic?"

Susanna blinked. "I thought I was to share my room."

"That you are. You just won't be *in* it. I realized your room is quite inadequate for five girls."

"What about the dawdi-haus?"

"My boys will be in there."

"Maybe I could sleep in the cot in the little room off the kitchen. Grossmammi used to keep a sofa in there for when she grew fatigued."

Irene frowned. "I suppose that would work. If your daed agrees."

He would. Susanna would see to it. She pulled in a deep breath. Exhaled slowly.

"Do you need any help?"

Irene batted her eyelashes. "It's your home, Rose. What do you usually do for Thanksgiving?"

Why did she want to know? Was she going to prepare Daed's favorites? Why? To put Susanna to shame by making better versions of them?

Thanksgiving preparations usually didn't cause Susanna a tension headache. But even though Irene had conceded on the sleeping arrangements, the throbbing in Susanna's head spelled the prelude to a major migraine.

Benaiah poked at the fire, then shut the oven doors. "What's going on, Peter?"

Peter shrugged. "I'm getting remarried. Told you that."

"To a woman who seems set on completely ostracizing your dochter."

"Ach, I'm sure it's not all that bad. Just a slight learning curve. They'll adjust." Peter's chuckle had a nervous edge to it.

Benaiah frowned. *Slight* learning curve? More like a huge one. And why did it seem Peter himself wasn't convinced, either? Benaiah would have liked to try to talk Peter into letting Susanna go to his haus to help, but she might truly be needed here—not only for kitchen duty, but also to assist with Irene's eight kinner. And running off would likely just cause more problems between Susie and her future step-mamm.

On the other hand, how much was Susie supposed to take before she cracked?

"Kum on," Benaiah muttered. "You saw her attack Susie at dinner. You know those gifts were personal."

Peter grinned. "Jah, I know. And it makes me wonder when you will step forward and admit that you still care for my dochter."

"Is that what this is all about? That's not going to work. You cannot force me to make promises I can't keep." Oh, how he wished he could promise to love and cherish her. The problem was, he wouldn't be free from his family obligations for ten years or more, and it wouldn't be fair to ask Susie to wait that long to have him to herself. She deserved better.

Unbelievably, Peter's smile widened. He calmly got up. "Take Susie and go. You're getting too stressed, and you're liable to break something. Besides, you're right. Irene overstepped her boundaries at lunch, seizing Susie's personal items. We can probably compromise on her name, too. Susanna is different enough from Susan, especially if we use both girls' first and middle names: Susanna Rose and Susan Marie."

"Danki." Benaiah nodded gratefully. "I'll deliver Susie to Mammi and kum right back. We need to get these lilies finished."

Peter shrugged. "If you're sure you'll be able to focus."

"I'll be fine." *Once Susie is safe from the sharp tongue of her future step-mamm.*

"I'll go with you to the haus, and we'll see how the situation looks."

Benaiah put his tools away. "Did you say you're listing the business for sale?"

"Jah. If it doesn't sell, you can keep working here long enough to fill the outstanding orders, then close it down. Unless the new property owners object to that."

"Let me know what you're asking for it." He needed to support his family somehow. Though taking on a bank loan wouldn't be a gut way of doing it. Maybe it'd be best to help Daadi with the small garden whose harvest supplemented his income. Enlarge it, and....

Would it be a viable enough business to make a living on? Not even close. His lips curled.

Well, that area obviously needed some thought and prayer.

"We'll talk." Peter climbed the porch steps.

Benaiah followed him into the haus. Susie and Irene sat at the dining room table, sipping something from steaming floral mugs, a plate of Susie's chocolate chip walnut cookies between them. Susie had a notebook in front of her and a pen in hand.

The two women appeared to be getting along. Would wonders never cease? Benaiah half expected a cookie to stand up and wave at him.

He took off his shoes, set them next to Peter's, and, in stockinged feet, crossed the floor to the sink. He washed his hands thoroughly, dried them on the towel Peter handed him, then turned to the table and dropped into the seat next to Peter—across from Susie.

Eyes fixed on the plate of cookies, he reached out to snag one as Susie pushed the platter toward him. His fumbling grasp sent several cookies tumbling to the table. He swallowed hard and picked up the fallen cookies. They totaled three. Not a worry. He could handle three cookies, easily. It was Susanna he couldn't handle. Her, and change.

"Ben and I thought we'd take a short break." Peter reached for a cookie. "What are you having that's hot?" He leaned toward the mug in front of Susie and inhaled. "Tea? Some of that herbal stuff?"

Irene looked up at him. "Mint. Brought some leaves with me." Irene stood and fetched the teakettle and two mugs. "Sugar or cream for either of you?"

"Nein, danki," Benaiah said in unison with Peter, who simultaneously gave him a sharp nudge to the knee. Benaiah glanced at his boss. Received a wink and a grin that communicated his impression that the rough patch was already smoothed over, and the ladies were getting along.

Which meant Benaiah would likely not need to put himself through the sweet torture of taking Susanna home to help Mammi. A blessing.

"And what are you two beauties working on?" Peter peeked at Susanna's notebook.

"We're trying to finalize the menu for Thanksgiving," Irene told him. "Comparing our traditional feasts. They're basically the same, except that Rose fixes bread stuffing, while I prefer corn-bread stuffing. And she makes cranberry salad with oranges, whipped cream, and miniature marshmallows, while I prefer cranberry gel. We differ some on desserts, too, so we are going to compromise and serve your favorites and ours."

"Compromise. That'll make for a solid marriage." Peter poured some steaming mint tea into his cup. He grinned at his frau-to-be. "And, speaking of compromise…might I suggest calling my dochter 'Susanna Rose' and yours 'Susan Marie'? Then it'd be easy enough to differentiate between them. Plenty of blended families have some difficulty with similar names, and I don't see reason for anyone to have to sacrifice her given name."

"Hmm." Irene pursed her lips. "I guess we can do that. Especially since you said your dochter is spoken for. If she marries, she likely won't be moving to Iowa with you."

Susanna's lips parted, denial rising in her eyes, but Peter shook his head at her. She remained silent.

"When is the wedding day? Is it soon?" Irene sank down into her chair once more, a gleam in her eye. "If it is, perhaps I can kum back and help with the preparations."

Susanna glanced at her daed.

Benaiah focused his attention on his weak-looking tea. His face burned. He hoped that his uncensored reaction didn't give anything away to Susanna. Then again, he hadn't expected his anonymous gifts to lead everyone on, like a lie. He'd only wanted to comfort the woman he loved.

He felt a chill, and not from having been outside in the cold. He wasn't a huge fan of tea, but the warmth would be gut. He wrapped both hands around the mug and let the heat seep into his skin.

"I don't believe a date has been set. Maybe next year." Peter took another cookie. "Ben suggested taking Susanna Rose to his haus to help his mammi with her Thanksgiving baking, since she's been feeling poorly. How have the preparations progressed here?"

Silence.

Benaiah raised his eyes from his tea. Susanna's cheeks were stained red, but whether she was embarrassed by the wedding talk or by the lack of dinner preparations, he had nein idea.

Irene rubbed her hand over her chin and looked at Susanna.

"Aenti Sarah is bringing lettuce salad, Jell-O salad, winter squash, sweet potatoes, pumpkin pies, and coconut cake, as well as an extra turkey, since she has such a large family. Benaiah's mammi will bring some schnitz pies. I'm doing the turkey, bread stuffing, regular mashed potatoes, and the cranberry salad. Irene said she'd prepare corn-bread stuffing, peanut butter pie, pecan pie, and cranberry gel. And most of my cooking will be done tomorrow morgen. I'll make the cranberry salad when I get home to-nacht."

"I don't need help with the pies," Irene put in. "My girls and I can handle that. So, if she needs to help the grossmammi, it's a gut day for that."

Peter beamed. "So nice to see my favorite ladies getting along. Susie, you'll go help Ben's mammi today, then. Ben will take you over."

A rock settled in the pit of Benaiah's stomach.

SUSANNA SETTLED IN next to Benaiah on the narrow buggy seat for the third time that day. She'd already placed the heated brick on the floorboard and spread the old, worn quilt over her lap and legs, hoping to keep the warmth contained.

Benaiah clicked his tongue, and Peppermint Twist pulled the buggy toward the road.

Susanna folded her hands together in her lap and looked out the small square window on her side of the buggy.

He cleared his throat. "Things, uh, improved somewhat?"

She shrugged. "Irene was more willing to compromise this afternoon. After I gave up my bedroom."

He gave her a quick, startled look. "Thought she said you were going to share."

"Jah, well, her definition of sharing was for me to vacate my room completely and go sleep in the cellar or the attic. My choice. I suggested the mudroom, off the kitchen. And then, she wanted to discuss the Thanksgiving menu. I know what we always serve. She has her own way of doing it. And she was willing to serve both menus. I had already made arrangements with my aenti regarding what she would bring. It was just your family I hadn't counted on, since you and I had broken up...." Her voice caught. Broke. And stubborn tears burned her eyes.

If Benaiah hadn't broken up with her, this would've been their second Thanksgiving together.

She swallowed the lump in her throat.

He released a heavy sigh. "Would it be easier on you if we didn't kum?"

Jah. But.... "Nein, nein. You said your mammi was going to cook boxed pizzas since she was sick. And your family has always been with mine—"

"Jah, but that was when we were planning on marrying. Now, we're not." His tone was flat. He flicked the reins.

Way to drive the knife deeper into her heart. If she could've shifted further away from him, she would've.

She made another effort to swallow that stubborn lump. "There is that."

"And you have that secret admirer. Or not so secret, since your daed says there's intent and a promise. Do know who it is?"

You? But it couldn't be. Not considering the casual curiosity lacing his voice. It sounded genuine.

"Daed assumes too much." Would it be wrong to admit she had a wish as to who he might be? But then, why did she want *him*, when he so willingly handed her back her love, torn and tattered? He didn't want her anymore, and he'd given her nein reason. Just the cliché "It's not you, it's me."

That was nein excuse.

"Ach, kum on. Nein guesses? What'd he give you so far? From what your daed said, he's invested a lot. A package every single month. Tell me about them."

"Why? So you can do the same for your chosen girl?"

He shrugged, his arm brushing hers. "It is a unique idea."

Jah, that was true. She inhaled. "Each month has a theme. January was 'I'm frozen without you'; he gave me a stuffed snowman. Mittens. A scarf. Sugar cookies in the shape of snowmen. February was 'I'll always love you,' and it included toy plush hearts like they gave away at a fair a couple of years ago. One said 'I love you,' the other, 'Be mine.'"

"Nice. I saw an umbrella in the bag you carried out."

She nodded. "April. 'I'm so blue without you.' In September, he gave me apple cider, apple fritters, and an apple-cinnamon-scented candle, since the theme was 'You're the apple of my eye.' All I have left from that month is the card."

He chuckled. "Wonder what next month will bring." He turned the buggy down the road leading to his haus.

Hopefully, a proposal. From the man sitting next to her. But how could she convince Benaiah that he still loved her? That she didn't want anyone but him? And she would be more than willing to care for his family?

Maybe Mammi Wren would have some ideas.

Or maybe not, since she seemed to be under the mistaken impression that Benaiah had never stopped courting her.

CHAPTER 6

*B*enaiah refrained from urging Peppermint Twist to pick up the pace. Reluctant to hurry away from Susanna, he let the horse select the speed for the trip back to the Kings'.

He couldn't keep from smiling as he recalled the animation in her voice while describing some of the gifts he'd given her. She hadn't said anything about October's theme, "I've fallen for you," featuring more apple cider, a large pie pumpkin, and a couple of colorful mums. Or June's theme, "You are my sunshine," with a big bag of yellow M&Ms and a daffodil notebook—the one she was using today for menu planning—along with a bouquet of sunflowers. Some months, he'd struggled for creativity. "Life is a picnic with you in it" for August. "You light up my life" for July. But May? Wow, that was hard. He'd finally settled on "Where flowers grow, so does hope." He'd given her flower seeds and a watering can. She'd planted the moss roses next to the haus, and her clear enjoyment of them had made him smile.

Not that he himself had any hope. But she'd seemed to anticipate great things all that month. All smiles, with the light of expectation in her eyes. That light had died toward the end of the month, though, when she'd apparently realized her secret admirer wasn't going to step forward. Benaiah had scrambled for excuses to keep his distance from her so he wouldn't give in to the temptation.

Now, December was mere days away. December, when they celebrated Jesus's birth. It was a magical season of wishes and dreams kum true. And it was pure torture to devise a fitting theme for Susie's gift.

Christmas would be a major challenge. Benaiah's only idea so far was to repeat January's frozen theme. Especially because this had been the coldest year of his life without the warmth of her love, the heat of her kisses and snuggly hugs, and the burning anticipation of starting a life together.

He closed his eyes. Whatever he came up with, it would have to signal a clear end to this succession of gifts, because he wouldn't be getting down on one knee to declare his undying love and ask for her hand in marriage. Instead, he'd have to figuratively kiss her good-bye as she moved to Iowa with her daed. As she should.

Iowa. Where her step-mamm would work her to the bone caring for her step-kinner, force her to sleep in the attic, isolate her from her friends and the community, and constantly put her down with verbal digs at her competency. Iowa, where Benaiah would never see her smile again or hear her laughter or taste her addictive cookies. Where a new beau would take her home from singings. Hold her hand. And kiss her soft lips while the two of them cuddled under the stars.

Honk!

The reins slipped through his hands. Benaiah snapped his eyes open in time to grab the reins once more as a black pickup truck roared by. Peppermint Twist reared and headed for the ditch alongside the road. Benaiah tugged on the reins with white-knuckled fingers. "Whoa!"

Peppermint Twist came to a stop on the shoulder, inches away from a steep drop-off.

Danki, Lord, for watching over me.

Once the traffic had passed, he clicked his tongue, and they started on their way again.

Maybe he should pray some more, for guidance about how to provide for his family once the glass shop closed. He expelled a sharp breath. And Peter expected to force Benaiah's hand by announcing the intentions of Susanna's secret beau? Nein. She would just be another mouth to feed in one month's time, when he was out of a job. More than one mouth, when their inevitable boppli was born.

He needed to apologize to Peter for misleading him. Apologize to Irene for giving her the false impression that Susanna wouldn't be moving to Iowa. And apologize to Susanna for fueling her dreams that someone loved her.

Well, someone did. But his love solved nothing. Absolutely nothing.

He growled deep in his throat as Peppermint Twist made the turn into Peter's drive without requiring a tug on the reins to direct him. Habits were often a bad thing. The habit of reporting here to work daily gave rise to the habit of seeing Susanna on a regular basis. Pure torture.

He couldn't go on like this. Either he was going to give in by declaring his undying love and begging her to consider marrying him, or he'd completely kill the relationship—stop encouraging her with gifts, stop eating meals with the family, turn his back on her when she came into the shop, and...he didn't know what else. But since he couldn't marry her, not with pending unemployment and his other reasons, he had nein choice.

His love for her had to die.

Susanna rolled out some pie dough on a floured cloth while Mammi Wren poured boiling water from the kettle over a bowl of dried apples to soften them.

"It is so gut that you and my Ben are together again. We surely did miss you around here." Mammi Wren returned the kettle to the stove, then patted Susanna's shoulder. "And with your daed remarrying, I'm thinking we ought to plan a winter wedding for you, too."

"Benaiah and I aren't together." Susanna struggled to keep her voice calm. "He's still being stubborn."

Mammi Wren frowned. "But I thought...when you came in together this morgen...the way he looked at you...."

"Probably looking like he'd had enough of me. Daed had just sprung on me the news of his upcoming marriage, and I lashed out irrationally."

"Hmm." Mammi Wren shook her head. "Nein, that's not it. He looked at you as if you made his heart sing."

The blues, maybe. Susanna shrugged.

"And do you mean that your daed hadn't told you about his marriage before this morgen? As his dochter, you should've been the first to know."

One would think.

"He made a special trip out here about a month ago to tell Daadi Micah and me." A gleam lit Mammi Wren's eyes. "We had a gut long talk. Too bad Benaiah wasn't here for it. But he'd taken off without a word, and I figured he must be with you."

The crack in Susanna's heart widened. She shook her head. "Nein. He must've been with another girl."

"Hmm. He's definitely courting someone. Buying gifts and sneaking out late at nacht." The gleam clouded into a look of confusion.

Buying gifts? Susanna couldn't help but hold out hope that he might be her admirer, after all. But if he were, why didn't he kum forward and declare his affections? Maybe he had found someone else and just didn't want to let her down abruptly. "I need to know how to win him back, Mammi Wren."

The older woman laid her gnarled hand atop the rolling pin, halting its movement. "Here, take a break. Have a glass of water. We'll discuss this."

Susanna sat in the chair Mammi Wren indicated. "Has he said anything to you? Who *is* she? What has she got that I haven't?" She hated how whiny she sounded.

Mammi Wren's bones virtually creaked as she lowered herself into a kitchen chair. She grimaced. "I don't know who. I assumed it was you, but I haven't asked. It's wrong to tamper with matters of the heart, Susie. I know he had his reasons, but whatever they are, I surely wish he'd reconsider. Ich liebe dich as if you were my own grossdochter."

That was sweet. Susanna beamed at the woman, then resumed frowning. "I'm not sure how to change his mind. If only I had a fairy godmother to grant me one wish. Ach, I know. A girl in my round-robin letter-writing group—she's from Wisconsin—says there's a love potion that's guaranteed to work. I think she said it has ginger, cloves, cinnamon—"

"Susanna, for shame." Mammi Wren thumped her hand on the table hard enough to rattle the lid of the sugar bowl. "That's witchcraft. You can't make a man fall in love with you by mixing a bunch of spices together. You might smell gut enough to cause his stomach to rumble, but it won't make him love you. And even if it did, what would happen once his hunger was sated? Would he wander off in another direction? Find some other girl who smells like food the next time he's hungry? What will be, will be. You can't force love."

Mammi Wren made the idea of a love potion sound sinful, as well as beyond ridiculous. But Cinda Yoder had promised gut results in her letter. And all the other girls who'd responded said they were going to try it. Maybe Susanna would attempt it, too, just for fun. To-nacht, she would reread the letter and see what the recipe called for.

"You go ahead and rest." Susanna popped out of the chair. "I'll check the apples and finish the crust. We'll have those pies done in no time. I'm so glad you and your family are joining us for Thanksgiving again. It wouldn't have been the same without you." She could use some friendly faces in the crowd, and a buffer between her and Irene. Yet it wouldn't be the same, even with them there. Last Thanksgiving, she and Benaiah were courting. His parents were still alive. He'd gotten down on one knee that evening and asked her to marry him.... Things were gut. But this year, everything had changed.

She simply *had* to win him back. And if it took a love potion, then so be it. For the balance of her time here today, she'd do as many chores as she could to help Mammi Wren. Then she'd try to convince Daed to allow her to work here for more than a few more days.

For as long as it took to win Benaiah back.

THE SHOP WAS empty when Benaiah returned. The fire had died down, as if Peter had decided to take the afternoon off.

After hanging his coat by the door, Benaiah added wood to the furnace, and examined the last lily that had been made. It looked gut. Too soon, this order would be filled, and then…what? If another one came in, would Peter accept it with Benaiah in mind? Or would he say, "Sorry, but I'm going out of business"?

His stomach churned. He went out the back door to bring in another load of wood. That's when he noticed Peter and Irene walking hand in hand by the pond. Irene's younger kinner bounded through the weeds, while the older ones skipped rocks on the water.

Seemed his boss couldn't stop smiling now that Irene had arrived.

At least one of them was happy.

Benaiah's frown was beginning to feel permanent.

He carried the wood inside, then prepared to start work again. Laboring on his own made the process slow going, but he made significant progress before the door opened and Peter came in, whistling.

Benaiah put the lily he'd just finished with the rest waiting for pickup. "I need to talk to you."

"Right. About the business." Peter strode over to his desk, where he handled the bookkeeping. He shuffled through a pile of papers, picked up a folder, and handed it to Benaiah. "This is the appraised value of the business. I've included a sheet of profits and expenses. Take a look, think it over, and let me know if you want to make an offer. I'd really rather it go to you than to strangers. If you buy the haus and land, too, it'd be real convenient for you. You and Susie and the rest of your family would have plenty of room. There's another page in there about that."

"Me and Susie…." Benaiah coughed. "I'm…uh, I need to apologize. Suz and I broke up, you know. Back in January, when my parents died. The anonymous gifts were intended to ease her broken heart, not to imply a hope that isn't there. I still can't marry her." He held the folder out to Peter without opening it. "I'm sorry if my eventual union with her was a condition for buying the business from you. I never meant to mislead you or Susie."

Peter plopped down on a stool, his expression one of warring surprise and disappointment. "But you love her. You said so yourself."

"Jah, but love's not enough. Love doesn't pay the bills. Love doesn't make unnecessary demands on a person. Love doesn't—"

"Love gives the other person a choice," Peter said quietly. "And it often requires sacrifice. I love my business. But Irene doesn't want to leave her family. I have nobody here except my sister and her family. And my dochter, of course. Irene has parents who need her. Older kinner and grosskinner. I'm sacrificing my creative outlet to be with her. Something to consider."

"Why sacrifice the business? Why not relocate it?" That would still put Benaiah out of a job, but at least Peter wouldn't be giving up everything in the process.

"Her bishop has nein tolerance for art of any form, except quilting. It's verboden in her district. The sale of the business will keep us comfortable until I master the skill of farming." He chuckled. "Maybe. Did you know Irene and I used to be sweethearts?"

"Nein."

"We were, long ago. But at the time, I wasn't willing to sacrifice my desires to be with her. Maybe I loved myself and this area more than I loved her. We both fell in love with and married other people, and I was very happy with Rosemary. Don't want you to think otherwise. But now Irene and have I found each other again. And this time, I'm willing to do whatever it takes."

Maybe that would be what would happen with Benaiah and Susanna. She'd move to Iowa with her daed, marry another man, and have a family. He'd eventually marry someone, after his siblings were grown and he was no longer responsible for them. And, Gott willing, someday in the future, he and Susanna would meet again....

"Remember, Ben, that love gives the other person a choice. I don't know your reasons for breaking up with Susanna, and I'll admit that I'm greatly disappointed that this secret-admirer business doesn't mean what I thought. But...." Peter shrugged, then waved dismissively at the folder still in Benaiah's extended hand. "Keep that. Look it over. And pray."

Benaiah let his hand holding the folder fall to his side. "Danki for your words of wisdom. I will. Pray, that is. But regarding Susie, I... well, I was wrong to mislead her. I'm sorrier than you know."

Peter nodded. "Prayer is all I ask."

"But until I decide, I won't be eating my meals with you anymore. Starting after Thanksgiving, that is."

Silence prevailed while Peter surveyed him. Then he clasped Benaiah's shoulder before turning away. "Suit yourself. But you should explain yourself to her." He walked out of the shop again. Shut the door.

"Jah. And say what?" Benaiah asked of the empty room. The same lame excuse he'd given before? *It's not you, it's me.*

That might work.

But after Thanksgiving. So he wouldn't ruin her holiday.

If only things could be different.

CHAPTER 7

Susanna trod the last half mile of her hike home feeling tired and more than a little irritated. Her arms ached from carrying the pies. Hadn't Benaiah said he would pick her up and take her home? She'd refused Daadi Micah's offer, figuring Benaiah would be along shortly. She'd waited to leave until Daadi Micah had gone into another room, so he would assume he'd just missed Benaiah's arrival and immediate departure.

As she lugged the pies up the driveway, she noticed the gaslight still on in the shop. Through the window, she spied Benaiah holding a pole into the hot fire. He probably hadn't even realized nacht had fallen, in his hurry to get those wedding lilies done. Why wasn't Daed in there helping him?

She entered the kitchen, set the pies on the counter, and peeked into the living room, where a lantern burned. Daed and Irene snuggled side by side on the loveseat, Daed's word search puzzle book in front of them. Irene held a yellow highlighter in her hand as they sat cheek to cheek, trying to solve a puzzle. Sweet—in a weird sort of way.

Daed looked up and glowered at her, paused in the doorway. "Where've you been? You weren't here to fix dinner. Irene had to do all the work, and she's a guest. Did you stay to eat at Benaiah's haus?"

"Nein. I thought Benaiah was coming to take me home, so I waited at his haus and visited with his großeltern and sisters until they went to bed. Then I walked home." She stepped closer to the fire to warm up.

"Hmm." Daed frowned. "Where is Ben?"

"In the shop. Guess he lost track of time." Susanna turned at the sound of the kitchen door clicking open and shut.

Benaiah entered the kitchen and looked at her. "Gut. You're home. I didn't realize what time it was. Sorry I forgot to kum get you. I was busy, but that's nein excuse."

"I would've picked her up if I'd known," Daed said. "I guess I thought you two were together."

Why would Daed have had that idea? Susanna frowned. Of all people, he knew the truth of the relationship—or the lack thereof— between her and Benaiah.

Benaiah cleared his throat and looked at Daed. "I finished the wedding lilies and closed up the shop. Called the bride. Someone will pick them up first thing Saturday morgen, she said."

Daed grunted. "How are we with the Internet orders? Up-to-date?"

Benaiah sighed. Shrugged. "Might be a week or two yet. I can handle them." He glanced at Susanna but didn't make eye contact. "Sorry again for losing track of time, Suz."

She forced a smile. "It's all right. I'm going to bed. Gut nacht." Turning, she headed toward the small room off the kitchen, imagining Benaiah's eyes on her. But when she glanced over her shoulder, he was facing away from her, his hand on the kitchen doorknob.

She went into the mudroom. Someone had positioned the musty, dusty cot against the wall—cobwebs intact—and dumped a sel-dom-used army-green sleeping bag on top of it, still rolled up. A tiny orange foam pillow had been laid next to the sleeping bag. This was what Irene called "getting it set up and ready" for her? She hadn't. It made the sting of rejection worse.

It was almost like camping, except she wasn't entirely out in the cold wind with nothing but tent fabric separating her from any nearby bears, or a half-mile hike to the nearest outhaus. But the room was still colder than the rest of the haus. Maybe the sleeping bag would be enough to keep her warm. She grabbed a damp washcloth from the edge of the laundry basket and used it to brush off the loose dirt from the cot, all the while checking for spiders and other creepy crawlers.

Then she sprayed the mattress with Lysol before rolling out the sleeping bag and climbing inside, tears stinging her eyes.

Giving up her room for their guests was the right thing to do, it just would've been nicer if she'd been asked. She certainly would've volunteered if she'd known in advance. But she wouldn't go down that road again. Daed had his reasons for not telling her about his fiancée's visit until just before her arrival. Just as Susanna had reasons she would never divulge for volunteering to help at Benaiah's haus.

Unfortunately, she hadn't been able to learn from Mammi Wren the real reason behind Benaiah's decision to break up with her. Either Ben had never shared it with her, or the woman had stubbornly decided to withhold it from Susanna.

Earlier, she'd brought in a clean dress for the next day, along with all the letters from her pen-pal group, having planned to write a response that evening. But now, with it so late, she would just locate and reread the letter about the love potion. She lay in the musty sleeping bag, lantern still glowing, and scanned the recipe. Read it over and over again, until she probably could've made the concoction in her sleep. Then, she closed her eyes, pretending that Benaiah still loved her and wanted to marry her.

The love potion simply *had* to work. Or else she'd find herself in a similar sleeping situation in Iowa.

Thanksgiving dawned earlier than Susanna would have liked, especially after a bad nacht's sleep, but she had to get the turkey in the oven, and those birds always seemed to take forever to prepare and roast. She cleaned out the innards in the still quiet of the early morgen, the fire in the woodstove crackling behind her, steam rising from the teakettle on the hot stove. She filled the turkey's cavity with bread stuffing, since Irene had prepared her corn-bread version in a disposable foil pan. Smart. It'd make for easier cleanup.

Daed came into the kitchen, rubbing his eyes and stretching. "Gut morgen." He poured himself a cup of koffee and settled in a chair near the stove. A break from his usual routine of going straight out to the barn and starting the chores.

"Happy Thanksgiving, Daed." Susanna slid the turkey into the hot oven, then reached for the peeler to start on a mound of potatoes. She didn't hear anyone else stirring.

"What time is everyone arriving today?" Daed stirred a spoonful of sugar into his koffee. Another change, thanks to Irene, from his usual "unpolluted" way of drinking it. He grimaced but drank half the mug's contents in one gulp, anyway.

"Sometime before we eat. Aenti Sarah was going to prepare her contributions at home and transport them over here ready to eat. I brought the schnitz pies from Benaiah's mammi when I came home last nacht."

"Did Ben talk to you?"

Susanna jumped and turned to glance at Daed. "About what?" And when would that have happened? Daed had still been in the kitchen last nacht when she'd gone to bed before Benaiah's departure.

He frowned. "Anything."

"Other than the brief conversation you heard last nacht, I haven't talked to him since he took me to his haus yesterday afternoon. And then he asked about the gifts from my secret admirer."

"Asked. About the gifts," Daed repeated. "As if he doesn't know anything about them?"

"I wanted them to be from him, but they aren't." Susanna's lips flattened. If Benaiah was going to treat her like he did yesterday, making her walk home in the cold and avoiding eye contact, maybe she should reconsider her wish.

"Hmm." Daed set the mug, still half full, on the stove and stood up. "Best get started on the chores."

"Whoever it is had better get his courage worked up and approach me quickly, or he'll miss his chance."

"Jah. You'll move to Iowa as soon as Irene and I marry." Daed slid his feet into his boots.

"Actually, I was thinking of maybe getting a job in town. I heard the restaurant is hiring. And the quilt shop. And the cheese factory."

"And you'd live where?" Daed shrugged into his coat.

"Here?" At least then something in her life would stay the same.

"Haus is going up for sale, remember? I expect it'll sell fast."

A fresh round of tears burned her eyes. "Daed…."

But with those not-so-cheery words, Daed walked out the door and shut it behind him.

Didn't he care?

The next thing she heard was the faint sound of whistling.

Guess not.

Either that or he didn't think she was serious. She'd need to prove him wrong. Monday, she'd head to town and find a job. She'd look in *The Budget* or the local newspaper for a room to rent. Or maybe she could stay at Benaiah's haus in exchange for helping Mammi Wren with kitchen things and haus-work.

The door opened, and her cousin Chloe dashed inside, carrying a wicker basket. "Mamm said I could kum over early to see if you need any help." She set the basket on the table, unloaded a green plastic dish, and jammed it into the already crowded refrigerator. Then she took a folded sheet of paper from the basket. "Did you see this? Mamm says it's sinful, but I'm thinking it's worth a try." She shook the paper open and held it out to Susanna. "It's a love potion. I'm going to use it on get Paul Hostettler. My sister Amanda has her eye on someone, too, so she plans to try it out."

Susanna glanced at the recipe. "Looks like the basic ingredients for gingerbread." As if she hadn't almost memorized the same list the nacht before.

"Jah, that's what I thought. And what an ingenious way of getting a man to take it without his knowing what it really is. I'm going to make a batch of gingerbread men."

"Ach, gut idea. Except…wouldn't it be more fun to make a gingerbread haus?" Susanna set down the peeler beside the stack of potato skins. "We could each make one, and decorate them with candy canes, gumdrops, chocolate kisses…maybe a marshmallow snowman out in front."

"We should!" Chloe squealed.

From up above came a thump. Irene—or someone else—was awake.

"Oops." Chloe refolded the paper and stuffed it back inside the basket.

Susanna returned to the potatoes. She'd give her gingerbread haus to Benaiah's family. And pray he would eat some of it.

BENAIAH SAT AT the dining-room table and opened the folder from Peter. He'd glanced at it earlier but didn't hold out much hope that the numbers had changed any. Still, he wanted a second opinion.

Daadi leaned closer. "How much is he asking for it?"

"He just told me to pray and said he'd give me a gut price. Although I think it might depend on whether I marry Susanna." Benaiah slid the folder toward Daadi. "Here's all the information." He waited for the verbal rejection that was sure to follow.

Mammi poured three cups of English Breakfast tea and delivered them to the table, along with a platter of pastries, before sitting next to Daadi. "Have a cranberry orange scone while you look it over. Susanna made these when she was here yesterday. She also made the butter."

Benaiah glanced at the white substance in the butter dish. Nein yellow food coloring, as opposed to the store-bought kind. Even though his stomach rumbled, he didn't reach for a pastry. The members of their district observed a fast all Thanksgiving morgen, though the young kinner and the elderly with health concerns were allowed to eat breakfast. As a diabetic, Daadi needed to maintain a consistent meal schedule.

"He's selling the haus, too?" Daadi lifted a page.

"Jah, but I wasn't thinking about that. Just the business. And that, not even seriously. It scares me to think of having to go into debt to keep my job. But I need the job to keep a roof over our heads."

Mammi tsked with her tongue. "You have so much responsibility for a man your age. Things you shouldn't have to worry about."

Benaiah shrugged. "I don't mind." *Much.* Though it would be nice to be able to walk confidently into marriage without having to worry about how he would support a wife and eventual kinner, not to mention his siblings and aging großeltern. He sighed.

Daadi frowned and put the paper down.

"Jah, that's what I thought." Benaiah reached for the folder. "I'll find something else to do to earn enough to support us. Maybe the lumberyard will have need of a—"

"Do you know where your name came from?" Daadi slid the folder out of reach.

"The Bible." Most likely. Seemed 90 percent of Amish people had biblical names. Benaiah resisted the urge to roll his eyes.

"Right. Tell me the story."

Benaiah sighed. Daadi would go there. "King David's bodyguard."

"Jah. And how'd he get to that position?" Daadi stood and walked into the other room. A few seconds later, he returned with his Bible and flipped through some pages as he sat once more. "Second Samuel twenty-three, verse twenty, says, '*And Benaiah the son of Jehoiada, the son of a valiant man, of Kabzeel, who had done many acts, he slew two lionlike men of Moab: he went down also and slew a lion in the midst of a pit in time of snow.*' Loosely translated, that means he killed two very strong Moab warriors—and then he went down into a pit on a snowy day and faced off with a lion. And won."

Mammi nodded. "He was a very brave man."

"If he was brave enough to go into a dark pit with a lion with nein guarantee of survival, can't you be brave enough to take the chance Peter is offering you? A chance to buy the business?" Daadi patted the folder.

"I promised him I'd pray about it." Benaiah glanced at the clock. They needed to do the daily chores, then get ready to head over to the Kings' for Thanksgiving dinner. Despite Mammi's weakness, she'd still want to sit in the kitchen and visit with the other ladies while they cooked. "And I will. But right now, I don't feel a sense of peace about it. And Peter's haus and land will have to go to someone else. I know we can't afford them." Not when he had a hard enough time paying the rent on the haus where they lived, which wasn't as nice as Peter's.

It would make sense for the business owner to also possess the land where the building was located. It'd be nice if he could buy the whole package. But the price would be too high. Plus, he had nothing to offer as collateral for a loan.

"You know nothing." Daadi's words were softened by a sympathetic look. "Pray, jah, and then live up to your name, Gross-sohn." He pushed to his feet. "I'll go milk the cows."

Pray, and then live up to your name.

Benaiah followed Daadi to the door. Slid his stockinged feet into his boots and then tied the laces tight. "Mammi, I'll collect the eggs, if there are any, and feed the chickens. Tell Ellie to stay inside where it's warm."

Pray, and then live up to your name.

Benaiah trudged across the drive to the small barn. The hens roosted on one side of the dilapidated structure. The landlord didn't seem to care whether the building stood or fell, but he had forbidden Benaiah and Daadi from attempting any repairs. Something about insurance and liability. So, they repeatedly reported the problem to the landlord, and nothing got fixed. More evidence that if he could barely afford the rent on this dump, there was nein way he could manage to buy a well-maintained, larger place like Peter King's.

Pray, and live up to your name.

What would his biblical namesake have done? Personally, Benaiah would rather take on a lion in a snowy pit, even with an uncertain outcome, than face the possibility of risking his family's precarious financial health and ultimately leaving them homeless.

And Peter thought he should take Susanna home as his bride. He snorted. As much as he wished he could, he loved her too much to subject her to his reality.

He grasped the flimsy wooden door of the barn and shoved it open. *Lord, help me to know what Your will is. And give me the courage to follow through on it.*

SUSANNA LOOKED UP as the door opened and Mammi Wren shuffled inside, supporting herself with a wooden cane. She was followed by Benaiah's sisters: Lizzie, Becca, Ellie, Jackie, and Molly. Aenti Sarah bustled in a moment later with another basket. "I decided to cook everything here on the stovetop, since it all would've been cold by the time we transported it. Elizabeth will bring the extra turkey over when it's finished roasting."

Susanna hurried to help get Mammi Wren settled in a chair at the table. Then she directed the girls to hang their coats on the hooks by the door, and to leave their empty baskets on her cot in the mudroom, before she began assigning them tasks to do.

After grabbing a pot holder, Susanna slid the big kettle of potatoes to the side to make space for Aenti Sarah's dishes on top of the woodstove. Then she checked the fire and added another log. Gut thing it was cold enough to use both the woodstove and the gas stove, since both were needed.

"Can I get you something to drink, Mammi Wren?" Susanna asked.

"A glass of water would be nice, danki."

Irene came into the room and sat down next to her. "I'm Peter's bride-to-be, Irene. So, Peter says you've been sick?"

"Nice to meet you. Jah, I caught the flu, and it isn't leaving as quickly as I'd like. Plus, my hip has been giving me a lot of pain. But that's what I get for growing older and developing arthritis. I really can't complain. Much." She chuckled. "Peter must be very happy to have reconnected with you after all these years."

Reconnected? What? Susanna stared at Irene.

"We never truly forget our first love." Irene looked to Susanna. "Could you get me a glass of water, too, Susanna Rose? I've been on my feet all morgen. I could use a break."

That was untrue. Irene hadn't been in the kitchen at all that morgen—until just now.

"Jah." Susanna turned away and stumbled to a stop. Outside in the yard, her cousin Amanda stood next to Benaiah, her hand on his arm. She gazed up at him with a flirtatious smile.

He grinned back at her.

Susanna's heart shattered.

Mammi Wren had said he'd been buying gifts and sneaking out at nacht. But Susanna had never dreamed it was her cousin who'd been on the receiving end of his affections.

Chloe had told her that a certain man had caught Amanda's attention. Maybe he wasn't in love with her. Yet.

Susanna had to make her gingerbread haus soon. And a dozen gingerbread cookies for gut measure.

CHAPTER 8

*B*enaiah stepped away from Amanda, dislodging her hand from its possessive grip on his arm, and shifted enough so his horse's head bobbed between them. Hopefully, Susanna hadn't been watching from the kitchen window. He didn't want to cause her any more pain than he already had by allowing her to think he might be interested in her cousin.

"Heard they're having blizzards out west," he said, hoping the mundane subject matter would soon bore Amanda. "When I caught a ride into town last week, I heard a weatherman announce we'd have a foot of snow here by week's end. Might need to install sled runners on my buggy to get around."

Amanda giggled. "Maybe you could kum to a singing and take me home in your makeshift sled. That'd be so romantic."

Romantic? He hadn't been going for romantic. Just looking for a safe topic of conversation. Besides, he hadn't been to a singing since breaking up with Susanna. He wasn't looking for a frau and didn't want to see his one true love getting rides from others. Not that he'd spared himself from witnessing any of them. Somehow, he'd either seen or heard about all the rides Susanna had gotten—and from whom. And his heart had broken a bit more each time.

He wasn't in any position to marry, and he wouldn't want to rob her of happiness. The one gut thing about Peter's plans to remarry was that he'd take Susie with him, meaning Benaiah wouldn't be in the front row to watch her fall in love with another man.

But that didn't solve his current problem of what to do with the still-giggling Amanda. He looked around, trying to think of something to say. Nothing came to mind. He just wanted to join the other men in the barn, thereby minimizing the risk of Susie seeing him talking to Amanda.

"I'm going to put my horse out to pasture." He unhitched Peppermint Twist.

"Your horse looks so big and strong. And such a unique name! How did you kum up with it? You must be creative," Amanda cooed, edging around the horse's snout and running her hand from Benaiah's shoulder to his elbow.

Benaiah almost snorted. As if he'd named the horse. "He's a retired racehorse. I liked his papered name and chose to keep it." Well, part of it, at least. Every racehorse had too many names, and he didn't want to have to keep track of them all.

She giggled again, as if he'd said something brilliant.

He managed what was probably a sick-looking smile, then led his horse off to the pasture while Amanda went inside to join the rest of the women fixing Thanksgiving dinner. *Danki, Gott, for hearing my silent prayer.* He joined the men in the barn who were shooting the breeze and watching the male youngies wrestle while waiting to hear the dinner bell ring.

Amanda's daed—Susie's onkel Nehemiah—gave Benaiah's arm a playful shove. "Got your eye on my girl, ain't so?" he said with a wink.

Benaiah swallowed the bile that rose in his throat. He didn't want the other men drawing incorrect conclusions from a girl's flirtatious advances, but he didn't know how to set Nehemiah straight without hurting his feelings.

When his gaze landed on Peter, the man was scowling at him, as if he believed Benaiah had deliberately encouraged Amanda in order to hurt Susie's feelings. Or was Peter thinking Benaiah could have put a stop to her flirting and escaped earlier if he'd really wanted to? That if he hadn't been so concerned with being nice, he would have told her if he ever took someone home from singing again, it wouldn't be her?

This whole breakup with Susanna had opened a mess he hadn't anticipated. Back then, all he'd wanted to do was to....

He sighed, looking around for something to talk about, something to get his focus off himself. He glanced out the open barn doors at the gray sky. At the chilly wind tearing away the stubborn leaves that hadn't yet released their tenacious grip on the tree branches.

Movement across the dirt driveway caught his attention. Susanna—the one he really wanted—carrying a dishpan out to dump.

And even though he saw her almost every day, the first sight of her in the *morgen* always made him catch his breath and look his fill until she disappeared from view.

She was beautiful, inside and out. Slim and graceful. Caring and gentle.

Someone he wanted to look at every *morgen* for the rest of his life.

Someone he still loved.

And always would.

Susanna dumped the dishwater in the flower bed. The mums she'd planted there earlier that autumn, as a replacement for the flowers from the anonymous gift that had kindled her hopes, only to leave her hopelessly alone, had long ago gone to seed. Hopefully, she'd end up with enough mums to sell some at one of her friends' roadside stands or at the farmer's market in town. If—and that was a big *if*—she still lived here when they bloomed again next fall.

It didn't seem likely.

Ach, Benaiah. Why? What did I do wrong? Why don't you love me anymore?

She needed to stop mooning over him and focus on moving on. She'd moped enough, openly wearing her torn, bruised, and battered heart on her sleeve. According to Gizelle Miller, men responded better to a heartbroken woman if she acted like she couldn't care less and started flirting with and dating other men. Gizelle should know. She flirted with most of the men in their district and also in the nearby communities.

Then again, it must not work as well as Gizelle claimed, because she was still trying. And she'd earned the reputation of being desperate.

A reputation Susanna didn't care to build for herself.

But she needed to move on, without having to move to Iowa to do so. If Daed didn't care about her enough to ask for her input before proposing marriage to a woman with eight kinner—more than eight, since Irene had mentioned older married kinner and grosskinner....

That was unfair though. Daed would remind her that he never asked her opinion about marrying Mamm and she'd never asked his opinion about Benaiah. He'd be right. But that aside, she loved Mamm. And Daed loved Benaiah.

Susanna didn't love Irene.

She didn't even like her. Much.

"As ye would that men should do to you, do ye also to them likewise."
Do unto others as you would have them do unto you.

The Golden Rule. Where had *that* kum from? Such a simple verse, often seen on wall prints and cross-stitch samplers. But had she really put it into practice?

"How do I want Irene to treat me?" she whispered to herself. "How have I been treating Irene?" It was something to consider and pray about.

She'd done what Irene wanted, but grudgingly. And probably with a show of attitude.

She shook the few remaining water drops from the dishpan and turned away from the seeding mums. Her gaze traveled across the yard and focused on the group of men standing in the open doorway of the barn. She caught Benaiah's intense stare.

He didn't look away. Instead, he held her gaze for a long, heart-pausing moment, a muscle jumping in his jaw. Was he judging her for the thoughts she'd shared with him yesterday? Her actions? Because he'd seen the tenuous control she kept on her temper?

Suddenly realizing she'd been holding her breath, she forced herself to inhale deeply, then lifted her chin and turned away. Ignoring him.

Today would begin her exercising her resolve to get over him.

BENAIAH'S SHOULDERS SLUMPED as Susie disappeared inside the haus. He wished she would've found some excuse to run over and greet him, as she'd done last Thanksgiving.

Last year, she'd kum out and said hallo to both Daed and Daadi, even though Peter had frowned at her for invading the men's realm on Thanksgiving Day. She hadn't stayed long. Just long enough to grasp Benaiah's fingers and flash him her beautiful smile. He'd winked at her and whispered, "Take a walk with me later."

And she had. A nacht not to be forgotten. He had gotten down on bended knee in the middle of the dirt road and asked her to marry him. She'd cried and whispered, "Yes."

They'd planned to be married by now. Maybe even expecting their first boppli. His heart cracked. She'd be sure to remember. And seeing him here in the barn this day must have reminded her of the same special moment. Of the lost opportunities. Nein wonder she turned away from him.

How could he let this special day go by without remembering—and helping her mourn the loss? He grimaced. Then again, how could he get a gift to her? With Irene and her eight kinner staying at the haus, there'd be nein easy way of sneaking a gift inside.

But Irene was leaving Friday—tomorrow—and he thought he remembered Peter saying he was going, too, and taking Susanna along to see their future home. They were to stay there over-nacht. Which meant the haus would be empty.

It would be the perfect time to leave a gift commemorating this special day. And Benaiah had already crafted the perfect thing. A glass rose, red for love. It wasn't the kind to display in a vase, but rather to lay in a place of honor, such as on a windowsill, a fireplace mantel, or a specially designed curio shelf.

He had another bottle of one of those special frappuccino koffees she liked so much. And one of his sisters had baked a batch of heart-shaped sugar cookies. Jah, a gift in honor of this significant day was in order, even if it would give away his identity.

And even though it wouldn't change a thing between them.

CHAPTER 9

Susanna stepped out of the shower and relished the silence. Something she'd never noticed before but now enjoyed, even if it made her feel a bit lonely. She liked being around people when they were the right kind of people, such as Benaiah and his family. Irene and her eight kinner had *finally* left for home just after lunch, and Daed had gone with them, having reluctantly accepted Susanna's decision not to join them in Iowa for the weekend. But she'd made the decision for Irene's sake. And maybe more for her own.

Susanna had spent the afternoon cleaning: stowing the sleeping bag, washing the sheets, and reclaiming her own bedroom. Also returning her kitchen to the way Grossmammi had arranged it. She'd also brought the gifts from her secret admirer to the haus again, and hung mistletoe in various places. While she'd worked, she'd prayed about her attitude, asked Gott for the grace to accept the changes that were ahead, and pleaded that He would make a way for her and Irene to form a friendship. For Daed's sake.

Never again would she take the quiet for granted.

After drying off, Susanna pulled on a pair of short cotton shorts and a tank top that Daed would have made a fit about. But he wasn't home. Besides, they were more comfortable for sleeping than long nacht-gowns that tangled around the knees and made it hard to move. Susanna tied her robe over her outfit and carried the flashlight lantern down to the kitchen.

She wasn't sleepy yet, so maybe she could at least mix up the gingerbread dough to start on her candy-covered haus tomorrow. Daed didn't mind when she stayed up late, as long as she did all her chores the next day. And he wasn't there to object, even if he did mind.

Once Susanna was finished mixing the dough, she scraped the wooden spoon clean with her finger, then stuck the dollop of sweet, spicy goodness into her mouth. *Yum.*

The back door opened. Closed.

Daed? Had he decided not to travel to Iowa, after all? Or was it an intruder? Fear snaked through her.

Susanna picked up her lantern and spun around, holding the wooden spoon as a weapon.

Benaiah? What was he doing here?

The light of her lantern reflected off something shiny before he slipped whatever it was behind his back.

Relief flooded through her, replacing the fear, and she had to force herself not to launch herself at him with a grateful hug that he wasn't a scary intruder. She balanced the wooden spoon along the edge of the mixing bowl and returned the lantern to the middle of the table.

"Susanna." Her name came across his lips as a gasp. "I thought you were…I thought…." His voice caught and broke as his eyes scanned her damp hair, unbound and uncovered, then drifted lower. His eyebrows rose, and his cheeks turned red, as his gaze rested on her robe that seemed to be covering nothing. Susanna checked to make sure nein part of her verboden Englisch clothes peeked through, just as she'd done the first few times she'd dared to follow her friend's suggestion for ditching the hated nacht-gown. Not that Daed had ever seen her wandering around in her robe after he went to bed. He went deaf when he was asleep, it seemed. Nothing woke him. Not even storms.

"I…um…I…." Benaiah's gaze rose to a spot somewhere above her head. A muscle jumped in his cheek.

She looked upward, following his gaze.

Right above her head dangled the sprig of mistletoe she'd hung as soon as the driver's van had left to transport Daed, Irene, and her eight kinner home to Iowa.

Convenient. She could've laughed. She hadn't intended to stand beneath it. Should she tell Benaiah that he didn't need to honor the time-worn custom of stealing a kiss under the mistletoe, all things considered? She was hesitant to look at him again, because his facial expression would either corroborate or undermine the legitimacy of the excuse he'd given when breaking up with her: "It's not you, it's me."

When her vision fell on him again, his gaze lowered to her lips, his blue eyes darkened, and, still hiding one hand behind his back, he approached her. Silently. His eyes rose to hers and captured them as he leaned in and, without otherwise touching her, brushed her lips with his.

Lights flashed like fireworks in July. She trembled, and couldn't keep from surging toward him, meeting his reluctant kiss halfway. Her eyes drifted shut as she wrapped her arms around his neck and held him tight. It'd been too long.

Something thumped on the tabletop beside her. Then she felt one of his arms wrap around her waist and tug her closer, while the other hand, shaking, rose to tousle her damp hair. And without invitation—or maybe the invitation was tacit—he took control of her parted lips, deepening the kiss. He tasted of peppermint, coffee, and desperation. Of a man too long denied the object of his desire.

A violent shiver worked through her. She pressed herself nearer, a groan escaping her lips.

He moaned in response, starting a fire deep within her. His hand slid down the length of her hair, came to rest at the small of her back, then gripped the belt secured at her waist, pulling her tighter against him.

Ach, jah…heaven….

His kiss hardened, becoming more demanding. More…more…. His hand wandered upward from her waist. Then, with a gasp, he released her.

Her eyes flew open, and she reached for him, even as he stumbled backward. This time, there was an unmistakable expression of horror—the look she'd expected to see earlier. "I'm sorry, Suz. So sorry. I never meant to do that. Wrong of me. Won't happen again."

Then he turned and ran out the door, letting it slam behind him.

Susanna grabbed the nearest chair and, as her knees gave out, collapsed into it. Benaiah had never before kissed her with such unrestrained passion. Such unchecked desire. Previously, his kisses had been gentle. Teasing. Wunderbaar, to be sure, but lacking the fire and unbridled force of this one.

"Wow." It was all she could manage to say, considering the thimbleful of air she'd pulled in. She released the tiny inhalation with a breathy sigh.

"Won't happen again"? It *had* to. Simply. Had. To.

She glanced at the cookie dough sitting uncovered in the mixing bowl beside her.

If gingerbread worked like that, it was potent stuff. She'd serve it at her wedding. During her honeymoon. Every day for the rest of her life. "Wow."

Outside, a horse snorted. Then, all was quiet. Susanna jumped to her feet, intent on running outside to catch him. He couldn't leave like this. A man wouldn't kiss a girl like that if she meant nothing to him, would he? Surely not.

But by the time she made it out to the front porch, the taillights of his buggy showed that he was turning onto the road.

She went back inside. And there on the table, behind where she'd stood, sat a sparkly silver gift bag, the words "Especially for You" printed across the front, tufts of glittery white tissue paper peeking out the top.

Mammi Wren's words replayed in her mind. *"He's definitely courting someone. Buying gifts and sneaking out late at nacht....I assumed it was you."*

A smile formed. Grew.

It *was* her.

Benaiah was her secret admirer.

THAT HADN'T GONE as Benaiah had planned. Far from it. He hated that he'd given himself away in such a manner. In addition to the gifts, he'd given her a kiss that testified of his affections. He still trembled with the strength of his desire, wishing he'd been free to dare to do more. If only he could love her as an ehemann loves his frau. If only he was free to claim her. But he wasn't.

Why had Peter told him he was taking Susanna to Iowa with him? Benaiah had clearly overheard the man asking his young nephew to kum over to feed the livestock and check things over while they were away, adding that he and Susie would return Sunday nacht.

His secret was out now. She'd caught him. And he'd been lured in by the mistletoe she'd hung throughout the haus and barn—her annual tradition, one he'd enjoyed and even taken advantage of last December.

Even though he'd intended the obligatory kiss to be a peck, his long-denied passion had taken control, and....

He had yet to stop trembling. Of course, the cold that permeated the inside of the buggy might be partly to blame for that.

Home once more, Benaiah parked the rig in the main room of the barn, stabled his horse, and headed toward the dark haus, shoulders hunched against the chilling wind. Snow was supposed to start falling sometime in the early hours of the morgen.

He kicked off his shoes just inside the door and hung up his coat and hat before flipping his penlight on. When he turned, he saw Daadi seated at the table in the darkness, head bowed, soft snores crossing his lips. His hand rested on his open Bible. The candle had burned out.

Benaiah put his hand on Daadi's shoulder and gently shook it.

Daadi's head snapped up, and he blinked for a moment. "You're home." His voice was groggy. He cleared his throat. "We need to talk."

"Maybe it'd better be in the morgen. You're tired."

Daadi shook his head. "Nein. Your sisters are asleep. We'll talk now. Light the candle, please?"

Benaiah nodded, but he retrieved the lantern from the counter, lit that instead, and set it in the center of the table. Then he sat across from Daadi. "What do we need to talk about?"

Daadi lifted the Bible enough to pull out an envelope from underneath it. He slid it toward Benaiah.

Benaiah glanced at the return address preprinted on the envelope. "It's a bank statement." And it was addressed to Daadi. Why would he share that information?

Daadi nodded. "Open it."

Benaiah lifted the flap and slid out a slip of paper. He skimmed over it, then did a double-take at the amount. Frowned. "What's this?"

"Almost enough to pay for the glassblowing business. Maybe Peter might be willing to offer a discount for cash, if you were to make an offer."

Benaiah shook his head. "I can't take your money." He tucked the paper back inside the envelope.

"Nonsense." Daadi waved the envelope away when Benaiah pushed it toward him. "You've been supporting us for a year now, without taking a dime from us. Your mammi and I think it's time we did our part. Besides, looking over the financial report Peter included, he keeps the major portion of the money earned—as he should, since it's his business—and pays you only a portion. When he came over the other nacht, he mentioned that you do the majority of the work, while he mostly handles the financial side of things. What if you ran the business alone and maybe hired someone to do the accounting? I could take care of the day-to-day stuff, but we might require the help of a professional for the quarterly and annual taxes."

Benaiah rubbed his jaw, feeling the prickly five o'clock shadow against his palm. It seemed past the time of nacht for making big decisions, but he didn't want to repeat his refusal to take Daadi's money. Not when it was an answer to prayer.

Daadi fingered the edge of his Bible. "Have you prayed about it, Sohn?"

Not as much as he probably should have. He'd been mostly watching Susie. Daydreaming and remembering. And then, there came the kiss that had robbed him of all rational thought on the ride home. "I will. But the bank is closed until Monday, so we have time."

Daadi pushed to his feet and walked over to the small table by the door. He picked up a letter. "Hate to burden you with more things to pray about, but you got this from the landlord the other day. Probably raising the rent again."

Benaiah groaned. Just what they needed, with all the other things battling for attention right now. Though he might not find himself unemployed if Peter agreed to sell him the business for cash, with a discount. But better to get the bad news over with instead of setting it aside for now, as he'd done when Mammi had handed him the same letter a couple of days ago. He carefully loosened the flap, took out the trifold letter, flattened it out, and scanned it.

The glimmer of hope was snuffed out in a Scrooge-like bah-humbug-on-your-Christmas announcement.

"Worse. He's given us till the end of the year to find someplace else to live. He's reclaiming his property."

SUSANNA RUBBED HER eyes and peered out the kitchen window, which was wet with condensation. About eight inches of snow had fallen over-nacht, and it was falling even now, heavily. Despite the blanket of white, a buggy was parked in front of the glass shop, an Englisch four-wheel-drive vehicle stationed behind it. Gaslights illuminated the interior of the shop.

She hadn't taken the time to peek outside when she'd first kum into the kitchen to start a batch of cinnamon rolls. The sweets were in the oven now, filling the haus with a tantalizing aroma. The rolls she'd made before Thanksgiving had been inhaled by Irene and her kinner. Daed and Benaiah had eaten only one each, and Susanna had gotten not so much as a pinch. Even though nobody else would be home, Daed had asked her to make another batch while he was in Iowa, so he could have some when he returned home.

She glanced at the shop once more. There was definite movement inside. Her cousin Roger was coming over to do the chores, so she had nein need to go outside to check. Except....

Wait. Benaiah must be in there—but on a Saturday? Daed worked Saturdays only when they had an order that needed to be completed immediately. Of course, the vehicle might belong to a member of the wedding party here to pick up those lilies Daed and Benaiah had worked so hard on.

Maybe Benaiah would kum in for breakfast after the Englischers left.

Not "maybe." He would. He certainly couldn't have meant what he'd said when he'd apologized last nacht. And surely, that kiss had signaled an imminent end to their breakup. Soon she'd be Benaiah's girl once again.

But perhaps the kiss didn't mean they would get back together again, and was merely a side effect of smelling the love potion-gingerbread mixture. She'd roll out the dough later today, bake it, and then assemble it as soon as she was able to get to the store to buy an assortment of candy.

Susanna filled the teakettle with water, then put it on the woodstove to heat. Into another kettle, she measured water, oats, and salt. Given today's weather, oatmeal seemed appropriate. And maybe turkey noodle soup for lunch, if Benaiah stayed around till then. They had enough leftovers from Thanksgiving to make a couple of meals out of them.

She sliced up two bananas and chopped some walnuts to add to the oatmeal. When the buzzer rang, she slid her hands into the oven mitts and removed the tray of steaming pastries.

While the rolls cooled a little, she mixed up some cream cheese icing, then spread the pastries with the yummy goodness, which trickled down the sides as it melted a bit. With a glance out the window to make sure nobody would catch her being naughty, she pinched off a piece of one of the iced rolls and popped it in her mouth. *Heavenly.*

As the sugary sweetness worked its way into her system, she twirled around the kitchen, kicked up her heels like a spring filly, and belted out a song they'd done at the last singing she'd attended. It wasn't from the Ausbund, and a chaperone had called it a "golden oldie"—whatever that meant. Susanna didn't know the title, but the lyrics had something to do with a mockingbird hill. And she adored the chorus.

"Tra la la, tweedle dee dee dee...." Singing at full volume, she executed an Olympics-worthy move, twirling as she jumped into the air. When she came down, her right foot hit the floor wrong, causing her ankle to twist painfully. She reached out for something, anything, to stop her fall. What she grabbed was the table knife she'd used to frost the cinnamon rolls, which did nothing to help her situation, and she crash-landed on her right hip. The sticky knife jumped out of her hand and skittered across the floor, sliding under the hot woodstove. Her slippers flew off in the opposite direction.

She lay there a moment, assessing her injuries. Just then, a blast of frigid air filled the room.

She rolled over and glanced toward the door. It stood open. Benaiah hovered in the entryway, his eyes bulging, his mouth gaping, and his arms extended, as if he somehow hoped to catch her after the fact, preventing the ungraceful and undignified landing that had already occurred.

The heat of embarrassment burned its way up her neck and singed her cheeks. Tears stung her eyes.

She buried her face in her hands.

And laughed.

CHAPTER 10

*B*enaiah would never understand women, that much was certain.

He cautiously stepped inside, shut the door, crossed the room in three long strides, then knelt beside the laughing-so-hard-she-cried Susanna.

"Are you hurt?" He wanted to scold her for her foolishness, dancing about the kitchen with a knife in hand. What had kum over her? She could've been rendered unconscious, or worse.

She giggled. "I'm fine." But as she moved to a sitting position, she winced.

"What? Where does it hurt?" Benaiah couldn't stop himself from reaching toward her exposed legs and wrapping his fingers around her right ankle. Her skin felt soft and silky under his rough, callused hand. He slid his fingertips over the ankle under the guise of checking for injuries, but mainly enjoying the opportunity to touch a place on her body that was normally off-limits.

If they were together, and if it had been her hand she'd injured, he'd "kiss it better," the way Mammi did with his young sisters.

She sucked in a breath, her laughter fading, and stared at him with parted lips. A pink color rose to her cheeks.

He shivered with growing desire, nein doubt a remnant of last nacht's supercharged moments. He glanced up to see if they were beneath another sprig of mistletoe. They weren't. Too bad.

"Kiss…it…better?" She paused between each word as the pink of her face brightened to red.

Was she asking? Or…ach. Nein. He couldn't have spoken that phrase out loud. Right?

He must've.

He looked down at her trim ankle, glad to see nein discoloration, and traced over the curve with his fingertip once more.

She retracted her leg from his grasp. "It's my hip."

Huh? He stared at her, the meaning of her words getting lost in the jumble of emotions in his head. Too many emotions to name. Too many feelings to unpack.

"I think it's bruised." She extended her hand to him.

He stared at it blankly for a moment, then curved his fingers around hers, taking extreme pleasure in holding her hand as he rose to his feet, gently pulling her up with him.

Susanna winced. "You can't kiss that."

He blinked. "Can't kiss…? Wait. What?"

"My hip."

"I wouldn't dream of it." Except that he already was. He pulled his hand away from hers. Sucked in a gulp of charged air. And backed away. "We need to talk."

"I'm so happy we're back together." She beamed at him, but there was a hint of pain underlying her expression—whether because of her injured hip or because they'd been apart for the past year, which had been equally painful for him, he didn't know. "Want some oatmeal? It's ready." She turned and reached for a bowl. Two bowls. And a plate. "Cinnamon rolls are, too. Sit. Eat. Then we'll make plans."

Plans? Huh? He had missed something, somewhere. He replayed the conversation in his mind. *Ach, nein.* She thought they…he and she…. Plans?

Benaiah tried to formulate a response, but his brain cells packed up and left for vacation when he tried not to think about the implications of those plans for him, personally.

Because, jah, he wanted to make those plans. All of them. The sooner, the better.

Even though he couldn't see them through.

"I loved the anonymous gifts. All of them. You were right—it was a unique idea. And I'm so glad it was you."

He backed up, unable to think of what to say with her so near.

And not wanting to wipe the smile from her oh-so-kissable lips.

Susanna placed a bowl of oatmeal, sprinkled with bananas and nuts, at Benaiah's place at the table. When she looked at him, she must have seen something in his expression that communicated the words he couldn't speak, because her smile died. A frown appeared in its place. Deepened. Her sweet lips quivered.

A twinge of regret worked through him. He hadn't meant to break her heart again. Or to give her renewed hope, only to take it abruptly away.

"We aren't back together, are we." It wasn't a question. Her tone was heavy with resignation. "That kiss meant nothing."

Actually, it meant the opposite of nothing. It meant everything.

"You don't love me anymore?" The quiver in her lips increased to a distinct quaking.

He didn't love her any less. That was for sure.

Susanna snagged the bowl of oatmeal from the table and jerked it away. The contents sloshed over the rim and splashed her hand. She yelped and dropped the bowl, which landed at her bare feet, not shattering the bowl but dumping the rest of the steaming cereal on her toes.

She danced out of the mixture with an intriguing wiggle of her hips and legs. "Now look what you've done. I'm so finished with you. Go. Just…go."

And without waiting for him to obey, she hobbled hastily from the room.

His heart was torn in three different directions. Should he clean up the mess, go to her, or leave? Do two of the three? Maybe all three?

Susanna shuffled down the hall to the bathroom. She shut the door, sat on the edge of the tub, and put her feet in, then turned the cold water on. As she let it run over her burned hand and feet, she wished the water could soothe her aching heart, too.

He didn't love her.

The kiss meant nothing.

They weren't back together.

Tears burned her eyes. Leaked out the corners. Ran down her cheeks.

The day had gone from gut to bad to awful. She wouldn't think about the possibility of things going from awful to worse, because they could.

Probably would.

Maybe a bubble bath would prevent that. It would at least help to soothe her legs. It wouldn't make everything all right, but at least she'd feel better. She ran the hot water and poured a liberal heap of lavender bubble bath into the stream. Lavender equaled calm, ain't so? And the water, if warm rather than hot, should soothe her burned skin. And maybe, if she was lucky, it would wash away a little of her shame at having assumed Benaiah's kiss, added to his tender touch and care, meant he still loved her. Or maybe he did love her and just refused to make his feelings official or commit to a permanent relationship, so his attentions might make her seem like…not a gut girl.

She caught her breath in a sob. But that didn't stop the tears from cascading down her cheeks.

If only she had someone to wrap her in a hug, comfort her, and tell her everything would be all right.

As if.

Going to Iowa might be a gut thing, after all. Jah, she'd mourn her losses—her home, her friends, and her local family; but she'd be able to start over as the new girl, available for courting. Not the one discarded for unknown reasons and reduced to accepting mercy rides from buwe who were already spoken for.

She'd apologize to Daed when he came home, write a letter to Irene and tell her how much she'd enjoyed meeting her—Gott would forgive her for lying under the circumstances, right?—and start making preparations to move.

She took off her clothes, tossed them in a heap on the floor, then sank down into the tub, letting the bubbles cover her. She turned the water off.

Something clattered in another room, and then a door shut. It must've opened again, because a few minutes later, it shut again. Heavy footsteps thumped toward the bathroom door. Then came a knock.

"Suz? You in there?"

She didn't want to talk to him. Didn't want to acknowledge his question. Maybe if she didn't respond, he'd go away.

She slid farther down in the warm water.

"Susie?" Another knock. "Aw, kum on. I thought you went this way."

Silence stretched for another minute, and she waited for his footsteps to clomp away. He knew better than to wear his boots in the haus. She'd have that mess to clean up, too, in addition to the spilled oatmeal.

The ancient doorknob creaked as it turned. The door hinges squeaked.

Susanna sprang from the tub, reaching for her towel. She slipped on a wet spot and fell to the floor with a thud. Directly on her sore hip.

Whimpering, she grabbed the towel and covered herself as best as she could. When she turned, she looked up into Benaiah's red-cheeked face and wide-eyed stare.

Jah, she'd been right. This day could get worse.

It just did.

BENAIAH WIPED HIS hand over his face and aimed his gaze at the ceiling, trying to forget the brief glimpse of creamy skin he'd gotten. *Danki, Gott, there's nein mistletoe hanging in this bathroom.* With Susanna, he was never quite sure where he'd find it. "Are you…are you hurt?"

"Just my pride. And my hip. Again."

"You should have that checked out."

"Nein, it's fine. Just bruised. But if you wouldn't mind stepping out and shutting the door, I'd like to get dressed." She sounded resigned yet firm. As she had when telling him to go away.

"Right." He stumbled backward and shut the door, his face burning. *Mercy.* If Peter found out about this, Ben would find himself married to Susie by next Thursday.

Why'd he break up with her, again? The reason didn't surface.

Except that he'd kum into the haus that morgen to tell her his final farewell. To apologize for leaving the gifts and leading her on. For....

Well, for everything.

From behind the closed door came another groan. He started to reach for the knob again but stopped himself seconds before touching it.

"I'm right outside, Susie. If you need me."

A whimper. "I think I need my grossmammi's cane. It hurts to walk."

"Where is it?"

A sniffle. "I don't know. Daed gave most of her things to different people around the community. It initially went to the Mark Zook family, but they moved away. I'm not sure if the cane went with them or not."

"Are you dressed?" His voice was huskier than he would have liked.

"Almost, jah."

"Then I'll help you. I'll take you to my haus to recuperate so my sisters can help take care of you...after we visit the urgent care center." She could sleep in his bed, without him, of course. But the idea of her being tucked under his sheets, her head on his pillow.... Desire rose again. His belly clenched.

"Nein, I'm staying here. And I'm not going to the doctor."

She was a stubborn one. Benaiah pressed his lips together and nodded, even though the closed door kept her from seeing, then went outside. He pulled his cell phone from his pocket and called the driver.

"Benaiah Troyer here. Would you run by my haus and tell Mammi that Susanna King has fallen and needs help over here for a while?"

He would stay with her and take care of her, at least until evening.

Maybe being forced to play endless checker games would cure her stubbornness.

Or his.

CHAPTER 11

*S*usanna pinned her dress in place, then checked to make sure her hair was still secured before she put on her kapp. It was gut she hadn't taken her hair out of the bun and gotten it wet. Bad enough she hadn't answered Benaiah. She should've swallowed her pride and responded. Then he wouldn't have opened the door and walked in on her. Maybe—hopefully—he hadn't seen anything. She should've stayed beneath the bubbles in the tub instead of diving for a towel, but somehow she hadn't felt comfortable trusting water to conceal herself.

Lying naked on the floor with a towel draped over her was worse. She couldn't face him again. Ever.

She'd heard his boots clomp away ten or so minutes ago. They hadn't returned. A distant door had closed, and she hadn't heard it open again. So maybe he'd left. *Please, Gott.*

She would rest a bit and give the pain a chance to subside. It was gut Daed would be away all weekend. She could be lazy, if she wanted to, without him questioning her. She would eat some breakfast, as long as the boulder-sized lump in her stomach allowed it, and then get busy cleaning up the mess—both from the spilled cereal and from the baking.

Trying not to put too much weight on her sore hip, she limped down the hall to the kitchen and stopped, one hand gripping the door-jamb for support. The kitchen was spotless. The oatmeal had been cleaned up off the floor. The pot of oats still sat on the stove, steaming, waiting for her to dish out a bowlful for herself. Her stomach rumbled. Maybe she could eat.

Benaiah had cleaned the kitchen? Really? She hadn't imagined he'd ever do a woman's work. Daed never did.

A deeper understanding of Benaiah's willingness to set gender roles aside in order to care for someone caused fresh tears to burn her eyes. She'd lost so much in losing him. And her childish behavior of fleeing the scene, seeking comfort in a bubble bath, and refusing to answer when he came searching for her made him even less likely to pick her as his frau.

The door opened. Shut. Maybe it was her cousin Roger. Curious, she turned to find Benaiah shedding his shoes at the door. Her face flamed. But in spite of her resolve to avoid seeing him ever again because of her embarrassment, she couldn't look away.

He hung his coat and hat on a hook. His face pinkened, and he stared at his oft-darned multicolored yarn socks as if they were the most fascinating things he ever saw. "Your cousin Roger's here doing the chores. I'll stay for a while, in case you need me. Or I could take you to urgent care if you decide you need medical attention."

"You don't have to do that."

His shoulders twitched. He glanced up only as high as her chest. His face reddened, and he quickly looked down again. "Figured we could play checkers."

"Checkers." Really? They hadn't played checkers since their earliest days of courting. If one could call "courting" what they'd done when they were twelve.

"Jah. Checkers." He sighed, met her eyes, then abruptly looked away. "Listen."

Susanna frowned. That word never meant anything gut. It indicated that whatever would follow, she was sure not to like. Not one bit. She hobbled over to the table, one hand on her hip, and painfully lowered herself into a chair.

She'd take control of this conversation. Gizelle's advice replayed in her mind. *Never let him see your pain.*

Susanna inhaled deeply. Exhaled. "I understand that we're finished. Danki for cleaning up, but, as you can see, I can get around on my own." Never mind the pain. "I'll be *fine*. It's just a bruise." Maybe when he left, she would get the bottle of pain pills from the medicine cabinet, assuming she could bear the long walk to the bathroom. She should've grabbed the pills while she was in there before.

"I need you to know I meant every word in those cards I sent as your secret admirer," he said quietly. "Ich liebe dich. Always. I didn't want you to feel rejected just because I can't marry you."

"You didn't want me to feel rejected when you dumped me?" How else was she supposed to feel when he'd broken their engagement?

"I never meant to mislead you, or your daed, or anyone. But there is nein intent or promise anymore. As much as I wish there could be, there hasn't been since we broke up."

"But…but why, Benaiah?" She hated the catch in her voice. "You told me, 'It's not you, it's me.' That's not a reason."

He frowned, still maintaining his stocking-footed stance by the door, as if he might bolt outside and away from her again at any moment. Hopefully, he wouldn't bolt before she got some answers, especially since she was hurt and couldn't chase after him.

"At the time, it was the only reason I could give. My parents had just died. I didn't know how…."

She glanced at the silver gift bag still on the counter. At the glass rose she'd taken out and laid on the windowsill, where it would catch the sun—and her attention. Now, it only brought her more pain. She forced her attention back to him.

He shook his head. "I don't want you to feel bad for my family, but the truth is, we're struggling to make ends meet on my income alone. There's not always enough food to go around. That's why I ate so often with you and your daed." He hung his head.

She'd noticed that the cupboards and refrigerator were almost bare when she was there helping Mammi Wren the day before Thanksgiving. She'd assumed they just hadn't had time to go to the store since his mammi had gotten sick.

"If I can't buy your daed's business, I'll lose my job, and then we'll have nein income until I can find new employment. Besides, I have five sisters whom I will spend the next…I don't know, ten years?—maybe more, since Molly is only nine—raising and supporting. Plus, I have the care of my großeltern. I can't ask you to give up this"—he waved his arm around—"for my reality. You deserve so much better." Tears glistened in his eyes.

She hadn't realized he'd had it so rough. Or that he'd sacrificed so much, even his personal happiness, to avoid taking on more responsibility than he could handle. She wondered how many meals and personal conveniences he'd given up in order to purchase the anonymous gifts for her. But why did that have to be a barrier to a relationship between them? "What if I still wanted to be with you?" she blurted out. "I…I could find work and help earn money…maybe not a lot, but at least enough to buy groceries."

He snorted. "Danki, but it isn't that simple. I love my großeltern and my sisters, and I don't mind taking care of them, but you would— trust me. Our circumstances are even worse than I described, and ich liebe dich too much to make you suffer." He inhaled deeply, then exhaled slowly. "And that's why I needed to let you go. I just couldn't bring myself to tell you that until now." His voice broke as he added, "Another man will be blessed to have you as his frau."

"What if 'another man's' reality is even worse than yours? What if he ends up being abusive? Or unwilling to work to support a family?"

Benaiah grimaced. "I don't want that for you, either, so choose wisely."

"I don't want any man but you." She would wait as long as necessary. She'd stay in the area and work a job to support his family anonymously, if need be.

"Suz, that last nacht we were together, cuddling on the porch swing, you said you wanted to be *alone* with me. If we married, we'd still have ten or more years before we could be truly alone. And if we have kinner, it'll be even later."

Susanna blinked. Was he really so dense? "That's *not* what I meant."

But she couldn't explain what she had meant, because that would cross the lines of propriety. As if they hadn't crossed the lines already this weekend with their heated kisses, his caresses of her ankle, and the view he'd gotten upon barging into the bathroom seconds after she'd fallen, sprawled, on the floor.

And she didn't dare to ask what he'd seen.

Not knowing how to respond to his comment, she shrugged and pushed herself slowly, painfully, to her feet.

"What do you need? I'll get it." He bounded across the floor.

"I thought I'd try to eat some breakfast." She took a wobbly step. "But I'll get it. My hip will just get stiff if I sit around."

"I don't think it will, if it's only a day or two. Let me serve you, süße."

Susanna smiled at the endearment. It revealed how he really felt, and it would make it easier for her to feign helplessness for a few days, if only to have some time to pray and think about how to convince him that they could be together. She took the hand he held out to her, and let him help her back to the chair. She would eat her breakfast, play checkers, do whatever he asked. And when Daed came home, she'd ask him to somehow explain to Benaiah what she couldn't.

If, after their time together this weekend, Benaiah still wouldn't budge, she'd show him by her actions that she didn't mind helping to take care of his family, especially now that she finally understood the reality of their circumstances. Somehow, she would tear down the wall Benaiah had erected, especially since she now knew he hadn't rejected her love; he'd only wanted to protect her and make provision for her needs in a way he didn't think he could manage himself.

The knowledge that he still loved her gave her the courage to fight for their future, even she would have to fight both Benaiah and the financial mountain his family faced.

But if she didn't rest and recover, he'd never accept her help, because he'd worry too much about her fragile state.

BENAIAH LADLED HOT oatmeal into two bowls, which he then carried to the table. He fetched a couple of spoons and the pitcher of cream, and poured two glasses of orange juice. Then he stood back and surveyed everything for a moment. Something was missing. What was it? He frowned. "What else do we need?"

She giggled, and it warmed his heart to see her happy again. She'd handled the truth better than he'd thought she would.

"A plate, if you want a cinnamon roll. Brown sugar, if you want to sweeten your oatmeal. And mugs for koffee."

He retrieved two mugs and the koffeepot, then sat next to her, in his usual place, and reached for her hand. "Shall we pray?"

They didn't normally hold hands during prayer. Not at her haus, at least. Only at the Troyers'. But with Peter gone, he could do things his way.

She slid her soft hand into his, and a spark worked through his nervous system, shorting out all thought processes.

He probably shouldn't have initiated the holding of hands, because now his focus was on her and not on Gott.

Maybe if he prayed out loud, like his friend Josh did from time to time, it would help. He gulped in some air. "Lord Gott...."

She startled, her hand jerking lightly.

"Danki for this food. Danki for Susanna and our friendship. Take care of her injuries and her future, and watch over her wherever she goes. And take care of my family, Lord. Amen."

Outside, a car door closed. Benaiah released Susanna's hand as footsteps sounded on the porch. He rose to his feet seconds before the door opened. His seventeen-year-old sister, Becca, entered, taking a moment to stomp the snow off her boots. "Hi, Susanna."

"Becca. Nice to see you." Susanna's expression harbored confusion.

Becca lingered in the doorway. "Get me a broom, Ben. I'll clean off the porch."

"Sure, but what are you doing here?" He headed for the closet where the broom was kept.

"The driver said Susanna fell and needed help. Mammi told me to kum over here and see what I could do."

Ach. He hadn't meant for Mammi to send her best helper. Nineteen-year-old Lizzie and fourteen-year-old Jackie did their part, but Lizzie was babysitting this week for an Englisch family, and Jackie tended to spend more time daydreaming than working. "I sent the message via the driver because I wanted Mammi to know I wouldn't be coming home soon. I intended to take care of Susie." Embarrassment burned his cheeks.

Becca smirked. "Well, now you have a chaperone, ain't so?"

Ben wiped his hand over his face. Considering the supercharged moments between him and Susanna last night and this morgen, a chaperone was needed. Mandatory.

"Besides, you aren't a gut cook. You'd burn water, if that were possible."

"What do you mean?" Benaiah handed her the broom. "I can follow directions pretty well, as long as the person directing me knows what she's doing."

Becca rolled her eyes, then grinned at Susanna. "Ben and I will take gut care of you. You'll be feeling better in nein time." She turned around and went back outside.

He crossed the room to the stove. "There's not enough oatmeal left to offer any to Becca. Should I make more?"

"She likely ate already, but you can ask her," Susanna said. "Or she could have a cinnamon roll."

"I know she won't turn down a cinnamon roll." Benaiah opened the door. "Have you eaten breakfast?"

"Jah, I made French toast. Go ahead and eat. When I finish this, I'll see what Susie needs me to do next."

"Draw the line at hanging mistletoe in the shop," Benaiah whispered to his sister.

Becca laughed. "I'll make sure that's the first place it's hung, if she wants me to hang any." She leaned closer to him. "It's about time the two of you kissed and made up."

Ben forced a smile and shut the door. She didn't understand. Nobody understood. Why was he the only one carrying the weight, the worry, the responsibility?

Gott—

Why don't you trust Me?

I do, Lord. Well, mostly.

Enough to follow a lion into a pit on a snowy day?

Okay, so maybe he didn't trust Gott that much. A heavy weight descended as he reclaimed his seat at the table.

SUSANNA HATED BEING stuck in a chair and babied by others. She'd never felt so helpless. Not even when she'd fallen and broken her arm at the age of fourteen while racing to catch up with her cousins. Grossmammi had put her to work doing one-handed jobs.

Benaiah insisted on helping her from the kitchen into the living room, where he helped her to recline on the sofa. It was rather nice to tuck her hand into the crook of his elbow as he escorted her into the other room. While Becca folded the laundry that had hung in the mudroom to dry over-nacht, Benaiah set up the TV tray with the checkerboard, then dragged a kitchen chair over to the table and sat across from Susanna. "Red or black?"

"Red." Of course. He always asked, and she always picked the colorful pieces—had done so ever since she was twelve. Still did, if given a choice, when she played with her younger cousins.

He set up the game board and then looked at her, a strange expression in his eyes. "Remember when we were twelve, and we would say something like, 'If you win, I'll give you an orange; if I win, you'll give me a piece of saltwater taffy'?"

She nodded and swallowed. If they did that this time, she'd ask for a kiss.

He probably figured as much, because a muscle jumped in his jaw, and he looked away.

She'd go ahead and say it. If she was to have any hope of convincing him to take a chance on a future together, she needed to remind him of the associated rewards. "If I win, I get a kiss."

His gaze darted to her lips. Lingered there for a long, drawn-out moment. He swallowed. "On the forehead," he conceded, glancing quickly toward the mudroom, where Becca was singing the doxology at full tilt. At least she had a gut voice.

And she was not-so-subtly reminding Susanna that, jah, she was there, but she wasn't eavesdropping.

Still, Benaiah lowered his voice to add, "And if I win, you'll kiss me on the forehead."

He was likely playing with fire right there, because, even while seated, she could touch him, put her hands on his strong, muscular shoulders....

But that wouldn't be enough.

He firmed his lips and gave a slight shake of his head. "Silly kin-ner's games." But his voice was husky. "Smoke before fire." He moved one of his checkers.

Jah, it was smoke before fire...and the embers that remained from the fire last nacht still smoldered.

CHAPTER 12

*B*enaiah repositioned one of his checker pieces. Another bad move, but he couldn't focus on the game. Playing strategically had been easier when he was a sweaty-palmed twelve-year-old, because he hadn't been distracted by the curves or the lips of the beautiful woman now sitting across from him.

Susanna jumped his piece, then another, and finally a third, landing in the row closest to him. "Kiss me!"

His spine stiffened, and his belly clenched, as he stared first at the piece, then at the girl—woman—across the game board. "You meant 'King me,' ain't so?" His voice caught. Broke.

She blushed, red flooding her face. "Sorry. I'm a bit distracted."

His attention flipped back to the board. Funny, so was he.

Benaiah turned one of the jumped checkers crown-side-up, and lowered it onto the checker that'd reached his side. *Kiss me.* He shook his head but couldn't keep from stealing a glance at Susanna's lips. At the tiny tip of her tongue as it poked out to moisten them.

Kiss me.

Why not? Without allowing himself to list the many reasons why he shouldn't, he rose, moved around the game board, and leaned over her, planting one hand on the back of the couch, the other on the armrest behind her. He placed a chaste kiss on her forehead, then moved away before he was tempted to take things further.

Except now he was tempted to lose the game deliberately so he could kiss her again. Well, winning wouldn't be all bad. Then she'd kiss *his* forehead.

He cleared his throat. Now that they'd got that hive of bees out of the room, he could focus on the game. Maybe. But she kept stealing glances at him, as if she wanted to reciprocate his gesture. She made a few bad moves, and soon one of his pieces reached her side of the board.

The loud singing had ceased, and he wondered where Becca had gone. He glanced behind him to make sure they weren't about to be interrupted.

Not seeing his sister, he looked back at Susanna and hesitated. He really wanted to feel the touch of her lips against his forehead. A few other places, too, if he were honest. But the forehead would do.

He shouldn't encourage this.

Her eyes lit with expectation, and she scooted forward on the sofa.

Benaiah didn't want to hurt her. And if a few kisses made her happy... He grinned. "Kiss me." Then he stood, stepped around the game table, and bent over her. She encircled him with her arms and gathered him to herself before he knew what was happening. Her mouth touched his forehead briefly. Too briefly. Who knew that a kiss on the forehead could be so sweet?

He started to pull away, but his socks slipped on the hardwood floor. He lost his balance and fell forward, his upper body landing against her curves as she leaned back to accommodate him. His face was buried somewhere in the vicinity of her neck, and he inhaled a gentle floral scent.

She giggled and pushed at him, but he couldn't resist nuzzling her neck. Feeling her pounding pulse, he made a row of tiny nibbles upward to her ear. Underneath his body, she shivered. Her arms went around his neck, her fingers wove through his hair, and she emitted a tiny sigh as he explored her ear with his lips, then rained kisses down the curve of her cheek and across to her mouth.

She met his kiss with a passion that rivaled what she'd shown the previous nacht.

"Susie—"

Somewhere in the jumble of his thoughts, his sister's voice registered, interrupting what he shouldn't have started in the first place. He broke away from Susanna, pushed himself off her, and barely collapsed into his seat before Becca entered the room.

Merciful Lord, give me strength....

"I folded the clothes, washed up the remaining dishes, and scrubbed the kitchen floor. Was there anything you'd planned to do today that I can do for you?"

"Hang some mistletoe." Susanna pointed directly above herself.

Ben grunted. "Nein."

"I'll see what I can do." Becca giggled. "Seriously, though, how can I help?"

SUSANNA STARED AT Becca for a moment. Her plan had been to roll out the gingerbread dough and make a haus for Benaiah—and his family. But how could she admit that to Becca? Besides, Becca had probably heard about the "love potion" recipe that was making the rounds. Maybe she'd even seen it. If so, she likely knew of at least several girls planning to prepare gingerbread treats for their crushes, in hopes that the blend of spices would cause those buwe to fall madly in love with them.

Earlier, in the kitchen, Benaiah had readily admitted he still loved Susanna. But he couldn't be over-the-moon in love with her, or he'd cast away his concerns and marry her. She needed to make the gingerbread haus. Not Becca.

Susanna floundered for a moment. "I washed the sheets upstairs, but I haven't gathered all the bedding from the dawdi-haus yet."

"I can do that. I'll wash them, too, and hang them in the mudroom."

"Danki, Becca." Susanna beamed at her.

"Snow's picking up again. Did you notice?"

Frowning, Benaiah jerked his head toward the window. Susanna heard the wind howl and whistle as it raced around the haus, driving snow against the pane. "I need to take care of Peppermint Twist. Should've done that earlier, but I didn't think I'd be here this long."

Susanna squirmed. He'd probably intended to be there only as long as it took to break up with her—again. To insist once more that he hadn't meant to kiss her, and restate his vow never to do so again. But her fall in the kitchen—and the consequences thereof—had changed everything for the better, even if she was injured. Suffering pain was worth having more time to try to change his mind.

Becca shook her head. "Roger put Peppermint in the barn after he finished the chores. He said he'd feed her and give her water. That's gut, because we'll be here over-nacht."

Over-nacht. The word took shape in big glass letters as Becca smiled brightly before pivoting and scurrying back to the kitchen. Moments later, the door to the dawdi-haus shut behind her.

Susanna looked toward the window. The snow was coming down heavily. Her usual view of the barn was completely obstructed.

"Visibility's bad." Benaiah voice was pinched, strained. Was he thinking of the poor visibility of the storm last year that had caused the accident that killed his parents? Or was he afraid of the temptation he would face by remaining there? "I can't stay," he finally said. "I'll leave Becca with you, but I can't—"

"Jah, you can. Sleep in the dawdi-haus." Susanna wanted him to be safe. And she wanted to prove to him that she could stop tempting him, even if she relished the lingering taste of his passionate kiss from a few minutes ago. She couldn't let him put distance between them before she had a chance to convince him of the future they could have together.

Benaiah rubbed his hand over his face. Twice. "Fine, if I decide to stay. Maybe the snow will let up, and it won't be necessary."

He stood, paced over to the window, and stared out.

"I guess we can finish the game." Susanna moved one of her pieces.

He spun around and stalked back toward the board. "Absolutely nein more kissing." He plopped down in his seat and glowered at her. As if it were all her fault.

She nodded, not knowing what else to do. Maybe it was her fault. She *had* hung the mistletoe in the kitchen, even though she hadn't expected Benaiah to kum inside—not with Daed away. But she'd felt the passion in his kisses and knew she'd gotten under his skin. And the more they kissed, maybe the more willing he would be to marry her, after all.

"We shouldn't have started kissing in the first place." He moved one of his game pieces. A muscle jumped in his jaw.

Susanna made a countermove. And nodded again.

"In fact, as soon as the game is over, I'm taking down all the mistletoe you hung."

Her head jerked up. "What? Nein! It's a tradition. One my grossmammi started."

"Look, Suz, I get that. But we broke up, and I can't be lured into kissing you multiple times a day. Not now. Back when we were courting, it was nice. But now…." He sighed. "Nein. Just…nein."

"But…it's something that's been done here for almost too many years to count." Great. Now she sounded whiny. Tears burned her eyes. He wanted to do away with a special memory of Grossmammi, just as Daed was doing away with everything she knew—her home, her community, the only life she knew.

"I'll hang it back up before I leave." He jumped one of her pieces. "*King* me."

"You could've just stood your ground and said nein. I would've understood, ain't so?"

"Would you have?" He fixed his gaze on her. Hard. Unyielding. "I don't think so. You would've been hurt."

"Meaning, if you saw the mistletoe and didn't kiss me, then I'd be hurt? What's a single missed kiss compared to a missed lifetime together because you broke up with me?" She didn't know where her outburst had kum from.

Benaiah's eyes widened. "Suz—"

"Don't 'Suz' me!" If she had been standing, she would have stomped her foot. "I never asked you to coddle me and protect my feelings—not now, nor back in January when you broke up with me. I'm stronger than I look. I don't need to be babied. I'm capable of taking care of myself, and more than capable of caring for you, your sisters, and your großeltern. I am. But if you don't see me that way, it's gut that you broke up with me. Just take your horse and go."

He stood. "Suz—"

"Go."

He glanced outside at the whirling blizzard. "You don't mean that."

Wincing, Susanna struggled to her feet, knocking over the TV tray and the checkerboard in the process. She folded her arms across her chest. "Don't you dare tell me what I mean."

He frowned. "I'm sorry. The mistletoe can stay."

She glared.

"I really am sorry. For so many things."

She sighed. Felt her resolve weakening.

He looked out the window again. Then back at her. He left the room.

That hurt. Her heart ached as if he'd tromped on it with his heavy boots, even though she'd told him—multiple times—to go.

Susanna swallowed her tears. She'd cried enough over Benaiah Troyer. She firmed her jaw, blinked her eyes to soothe their stinging, and lowered herself to the floor to clean up her mess.

Her gingerbread haus would go to someone else.

But who?

BENAIAH HAD LACED his boots and buttoned his coat when Becca entered the kitchen from the dawdi-haus with an armload of bedding.

She stumbled to a stop, her eyes widening. "Where are you going?"

"Home." He pulled his gloves on his hands and slapped his hat on his head.

"Ben, why? Susie needs help, and, in case you forgot, we're in the middle of a blizzard."

"Susie doesn't need anything. She's more than capable of taking care of herself." That was true. Very true. "And I was being a jerk. She told me to leave."

Becca made a strange noise in her throat, as if suppressing a laugh. "She called you a jerk?"

Ben snorted. "Nein, she didn't need to. I know I was."

"Here, I thought she had the courage to speak the truth. I'll go talk to her. Just let me put these sheets in the mudroom. If she still wants us to leave, I'll get ready and go with you."

Ben shook his head. "I'm leaving. You're staying. I wouldn't send my sister out in this storm. Don't worry, I'll be fine. The horse knows the way home."

Becca frowned with a look of concern. "Call the phone in the glass shop if you get into trouble. Call nein matter what when you get home. I'll check for messages."

He glanced out the window at the thickly falling snow, being blown horizontally by the fierce winds. Probably zero visibility. "Maybe I'll just stay in the barn, just in case…. Ach, never mind. She doesn't need me. And she has you. Tell her I'm sorry for being a jerk."

"Tell her yourself."

Benaiah shook his head. His jaw was clenched so tight, it hurt.

Why did this latest breakup feel more permanent?

He jerked the door open. A blast of cold air and blowing snow rushed into the kitchen, and he had to fight the wind to get the door closed behind him.

Tucking his chin against the gusts, he struggled through the knee-deep drifts to the barn. On his way back to get his horse from his stall, he noticed Peter's sleigh. That would get him through the snow easier. He pulled it out, then moved his buggy into its place. He hitched Peppermint Twist to the sleigh, shut the barn doors, and climbed up. "Home, Bu."

Peppermint Twist whinnied, nodding his head. As the horse pulled the sleigh toward the road, Benaiah flicked on the battery-operated lights, grateful they worked. He hoped to make himself visible to any motorized vehicles that might be on the roads.

The wind chilled him, and he wished he'd wrapped a scarf around his face this morgen before leaving home. Hi eyes stung from the cold. Well, that, and from Susanna's words.

The roads were completely covered in snow. There was only one set of faint tire tracks from the driver who'd brought Becca over.

Benaiah hated leaving like this, but Susanna was right.

And he was wrong. He hadn't given her enough credit for being capable of taking care of herself and running a haus-hold. Hadn't she been taking care of her daed for years?

Suddenly, there was a loud thud as the sleigh struck something submerged beneath the snow. The force of the collision sent the vehicle skyward. It flipped and landed on its side.

Benaiah flew from his seat into a deep snowdrift.

CHAPTER 13

*S*usanna fought down the lump in her throat as she collected the checker pieces and board, righted the TV tray, and set the board back on it. Then she struggled to her feet, supporting herself on the chair Benaiah had sat in.

Fresh tears filled her eyes.

She should've called him back into the room when she'd overheard him confessing to Becca that he'd been a jerk, but she'd been too stubborn. Silence prevailed in the haus. Had Becca left, as well, without saying gut-bye?

That said a lot.

Though Susanna had overheard Benaiah telling his sister to stay. She be here somewhere, ain't so?

The haus was too quiet.

Pushing the chair in front of her, like a walker, Susanna hobbled into the kitchen. She checked the stove, added a piece of wood to the fire, then went to start some laundry.

When Susanna entered the room, Becca looked up from feeding a bedsheet through the wringer washer.

Ach, gut. Becca wasn't out in the blizzard. Maybe Benaiah had decided to do some work in the shop instead of traveling home. Hope flared. She needed to apologize to him, for being so unkind. He was the considerate one, looking out for her, and she'd rewarded him with hatefulness.

She sniffled.

Becca let the sheet drop into the basket. "Should you be up and about?"

"Nein reason why not." Her hip was sore, jah, but that was to be expected. At least it wasn't broken.

"I told Ben to call when he gets home."

"He left, then." A rock of dread settled in Susanna's stomach.

"Jah." Something in Becca's eyes condemned Susanna. Or maybe she was just condemning herself.

"I'm sorry." Susanna reached for another bedsheet. "Can I help?"

"Nein. Right now, I'd really like to be alone."

Susanna nodded. Benaiah was usually the same, needing some space until he felt calm enough to talk quietly. Too bad that trait hadn't stepped in today.

It was Susanna's fault. She'd been taught not to talk back to her elders or to men. And yet she had. Her shoulders slumped as she left the room.

Except that in the heat of the moment, they had actually started to speak the truth about what they felt instead of continuing to keep it hidden.

Maybe she would bake the gingerbread haus for Benaiah, after all, and offer it to him with an apology.

She needed to apologize to a lot of people besides him. Daed. Irene. Becca, for starters.

She got the gingerbread dough out of the refrigerator, uncovered it, and went to retrieve a rolling pin from the utensil drawer.

Gott, I've failed You miserably all this week. I should've spent more time listening for Your voice instead of trying to do things my way. I'm sorry. Please help Benaiah get safely home.

BENAIAH WASN'T SURE where he was when the blackness receded. He sat up, bracing himself with both hands, until the dizziness faded enough for him to look around. The blizzard still raged, and the wind-driven snow stung his face. He was sore all over. Probably as bruised and battered as Susanna's hip. And, for a wild moment, he wished she were there to finger the places where he hurt.

And maybe kiss them better.

Peppermint Twist was gone, not visible anywhere in the swirling whiteness. Nothing was, except for a dim gray luster of trees ahead of him and a line of sad, sorry-looking mailboxes to his right. They were marked with numbers only, nein names. And unfortunately, the nearest haus was about a mile down a curvy one-lane dirt road that crossed a low-water bridge that was underwater almost all the time.

Not a wise choice today.

He glanced ahead at the woods. Snowfall would be lighter in there, ain't so, since the trees would catch a gut portion of the stuff before it hit the ground? Might take less time to cut through the forest than to keep to the road. Should he head home? Or return to Susanna's? Kum to think of it, he was pretty sure Preacher Zeke's farm was just through these woods. Or was it? He looked around again, the heavy swirling snow causing him to second-guess his location.

Benaiah pushed himself to his feet. Nausea rose as his vision blurred again, and he reached out for something, anything, to steady himself. His hand gripped the nearest mailbox, and he leaned against it, keeping himself upright until the dizziness faded.

He should've stayed in Susanna's barn. Not risked his horse's life, or his own, by attempting to go home in a blizzard. Not only that, he'd jeopardized his family's welfare. If he landed himself in the hospital or ended up dead, who would provide for them?

He moved a few steps away from the mailboxes, then noticed the sleigh, lying on its side at the edge of the road. He moved toward it. Had he wrecked the vehicle? It didn't appear to be damaged, except for the broken straps that told him how Peppermint Twist must've gotten loose. He tried to tug the sleigh upright but couldn't get the traction he needed to pull it out of the ditch. At least it was out of the way of traffic—unless someone lost control. The battery-powered lights were still on, and he decided to leave them that way. Their glow might alert someone to the danger, and signal to whoever might find the sleigh that the driver was out in the elements somewhere.

What had he hit to cause the wreck, anyway?

He tramped through the snow, kicking as he went, and soon exposed a tuft of brown fur. He cleared away enough of the snow to identify the deer someone must've struck earlier. He tugged the carcass off the road next to the sleigh.

Another wave of nausea and dizziness hit him. He leaned against the sleigh until the feeling passed. Was it his imagination, or had the blizzard picked up? He couldn't see the row of mailboxes anymore.

Lord Gott, protect my horse. Provide for my family. And Susanna....

Benaiah reached beneath the seats of the sleigh for any blankets that might be there. He found one and pulled it out. Wrapped in the worn afghan, he finally decided he should call Becca, or someone else, and ask for help. He patted one pant pocket. Then the other. Checked his coat pockets. He didn't have his phone with him. Had it been flung into the air when he'd fallen from the sleigh? Or...he had used it that *morgen* at Susanna's *haus*. Had he left it there? He couldn't remember.

Gott, You alone know where I am. Help me.

He decided try flipping the sleigh the rest of the way over, so it would be upside-down, and using it as a makeshift shelter. If he packed enough snow around the sides and up the curved parts to form an enclosure, he could protect himself from the brunt of the frigid wind.

WHILE A KETTLE of broth, leftover turkey, and vegetables simmered on the stove for turkey noodle soup, Susanna rolled out the gingerbread dough, then used a knife to slice it into four squares and two rectangles, for the walls and roof of the gingerbread *haus*. Taking out the box of cookie cutters, she pressed out a couple of trees and made the remainder of the dough into gingerbread men.

As if drawn by the aroma of gingerbread, Becca came into the kitchen while the cookies were baking. She poured some hot water from the teakettle into a mug, then added a tea bag before sitting down at the table. "I'm sorry about earlier. I was so angry, I didn't trust myself to speak without exploding."

Susanna sat across from her. "I understand. I'm sorry, too. I should've held my tongue."

Becca shrugged. "Ben tells me I don't understand, and he's right. I don't. You two have been together for as long as I can remember. Everyone always figured you'd marry. I know you two love each other, but I don't understand what is holding him back. It can't be his family. We girls are growing up. Daniel Zook is courting my sister Lizzie, and I expect they'll marry next year."

"And you?" Susanna attempted a teasing smile. Wasn't his family a big part of Benaiah's refusal to marry her?

Becca lifted and lowered her shoulders again. "I've had a few rides home from singings with someone. But whether he'll ask to court me, I don't know."

"I'm sorry I sent Benaiah out into the blizzard. Honestly, I hoped he wouldn't go far. I figured he'd return to the glass shop and do some work."

Becca shook her head. "He's too stubborn. When he gets something stuck in his head, he's determined to do it, whatever it takes. So, he was going home. Period. I was mad at him, too. It wasn't just you."

There was the sound of a bird chirping. Definitely not a real bird. Susanna looked at Becca with raised eyebrows.

"It came from over by the door." Becca stood and moved toward the sound. She looked around for a moment, then bent over and picked up something from the floor near the wall. "Ben's cell phone." She swiped her finger over the screen and held it to her ear as she headed for the other room. "Hallo?"

Susanna slowly pushed herself out of the chair and hobbled to the stove. She stirred the soup, then ladled out a carrot slice to test its tenderness. Satisfied with the texture, she added a pound of dried egg noodles to the pot, then stirred it again. Next, she peeked in the oven to check on the baking cookies, the gingerbread-haus components, and the loaf of bread she'd put in there earlier.

Becca returned to the kitchen and set the cell phone on the table.

"Lunch will be ready in about ten minutes," Susanna told her. "Was that Benaiah, safely home?"

"Only his horse made it home. Daadi said Peppermint Twist came running into the open barn, dragging broken reins and the harness. He wanted to know if Ben was here." She gave a glum smile. "If he doesn't show up by the time the blizzard lets up, they'll form a search party. I'm going to finish hanging up the laundry."

Susanna stiffened. Frowned. "They're going to wait to look for him?" What if he froze to death before she had a chance to apologize? *Lord, please spare his life.*

"Nothing can be done right now." Becca gestured toward the window. "There's zero visibility."

"Then how'd your daadi get to the barn to call Ben's phone?" Susanna knew that being ornery wouldn't solve anything. But she needed to do *something*.

Becca shook her head. "You know as well as I do there are always chores to be done. And Mammi always ties a clothesline from the barn to the haus at the first threat of snow, so Daadi and Ben won't get lost traveling back and forth in blizzards."

"But what if Ben was in an accident?" Susanna pivoted and paced over to the window, ignoring the pain in her hip.

"Pray. All we can do is pray."

Praying to Gott and waiting patiently for His answer wasn't something she was very gut at. Working and getting results was somehow easier.

"We need to work through this," Becca counseled her.

As if in agreement, the buzzer went off. The cookies and bread were finished, and the noodles likely were, as well.

But how could Susanna eat at a time like this?

Becca changed course and went to the stove. "You have to maintain your strength. You won't be any gut to Ben if you starve yourself. You'll need the food for fuel to help search."

If she was allowed to help. Normally, the men searched while the women stayed home.

And if she had to stay home, she'd make it *his* home she stayed at.

CHAPTER 14

Benaiah shivered beneath the blanket for what seemed like an eternity. The makeshift shelter of the overturned sleigh packed with snow didn't provide much protection from the elements, even though it did keep him from direct exposure to the wind. The sleigh was most likely covered with snow by now—and if that were the case, it'd eventually warm up, and he'd be safe—unless he ran out of oxygen first. Being buried alive in a blizzard was something he'd never before considered. Maybe he should dig out an airway.

The howling wind outside his makeshift shelter was spooky, especially when mixed with a rat-a-tat sound that he normally would've attributed to a woodpecker. But nein self-respecting bird would be out in this weather. It must be a part of the sleigh that repeatedly struck something else when blown by the wind. Or a tree branch, slapping against another one.

Either way, with all the noise, he wouldn't be able to hear if anyone drove by or came looking for him. How long would it be before someone noticed he was missing? His family at home would assume he was at Susanna's haus, and Susanna would likely believe he'd made it safely home.

There was nothing he could do but pray.

And yet he didn't know where to start, after *Lord Gott....*

That morgen, during the time of family devotions, Daadi had read from Psalm 91. *"Because thou hast made the* Lord*, which is my refuge,* *even the most High, thy habitation, there shall no evil befall thee, neither shall any plague come nigh thy dwelling."*

Strange how the passage sprang to mind with so little effort. Would Gott consider an upside-down sleigh to be a "dwelling"? "The Lord is my refuge," Benaiah declared out loud, just in case there was any question. His lips were dry. Chapped. Numb. His voice hoarse.

The passage continued, *"For he shall give his angels charge over thee, to keep thee in all thy ways. They shall lift thee up in their hands, lest thou dash thy foot against a stone."*

Were Gott's angels watching him even now? Guarding him, so he'd remain safe in the blizzard?

"Thou shalt tread upon the lion and adder...."

Was Daadi trying to communicate a deeper message with the text he'd chosen to read? It talked of treading on lions, and the fact that it came on the heels of their conversation about Benaiah's biblical namesake had an implication that was too strong to be ignored.

Benaiah forced air into his lungs. *Lord, help me to hear what You want me to. Help me to understand.*

"Thou shalt tread upon the lion and adder: the young lion and the dragon shalt thou trample under feet. Because he hath set his love upon me, therefore will I deliver him: I will set him on high, because he hath known my name. He shall call upon me, and I will answer him: I will be with him in trouble; I will deliver him, and honor him."

"The Lord is my refuge." He said it again, for gut measure. "Lord Gott, help me to make my dwelling in You. Please keep my dwelling from disaster."

A tear escaped his right eye without warning, and ran down his cheek. He wiped it away.

"Help me to trust You to keep me, to deliver me, so that I might have the strength and courage to tread upon the lions in my life. Amen."

WITH MECHANICAL MOTIONS, Susanna sliced the fresh-baked bread, transferred it to a cloth-lined basket, and set it on the table, even though her stomach revolted. How could she possibly eat a bite? How could Becca? It wasn't right. Everything within her wanted to go out into the storm and search for Benaiah. He could freeze to death if they waited for the blizzard to let up, especially if the grim forecast Becca had read using an application on Benaiah's phone was any indication: heavy snow every day for a week. That seemed a bit excessive, even to Susanna, who loved snow. Used to, anyway. Knowing that someone she loved was stranded in the snow made her wish it would go away and never return.

"All the laundry is hung." Becca came back into the room and rubbed her hands over the woodstove to warm them. "I think the wind is coming through the windowpanes, but at least your haus is warmer than ours. Daadi blames poor insulation."

"Hmm." Susanna forced herself to acknowledge the comment in some way. She didn't want to waste her energy talking when she could be *doing* something.

But even though everything within her longed to go out, find Benaiah, and rescue him, she couldn't follow through. How did she expect to locate Benaiah if she couldn't clearly see the barn from the kitchen window? Besides, he might have gotten home by now and had chosen to warm himself by the fire before calling to notify her.

Cheered some by that final thought, she set out the butter, then ladled turkey noodle soup into two bowls.

Becca closed her eyes and inhaled. "That soup smells so gut. Since we always kum to your Thanksgiving celebration, we never have left-over turkey at our haus. We never have leftover *anything*. Sometimes I dream of turkey cranberry sandwiches."

"We can make those to-nacht, if you want." Susanna set the full bowls on the table while Becca got out two spoons and a knife for buttering the bread.

"Do you think Benaiah would call his cell phone if he made it home?" Susanna glanced at the device, resting silently on the table.

"I think he intended to take it with him. He said he'd call the shop phone."

"I'll bundle up and check for voice mails before we sit down to eat." Doing something was better than nothing. "Daed would normally object, but under the circumstances, we could bring the phone into the haus, so we'll hear it if it rings, and have it if we need it. Maybe I could call my onkel and leave a message for him to tell Roger not to worry about the chores. That way, we won't have to worry that he'll get lost on his way over here."

"Gut idea." Becca glanced at Susanna's injured hip. "I'll go. You're hurt, and I'd hate to think you might fall again, maybe break something, when I'm supposed to be helping you." As Becca spoke, she hurried to the door and bundled up, shoving her feet into Susanna's work boots.

Susanna sighed. "Danki. The phone's usually kept on the long work bench in the middle of the shop."

Becca nodded. "I'll be right back."

She disappeared into the swirling whiteness almost as soon as she stepped off the porch.

Susanna stood by the window and gazed out at the snow. It seemed to take a long time for Becca to reappear. She climbed the steps, stomped her borrowed boots on the porch, and flung open the kitchen door, hustling inside.

"Wow. Snow got deep fast. Doesn't even look like I swept the porch this morgen." She kicked off the boots. "Your feet must be a lot smaller than mine. I would've worn my own tennis shoes, but didn't want to get them all wet." She hung up her coat, then took off her mittens and stuffed them inside the pockets.

"Any messages?" Susanna asked.

Becca frowned and shook her head, then laid the phone next to Benaiah's. "Nothing. Let's pray, and ask Gott to calm the winds long enough for Ben to be found. I know Daadi will start a search party then."

"Can we do that—ask Gott to calm the winds?"

Becca shrugged. "Why not? The Bible says that even the wind and the sea obey Him. And Daadi has been encouraging us to be bold in our faith. He talks a lot about fighting lions."

What? Susanna blinked. She would pray for Gott to calm the winds, but she wouldn't be so bold as to dare believing He would do so.

She poured glasses of water for Becca and herself, then took her place at the table.

Without a man there to say, "Let's pray," Susanna wasn't quite sure what to do. Becca, too, fidgeted a bit, then bowed her head. Susanna did the same.

Lord Gott, if You would please calm the blizzard so we can find Benaiah safe and sound.... Ach, maybe she should have started with praise. *You are the One who created the blizzard winds, so You can calm them if You want to....* Was that the same as making demands?

If only she'd paid attention last church Sunday when the preacher had used the acronym PRAY to spell out four essential components of prayer. She was fairly sure that the P stood for "praise." But she couldn't remember the other three letters. *Lord, forgive my ignorance.* Ach! R was for "repent." She smiled. *Praise and repent.* Maybe Gott would forgive her for not remembering the other two letters. *Forgive me for being so horrid to Benaiah today and for forcing him out into the snow. For tempting him to kiss me....* Okay, so she wasn't all that sorry about that. *Please bless this food to our bodies, and help us to find Benaiah alive. And please, please, please calm the winds. But only if it's Your will. Though I might be mad at You if you don't.* Oops! She shouldn't have thought that last part. *Forgive me for my disrespect.* Wow, she was really blundering this prayer. *Lord, I need help. I have to get my head on straight. Amen.*

She struggled to force down a spoonful of the lukewarm soup. If she saw Benaiah alive again, the first thing she'd do would be to apologize.

Once again, she worried she'd never have the chance. What if Gott let him die while they still had a gulf between them? And he was only twenty-two. His whole life was ahead of him.

Susanna swiped at the tears coursing nonstop down her cheeks. Her stomach knotted like a pretzel. She pushed her bowl away and struggled to her feet. She rubbed her right hip, hoping to ease the pain, but it hurt to touch it.

"I'll do the dishes," Becca said. "You sit and rest."

Susanna nodded. "Danki." She closed the lid on the butter and put away the uneaten bread. Then she glanced again at the two silent smartphones lying side by side on the table. Both Benaiah and Daed passed off their phones as business expenses. Daed's was basic black, while Benaiah had humored Susanna by ordering a holly-berry-red cover for his. He kept it well concealed, since red was flashy, and he didn't want to draw attention to himself.

Now Susanna glared at the phones. *Ring! Chirp! Buzz! Make whatever sound it is that you're programmed to make.*

Both phones remained still and quiet.

She hobbled over to the window again and stared out at the blinding snow. Her view of the barn, only fifty feet or so from the back porch, was blurred. Most of the time, she couldn't see it at all.

Wasn't her own inner vision a little blurred and unclear at times? For example, her decision to entice Benaiah to kiss her, as a strategy to win him back? She should've accepted Benaiah's decision as final, instead of begging and conniving in an attempt to change his mind.

Gott alone could see clearly. But it was so hard to trust in what was unseen.

The silence, from the phones and from Him, was deafening.

BENAIAH YANKED HIS hat down over his ears, glad to have at least a bit of extra protection for his head. Inside his gloves, he flexed his fingers to work the chill out of them. He wasn't sure if he'd dozed off or not, but something was different now. He listened.

The howling wind had stopped.

Should he give it some time, just in case it was a brief lull before a bigger surge of the storm? Or should he take advantage of the stillness, dig his way out, and head home?

The choice seemed clear.

He'd packed the snow pretty thickly around the edges of the sleigh, and the wind had blown bigger drifts across the space where he'd crawled in. He attempted to dig his way out, but being on the inside of the "cave" with nothing but a narrow spot to crawl through made escape nearly impossible. He grunted. Nein choice but to try. He stuck out his booted feet and kicked, but that didn't seem to accomplish anything.

At least the exertion warmed him a little.

He settled back for a few minutes, determined to praise Gott in the midst of his circumstances rather than focus on the negative. But that was easier to intend than to do. The weight of his problems was crushing.

Worry ends where faith in Gott begins.

One of the preachers had spoken those words recently, but Benaiah couldn't recall exactly who. He'd been distracted by a spider spinning a web beneath the wood bench in front of him. It wouldn't have been a very sturdy, forever-type home, but the spider didn't seem to care that in less than twenty-four hours, those benches would be loaded into the back of a wagon and stored in a barn until the next church Sunday.

He supposed he could learn something from that spider. If Gott was gut enough to provide temporary lodging for a spider, then He'd surely provide a home for Benaiah and his family. He'd provide a job for Benaiah, too.

If Benaiah got out of here alive, he'd talk with Peter on Monday and ask if he'd accept a cash payment for the shop, at a reduced price. Or if he'd consider letting Benaiah make a down payment of the money Daadi had saved, and pay off the remaining balance in a series of installments.

With a standing job, finding another home to rent would be easy.

He hoped. Maybe Peter would even let them rent the dawdi-haus attached to his home on a temporary basis, at least until the property sold. It'd be tight quarters, but they'd make it work. Somehow.

In spite of the tiny size, that dawdi-haus would be a step up from where they lived now.

And he'd talk to Susie. Give her the choice that Peter had accused him of denying her. *Love gives the other person a choice.*

Not that Peter really had given Susie a choice. He'd informed her that she'd be moving to Iowa with him to live with his new frau. But it was probably different for daeds and their dochters.

Love gives the other person a choice.

Benaiah loved Susanna, for sure and for certain. If he survived this, he'd talk to her. See if she would reconsider waiting for him.

He kicked at the snow again, then startled when the sleigh started to rise. He blinked against the snow drifting lazily from the gray skies. Thunder rumbled in the distance. Preacher Zeke Bontrager and his sohn Caleb stood on opposite sides of the sleigh, which they'd righted along the side of the road.

"Danki." Benaiah scrambled to his feet. "How'd you know to find me here?"

"We didn't," Preacher Zeke told him. "We were stranded at the former bishop's haus, where we'd been helping to get it ready to put up for sale. When the storm quieted, we decided it would be a gut time to head home. We saw the sleigh upside-down in the ditch, and Gott prompted us to stop and see if help was needed. Think the lull is temporary, though, so we'd best get you home. Are you okay?"

"Jah, fine. A bit cold, but I think I'll be okay." His headache had become just a dull throb, and the nausea was gone.

Preacher Zeke nodded. "Just make sure you get to the doctor if you notice any sign of frostbite."

"Will do. Do you have a phone? I've misplaced mine. Might've flown out of my pocket into the snow." He looked around at the whiteness surrounding them. The bright-red case of his device should be easy enough to find, but not if it were buried, like the deer he'd hit.

"Here." Caleb handed him his phone.

"Danki." Just in case his own phone was nearby, he dialed his number first. There were nein sounds of his ringtone—birds chirping—in the stillness. He ended the call, then dialed the number of the phone in his family's barn.

Someone picked up immediately, to his surprise. "Hallo?" One of his sisters. The older ones all sounded alike.

"Lizzie, you're home. Gut. Listen, I'm safe. On my way home."

A sob broke her voice. "Ach, Ben, hurry! It's an emergency!"

CHAPTER 15

Susanna hovered over Benaiah's cell phone, willing it to ring again. Becca tried returning the call, twice, but it went straight to voice mail both times.

"Did you recognize the number?" Susanna asked.

Becca sighed. "Nein. But the voice-mail message said it was Bontrager's Clocks."

"Should we go out looking for him?"

Becca shook her head. "Daadi will call us and let us know if a search party is formed. Though maybe that's why Bontrager's called. And you probably shouldn't be out and about, anyway, considering your injury."

"Jah, but I'm twenty-one. Not ninety. I didn't break my hip. It's just badly bruised. I won't even think about it while I'm searching for Benaiah, I promise."

Becca frowned. "I guess I'd rather be out looking for him, too. I need to know he's safe. But what if another blizzard blows in while we're out there?"

Susanna stared out the window at the snowflakes drifting lazily downward. The heavy gray clouds overhead looked ready to dump another foot or two of snow at any minute. Lightning flashed, and a moment later, thunder rumbled. That combination, during snow-storms, always freaked her out. "If we truly believe Gott calmed the wind, then shouldn't we believe He'll keep it calm until we've found Benaiah?"

After Gott had miraculously calmed the blizzard, it seemed wrong not to trust Him to do the rest.

Becca nodded slowly. "I guess you're right. But if you fall again, or get another injury, Ben will be upset with me. Besides, you don't have to be ninety to break a hip. I'm sure twenty-year-olds have been known to do that, too."

With a smile, Susanna quickly loaded the woodstove and banked it, as if preparing for nacht-time. Then she bundled up for venturing out into the elements. Hopefully, her hip wouldn't bother her too much, as they'd have a lot of walking to do.

"Do you think we could take a buggy?" Becca asked. "We have sleigh runners we could add to the wheels, but they're at home."

"We have a sleigh in the barn," Susanna told her. "I'll go hitch it up while you get ready."

She stepped outside with a gasp as the frigid temperature stole the air from her lungs, and began plodding through the deep drifts that were higher than the tops of her boots, sending snow down her socks and up under her dress. She shivered, but she wasn't going to wimp out over a little—make it a lot of—snow. Besides, it wouldn't be so bad in the sleigh. There should be a blanket stored under the seat that she and Becca could use to keep warm.

She entered the barn and stopped short, nearly losing her balance. The sleigh was gone.

In its place stood Benaiah's buggy. He must've stowed it hastily in the barn, for he hadn't taken the time to scrape the snow off the top and sides.

The buggy wouldn't maneuver well in such deep snow.

Walking was their only option.

THE AIR NEAR Benaiah's home was filled with black smoke as the sleigh carrying Benaiah, Preacher Zeke, and Caleb approached the property. Flames were visible through the upper-story windows, but the emergency bells were silent. A few Englisch neighbors with all-wheel-drive vehicles, and some Amish who lived close enough to arrive on foot, had kum to help. The fire department hadn't arrived yet. Had they been called?

Someone held a hose shooting a weak stream of water at the flames, doing nein gut at all. Those with buckets had ceased tossing water on the inferno and now stood by, watching as part of the roof collapsed in a shower of sparks. Flames shot high into the sky through the new openings.

Really didn't matter. The haus would be a total loss. All their belongings, clothes—everything gone due to the raging fire.

Seated beside Benaiah, Preacher Zeke said something, and Caleb answered. Their words were lost in the cloud of despair hovering over Benaiah.

So much for having until the end of the month to find a new home. They needed one now. This nacht. And that assumed everyone he loved had made it safely out in time. His shoulders sagged, the weight of this new worry crushing him, as Preacher Zeke directed his sleigh into the driveway.

Daadi—or somebody else—had gotten the cow and both horses out of the barn, just in case the building caught fire due to a spark shooting from the haus. Mammi and four of his sisters stood huddled in the pasture with the three animals. Nobody wore coats or blankets.

Benaiah clambered out of the sleigh and stumbled over to Daadi. At least it appeared everyone was safely out. "What happened?"

Daadi shrugged, his gaze flittering from Benaiah to the inferno behind him. "I'd say chimney fire, but you cleaned it out this year, since the landlord never bothered, ain't so?"

Benaiah winced. He'd intended to clean the chimney but never got around to doing so, since he'd been working so much to pay their bills. This fire was essentially his fault.

His jaw hurt from tension and frowning. Where would they go? Someplace temporary for the nacht. So much for his plan to purchase the business from Peter. They would need Daadi's money for a deposit and the first several months' rent at a new place—if they managed to find something suitable. They might be forced into an apartment or a single-wide mobile home in town. And what about their buggy? Their horses and cow? At least that was all the livestock they had to worry about.

The only place he could think of that might suit was the dawdi-haus attached to Peter's haus. But it wasn't ideal.

He had nein way of contacting Peter or Susanna. Well, he could use the phone in the barn, but there was nein guarantee anyone had braved the blizzard to get Peter's phone out of the shop. And what if Peter had taken it with him to Iowa? The possibility hadn't crossed Benaiah's mind till now. And Benaiah couldn't just show up at the Kings' with six additional people—seven, counting Becca—and expect Susanna to accommodate them.

It was bad enough she knew about their prior poverty, without witnessing their new neediness firsthand.

But that wasn't the main problem.

Nein, the big issue would be how close to Susanna he'd be staying.

It would be torture.

Pure and simple torture.

SUSANNA STOMPED BACK to the haus, not even trying to retrace her footsteps, or that breaking new trail was causing more snow to work its way under her dress and into her boots. What did it matter? She and Becca were stuck—unless they wanted to risk losing their toes, feet, and legs to frostbite.

What if they made some themselves snowshoes? Susanna seemed to remember Benaiah doing that once, using—if she recalled correctly—some chicken wire, wood, and laces. She frowned, trying to recreate in her memory just what Benaiah had done. And whether it had actually worked.

Nein matter what, she needed to try.

Susanna returned to the barn, ignoring her throbbing hip, and looked around for a roll of chicken wire. She found one in a corner of the lower loft. She rolled it to the edge and let it drop. It hit the top of

Benaiah's buggy, then slid off and landed on the dusty ground, sending up a puffy cloud of snow and dust.

Now to locate some thin, flexible pieces of wood. Daed surely had some stashed around here somewhere. Susanna searched the loft where she'd found the chicken wire, then painfully made her way up another ladder to the higher loft. She'd never before climbed to that dim, dusty level, mostly because she feared it was where the bats roosted.

The highest loft was filled with treasures. Wrought-iron bed-steads, an antique desk, a worn wooden table that used to be kept in the dawdi-haus kitchen. A hutch that was missing one of its lower doors. A rocking chair. More things she couldn't see, pushed back and clustered together in the darkness. How long had these pieces of furniture been here? And why? She didn't recognize even half of them.

She didn't see any stacks of wood, though. Bendable or otherwise.

"Susie?" Becca's voice was faint, as if she were yelling from the porch.

As quickly as she could, with plenty of groans and grimaces, Susanna clambered down one ladder and then the other, then went to the barn doors, which she'd shut almost all the way. She slid one shaky door open and peered outside.

Sure enough, Becca stood on the porch, her arms wrapped around her chest. The snow was falling more heavily now, and the wind had the whistling howl that meant a storm was imminent. "It's starting again," Becca shouted. "Ben's phone just received a text from the National Weather Service saying we're under a blizzard watch with additional accumulation expected. I opened the vents on the woodstove a little." With that, Becca disappeared inside the haus.

So much for her snowshoe-making aspirations. Susanna glanced over her shoulder at the interior of the barn and its inhabitants. A horse shuffled in its stall. Should she take care of the animals right now, in case the weather soon became too severe for anyone to get to the barn? They had hours to go before it would be time for the evening chores.

Deciding to wait at least a little while, she secured the barn doors and, with her head bent against the blinding snow, hurried to the haus, this time trying to follow one of the paths she'd broken earlier. Not that it did much gut. She still got plenty more snow under her dress and inside her boots.

Susanna had just reached the porch when a bigger sled, like the type the youngies used for sleigh rides, pulled up. The driver was Preacher Zeke, and his sohn Caleb sat beside him. As Preacher Zeke called out, "Whoa!"

Susanna blinked at the load of passengers: Mammi Wren and four of Benaiah's sisters. There was nein sign of Benaiah or Daadi Micah. "What's going on?"

Preacher Zeke jumped down from the sleigh. "Chimney fire destroyed the Troyers' home." He cleared his throat. "They need a place to stay, temporarily. We figured that since Benaiah is employed by your daed, Peter wouldn't mind if the family stayed here for the rest of the weekend."

"Of course." Susanna nodded emphatically. "You probably heard that Daed is in Iowa with his...girlfriend"—that still hurt to say— "but he wouldn't mind. We have plenty of room."

The two littlest girls were crying. Susanna reached for them. Where were their coats? Did they fail to grab them in their rush to escape the haus? One of the girls had flip-flops on her feet. Her toes must be nearly frozen. At least Becca had stoked the fire again, so they would warm up quickly.

"Where are Benaiah and Daadi Micah?" She clasped her hands together.

"Still at the farm. They'll be along as soon as they make sure the fire's extinguished. Danki for your hospitality, Susanna."

Fourteen-year-old Jackie helped Mammi Wren out of the sleigh. The older woman pulled Susanna into a hug. "Bless you, Susie. I knew you'd take us in."

"Of course! I'm so sorry about your home. But glad you're safe and thought to kum here." Susanna returned her hug as Becca opened the kitchen door.

"Gott has a plan, I'm sure," Mammi Wren said with a sniffle.

Susanna turned back to Preacher Zeke and Caleb. "Want to kum inside and warm up? We'll make koffee."

"Nein, danki," said Preacher Zeke. "We need to get home before the snow picks up again." With a click and a wave, he drove away.

Once Mammi Wren and the girls were inside, they family gathered near the woodstove, holding hands and warming up.

Susanna would figure out the sleeping arrangements later, though she had a feeling she'd find herself back in the cot in the mudroom. Funny, but for Benaiah and his family, she'd gladly give up her bedroom for a hard, narrow cot and a sleeping bag.

That thought pricked her conscience. *Lord, forgive me for failing to joyfully serve Irene and her family in this way.*

"Are you hungry?" Susanna asked the group. "We have some leftover turkey noodle soup and fresh-baked bread."

"Soup sounds gut, danki. The haus fire started while we were cooking lunch." Mammi Wren lowered herself into a chair with a whispered groan. "And with the strong winds, it was quickly fanned into an inferno."

"It's gut that Benaiah was there." Susanna grimaced at the reminder that he'd been there only because she'd sent him away in a blizzard.

Lizzie frowned. "He wasn't there. Not till the end. Daadi Micah did what he could, but…. This is so hard."

"I can only imagine." Tears burned Susanna's eyes. She quickly turned away and busied herself helping Becca get lunch ready. Susanna added more turkey and vegetables to the leftover soup in order to stretch it.

The wind resumed its noisy howling from earlier. Susanna looked out the window. The barn had blurred into nothingness.

She rubbed her hip, feeling more pain now than when she'd gone out in the snow and climbed the loft ladders in the barn. She might have overexerted herself. After her new guests had been served their meal, she lowered herself into a chair, trying not to wince, and helped herself to a cookie, even though she wasn't hungry.

They women had just finished eating when the door opened, and Daadi Micah and Benaiah came inside, both of them covered in snow, and kicked off their boots. A surge of relief washed over Susanna.

"Hope you don't mind, Susie, but we put our horses and cow in your barn," Daadi Micah said.

They'd brought their cow over during a blizzard? Nein wonder it'd taken them so long to get here. But that would save them from having to go back to their barn later to take care of the bovine.

"I don't mind at all." She turned to Benaiah. His blue eyes stared into hers. "I'm so sorry."

In the next second, she was in his arms as he held her against him.

CHAPTER 16

*B*enaiah quickly maneuvered Susanna into the other room, out of view from his family. With a sense of desperation, just to verify she was real and not a mere figment of his imagination, he allowed his hands to roam over her arms, back, and shoulders, then simultaneously cupped the back of her neck and raised her chin.

She clung to him, tears shimmering in her eyes. "I thought I might never see you again."

Jah, he'd been afraid of the same thing. And now he couldn't see enough of her. Get enough of her. He wanted to hold her, squeeze her, kiss her, and love her....

"I'm so sor—"

Benaiah silenced her by raining tiny kisses from her ear down her neck, then back up. He pressed his lips against hers, letting her feel every bit of the anguish, the pent-up passion, the longing, the...jah, the burning desire coursing through him.

She moaned as a shiver worked through her, then pressed herself closer as he deepened the kiss.

He didn't know—or care—how much time had passed before he finally lifted his head and simply held her in his arms until he—or she—stopped trembling. Then he ran a finger over her cheek. Traced her lips with his fingertip twice, three times.

She leaned toward him, her head tilted upward in an open invitation. But he'd kissed her enough, especially with his family in the next room. A couple of his sisters giggled, as if they'd peeked in on them during the course of their embrace.

"Take a walk with me later. I need to talk to you."

The wind howled in reply, reminding him of the blizzard raging outside. He shivered. "Or we'll just find someplace private in the haus to talk."

Susanna's smile faded, and her expression darkened, as if she feared their impending conversation.

She probably had gut reason to be afraid, considering how things had been between them this weekend—hot kisses, followed by his pulling away. Stir, repeat. He grimaced.

"I'm just so glad you're safe. Your family, too. It can snow all it wants to, now. We're all together." She backed away slowly, as if reluctant to leave his arms.

He didn't want her to go.

"Let me see if there's any soup left for you and Daadi Micah. If not, I'll fix you something else."

Of course she would, because she could. Her pantry was full. And her kitchen skills considerable.

As Benaiah watched her retreat to the kitchen, he forced back his feelings of inadequacy once again. She didn't understand what it was like to go without food. And he was supposed to give her a choice? If she chose him, it would be because she loved him even though he'd been a jerk. And she wouldn't be making a wise decision based on facts and figures.

Love gives the other person a choice.

Right. He'd lay things out for her. Let her see the grim reality he faced. Truthfully, though, he wanted her to choose him. He wanted to marry her, to hold her, to love her forever.

Benaiah followed her into the kitchen, ignoring the knowing looks from his großeltern and the smirks from his sisters. He belatedly shed the rest of his outerwear and hung it up. Then he stood as close to the woodstove as he could get, letting it warm his hands and his stocking-covered feet, while Susanna ladled soup into bowls for him and Daadi. Lizzie carried the dirty dishes from the table to the sink, for once doing a task without having been issued a direct order. Unless someone had asked her to do it while he had been in the other room. He smiled and mouthed "Danki" to her.

Susanna carried the bowls of soup to the table. Benaiah washed his hands, then took a seat beside Daadi, whose eyes were closed in silent prayer. Benaiah could guess what he was thanking Gott for—and he needed to do the same. Maybe with a slight addition.

Lord Gott, danki for providing shelter for us during this storm. For gut food and gut company. Please bless Susie for taking us in like this. Provide for my family's needs, Lord, and give me the courage to fight the lion I'm in a pit with. Amen.

Not unlike the Bible story. He glanced out the window. The snow still fell just as heavily as before, and the wind still howled. He was in a pit with a lion in the middle of a snowstorm. Had the biblical Benaiah been as scared as he was now?

SUSANNA GLANCED AROUND her crowded kitchen and smiled. It was so nice to have loved ones around her table, their chatter filling the warm room. Even if the talk wasn't exactly joyful. They talked of how they would need to purchase material to make new clothes, since their wardrobes had all been destroyed…that sort of thing.

Still, Susanna knew the community would kum through. As soon as the weather cleared, their Amish neighbors would stop by with donations—clothes that had been outgrown or were nein longer needed, pantry staples, meals, and more. They'd probably know of places for rent or for sale, too. Such as Susanna's own home.

The reminder pressed down on her like a heavy blanket soaked with water. If only she had a way of buying the house, the barn, and the land for herself—and for Benaiah. But she didn't.

On the other hand, maybe she could talk Daed into offering it to Benaiah as a wedding present. But would he need cash from the sale to start his new life in Iowa? Maybe selling the business would be enough. Or would he need more?

If Daed could swing it, she would be almost irresistible to Benaiah Troyer.

She brightened as she glanced at him across the table. He'd finished his soup and bread and now munched on a cookie—one of the iced heart-shaped ones she'd helped his sisters make the day before Thanksgiving, when she'd gone over to help Mammi Wren with the pies. They were the same cookies he'd brought when he snuck in on Friday nacht—was that just last nacht?—with the other "anonymous" gifts. If she hadn't caught him in the act of delivering them, the cookies would've been a dead giveaway. And if not those, then the blown-glass rose, fashioned in the shop right across the driveway. She'd seen it on the display shelf when she'd gone to the shop to fetch her stash of gifts from her secret admirer once Irene and her kinner had left.

Benaiah Troyer loved her.

It was too wunderbaar for words. Love without the love potion.

But that reminded her…she needed to get the gingerbread haus finished and decorated today, before her cousin Amanda discovered where Benaiah was staying and showed up with her own variation of the "love potion."

Except Susanna had nein candy to use for decorating a gingerbread haus. But she could make some. And she'd have plenty of help. Benaiah's five sisters and Mammi Wren would need some way to pass the rest of the afternoon, and making candy and icing for a gingerbread haus would provide a welkum distraction from the pain of their losses.

Susanna clapped her hands, excited about her idea.

The room fell silent. Everyone looked at her. Her face heated. Even more so when she realized that two of Benaiah's sisters already knew about the "love potion" and might have made plans, before the fire, to create their own.

She could work with that.

"This afternoon, let's have a gingerbread haus challenge."

Blank stares.

"It'll be fun!" she insisted. "We'll need to decide what kinds of candy we want to make to use as decorations." She hurried to the pantry and took out the shoe box where she stored her assortment of colored sugars, sprinkles, cookie cutters, and flavorings. "I have these that we can use, but you might have other ideas. I'll make more gingerbread if anyone wants to make her own haus...and, ach, we'll need icing. So, who wants to do what?"

More blank stares. She glanced at Becca, then at Mammi Wren. Maybe Benaiah's sisters had never made a gingerbread haus before, or at least since the death of their parents. It might've been deemed a frivolous expense in their cash-strapped family.

Then Lizzie raised her hand as if she were in school. "I want to make one." She glanced at Mammi Wren, as if expecting her to object.

"Maybe I would, too," Becca said, dipping her head. Red colored her cheeks.

Mammi Wren frowned. "What will we do with three?"

Since the two sisters obviously knew about the "love potion" recipe, they were probably planning to give theirs away, so Susanna could keep hers here—for Benaiah. The girls chewed their lips and exchanged glances, their faces still flushed, suggesting they had their recipients in mind.

Susanna's gaze darted to Benaiah, then to the floor. She swallowed. "We'll keep one. And...and we'll give the other two away. Christmas gifts."

"Ach. That'd be sweet." Mammi Wren smiled. "I'll take a look at your recipes, though I can't think of a homemade candy you could use for a gingerbread haus."

"Maybe a row of fudge bricks for a fence?" fourteen-year-old Jackie suggested.

"Or black licorice for a tree, with green gumdrops for leaves," nine-year-old Molly added.

Susanna didn't have a recipe for either licorice or gumdrops. But maybe they could make green and brown marshmallows. She liked their sense of creativity and wanted to encourage the start of smiles on their faces.

"A marshmallow snowman would be cute," Becca said.

"You girls are real creative." Daadi Micah pushed to his feet. "I can't wait to see the finished products. Benaiah and I are going to see how much wood is already stacked by the haus, and bring more in, if need be. But we'll be available to judge later."

"Taste tests." Benaiah winked.

Lizzie frowned. "You will *not*."

"You can taste mine." Susanna's face heated. Hopefully, nobody would notice. She blazed into a quick distraction. "Okay, Lizzie, you mix up some icing. You know how to make it, jah? Just butter and powdered sugar with a little milk and vanilla extract."

"Homemade?" Lizzie frowned. "I usually use premade icing."

"It's super easy to make butter-cream frosting," Susanna said with a smile. "Plus, it's cheaper and tastes way better. Both you and Becca should learn."

As the door closed behind the men, Becca found the recipe box in the hutch and gave it to Mammi Wren, still seated at the table.

Lizzie rolled her eyes. "I don't want to learn to make homemade frosting. The store-bought kind is perfectly fine. They sell so many different convenience foods nowadays that it really isn't necessary to know how to cook that many things."

"Which explains why you never want to help in the kitchen." Twelve-year-old Ellie planted her hands on her hips.

Mammi Wren sagged. "Girls, please, no fighting. Lizzie, it's always gut to know how to bake from scratch. Ellie, don't antagonize your sister."

Susanna turned away to hide her smile. She'd always wanted a brother or a sister. Then she frowned, remembering that one of Benaiah's reasons for being unable to marry her had something to do with his belief that she wouldn't want to help take care of his family.

Did he think she couldn't handle them? Was that one of his concerns?

Or was it that he didn't think she'd want to be around them when they started arguing?

BENAIAH STOOD ON the porch and stretched his sore muscles after moving at least half the woodpile from the stack in the shelter of the barn's eaves to the back porch, beneath the overhang of the roof. The new pile stood about five feet high and as many feet long. They'd have plenty of wood to keep them warm in the frigid temperatures and blizzard conditions. He and Daadi had also tied a rope from the barn to the haus so Mammi would be more confident about their safety going back and forth.

Daadi clapped him on the shoulder. "That ought to do it. Hope Peter won't object to our presence. Really was more than sweet of Susie to take us in."

Unselfish. Kind. Thoughtful. Jah, his Susie had the gift of service. And of mercy. Then again, she really hadn't had a choice but to take them in. Not when Preacher Zeke brought Mammi and the girls over and asked in their presence. But Benaiah didn't think she would've objected in any case.

He opened the kitchen door. Immediately, the spicy scent of gingerbread welcomed him. His sisters stood at either the counter, the stove, or the table, helping with the baking and decorating, while Mammi sat beside Molly, verbally guiding her as she measured a brown liquid with a spoon. Susie rolled out gingerbread dough. It warmed his heart to see his family working together in one room. That it was in *this* haus, with Susanna in the midst of them, gave him hope to dream more impossible dreams.

His stomach rumbled. "Don't suppose there are any samples yet?" He took off his hat and hung it on a hook by the door after Daadi had done the same.

"Nein, and don't touch." Lizzie didn't look up as she used icing to glue two pieces of gingerbread together. "I had nein idea how much work went into this. Daniel Zook had better appreciate it if he knows what's gut for him."

"Daniel Zook?" Benaiah's stomach knotted. Were Daniel and Lizzie courting? "Why wouldn't he appreciate it? It's a Christmas gift, ain't so?"

His sister glowered at him. "That's who I'm making it for, is all."

Benaiah accepted her statement with a shrug. He had nein issue with Daniel Zook, though he didn't know him very well. But wasn't he a couple years younger than Lizzie? He at least acted that way sometimes. His behavior tended to be immature. Rash. Impulsive.

"It's a *love potion*," Molly said in singsong.

All activity in the room came to a stop. Lizzie glared at Molly. Becca dropped the wooden spoon into the pot of whatever it was that she'd been stirring on the stove.

"A *what*?" He hadn't meant to bellow.

Mammi pursed her lips. "Gingerbread is not a love potion. It's just food."

Nobody answered.

"Susanna." Mammi's tone was somber and serious. "You didn't add that so-called love potion into the gingerbread, did you?"

Susanna shook her head without looking up. "Nein, the ingredients just happen to be the same."

"I told you that it's witchcraft, remember?"

Susanna nodded gravely. Her cheeks were bright red.

"Girls, listen close, now." Mammi's voice rose in pitch. "You can't make a man fall in love with you just by mixing some spices together."

Daadi chuckled. "But you will make him think about food. And eating."

"It is just for fun, Mammi." Becca resumed her stirring at the stove. "A Christmas challenge. I'm not even seeing anyone."

"Jah, and Susie is already being courted by Ben, so she'd be wasting time if she were making anything other than a fun treat." Lizzie returned to assembling her haus. One of the cookie pieces fell away from the rest of the structure, leaving her with gobs of icing stuck to her hands. She made a growling sound in her throat and tried again.

Benaiah cleared his throat. "Suz, can I speak to you? In private?"

CHAPTER 17

Susanna's shoulders slumped. *Here we go again. Breakup number...* *three? Four?* She wondered what the record was for number of breakups within a twenty-four-hour period. With a sigh, she set down the rolling pin and followed Benaiah to the basement door. He opened it, then pulled a small flashlight out of his pocket and flicked it on. There ought to be a lantern on the table downstairs, unless Irene had moved it. Susanna took the flashlight from Benaiah and led the way down into the darkness.

The lantern sitting just was where she'd left it. Benaiah lit it, and the flickering light chased the shadows into the corners of the room. He pulled out one of the spare chairs beside the table, but neither he nor she sat. "Listen."

There was that horrible, nein-gut word that meant she wouldn't like whatever it was that he planned to say. She shivered, and not just from the chilly air in the cellar, and searched for some way to get the conversation to go in her favor. She came up with nothing.

Why did she bother trying? Where was her pride? She quit. If he didn't want her, somebody else surely would.

But she still wanted him. With another shiver, she folded her arms across her chest and rubbed them vigorously.

He must've somehow read the panic building inside her, because his stance softened. "I know my track record. But, listen. I'm not breaking up with you."

"After those kisses, you'd better not." Ach, she hadn't meant to say that. If possible, her cheeks burned hotter now than when Mammi Wren had scolded her in front of everyone upstairs. How had Molly known about the love potion, anyway? She was only nine!

Benaiah chuckled. "Jah, about those kisses. I shouldn't have let them get so...."

Heated? Knee-buckling? Intense? Mind-meltingly passionate?

"...involved."

"Sure." Not exactly the word she would've chosen, but it worked. And she didn't know what the correct response would be. Telling him he was welkum to kiss her like that anytime would hardly be appropriate. And that would defeat the purpose of—

"A love potion, Suz? Really? What's this all about?"

"Ach, just something that was mentioned in a silly round-robin letter. Apparently the recipe's spreading like wildfire."

He shook his head. "Mammi is right. It's witchcraft."

"I happen to know someone else who's making you a gingerbread haus." She wouldn't say who.

"Someone else, other than you? With the motive being to cast a 'love spell'?" He frowned. "I don't want to be unkind, but one gingerbread haus is enough for us, and I'm not interested in any other girl. Whoever it is, I'll just tell her we already have one, and suggest she give hers to another family."

Jah, as if that would work. Amanda would be determined. And Benaiah would end up accepting it because it'd be the nice thing to do.

"Anyway, that's not what I wanted to talk to you about." He motioned toward the chair he'd pulled out and she'd ignored. "Have a seat."

She still wasn't sure if she wanted to, even if getting off her feet would be easier on her sore hip. Sitting down seemed to put him in control, especially if he remained standing. And even though he technically had control, she didn't want to acknowledge it, even nonverbally.

Benaiah shrugged, then slid out the other chair and arranged it directly across from the one he'd intended for her. Then he sat.

She inhaled a deep breath, gave in, and sat down across front of him. The chairs were so close that their knees touched.

Benaiah leaned forward and clasped her hands in his. "Suz...." He sighed. "I don't even know how to say this."

Ugh! He'd used the exact same words to preface his initial breakup with her, almost a year ago.

Should she give him the benefit of the doubt? Or....

His right thumb traced figure eights on the back of her left hand, sending her thoughts skittering in five hundred different directions.

He sighed again. "Suz...." This time, he released one of her hands and raked his fingers through his hair.

Susanna opened her mouth, ready to tell him to just say it already. But when he bowed his head, she pressed her lips together.

He grabbed her hand again. Squeezed. "Lord Gott, help me face these lions."

What? Susanna shivered.

His hands tightened their grip on hers. "Suz," he said again, "I...I know I've been a jerk lately. I didn't mean to be. The truth is...you know...." Another sigh. "Look, the truth is that I don't know how my family is going to survive. We have nein place to live. We have nothing of our own. Once your daed moves to Iowa and closes the shop, I'll have nein job. I thought maybe I could buy the business, but that would leave us homeless, and...I'm just not handling this well."

Susanna gave his hands a reassuring squeeze. "Ach, don't worry. I'm sure Daed won't mind if you and your family stay here until you find someplace to go. Or until the haus sells," she added glumly. "Maybe he'd even allow me to stay awhile, since I wouldn't be alone. I'd be living with you."

He chuckled, but there was nein humor in it. "I don't see that as a selling point. But that gives me the way to say it. See, the thing is, I want to live with you. As your ehemann."

Her heart skipped a beat—more like ten—at his admission. She opened her mouth to agree with him.

"But...."

And there was that other horrible word. Her heart stalled.

"I also know how hard my life is. How much we struggle. Ich liebe dich too much to ask you to go through that hardship. But I learned from your daed that love gives the other person a choice."

He'd talked with Daed about her? Did Daed know something she didn't? Had he encouraged Benaiah to make another move?

"And so...I guess what I'm asking is, can I court you again, even though I am homeless, jobless, and beyond poor?"

Wow. Such a statement must have taken a huge toll on his man-pride. And that made her love him all the more.

She wanted to get up and dance around the room, the way she had that very morgen before all the drama had started. Instead, she nodded calmly. He really didn't need to ask. He knew she loved him and would welkum him back into her life, ain't so? Or should she make sure he understood that she'd never stopped loving him?

"Jah," she finally said. "And don't worry so much. Gott will provide." She wasn't trying to repeat platitudes or to sound optimistic in general. But if Daed had talked to him, maybe there was a possibility he was planning to help them.

Benaiah's hands tightened around hers. "If we marry, you'll be living with my sisters and großeltern. I kum as part of a package deal. We won't be alone for a long time."

"That's fine. Ich liebe dich. Them, too." Did she need to convince him of the truth of her feelings? She really did love his family, squabbles and all. Okay, maybe not the squabbles so much. But she could handle them.

"And if we court, it has to be with the agreement that as soon as I find a job and a home, if you're still willing, I'll approach the preachers and ask permission to marry you."

"Jah." That was fine, too. More than fine. He could approach them now, as far as she was concerned. At least Benaiah was asking, albeit in an awkward, roundabout sort of way. It wasn't the romantic, swoon-worthy sort of proposal she'd sometimes dreamed of. Still, she wouldn't be picky. Mushy-gushy proposals were probably too fancy for plain Amish girls. His first proposal hadn't been flowery, either. Except now she *knew* how romantic he could be, thanks to his gestures as her "secret admirer." Maybe he just had a hard time expressing his feelings in person and spoke better with gifts.

"Take your time and think about it if you need to," he told her. "I know this is huge. And don't answer with your heart. Think about the facts and figures. Because the reality is—"

Enough talk. Susanna popped off her chair and onto his lap, wrapping one arm around his shoulders for support. "You aren't listening to me. I said jah." *Three times already!*

His eyes widened. "Suz!"

She snuggled against him. "Shut up and kiss me."

BENAIAH GAPED AT Susanna for a moment. And then, against his better judgment, he wrapped his arms around the very real, very warm, very willing woman in his arms, and his lips found hers. He'd never get enough of kissing her. Holding her. Touching her. Being alone with her.

Even in a dark, drafty basement.

He ached with desire. Tugging her closer, he deepened the kiss. She shivered in his arms and welcomed his embrace. Giving and taking.

There was a thud, followed by a series of thumps, as if something were falling down the stairs. And then came a crash. And a groan.

Susanna scrambled off his lap. As she did, she tripped over the legs of the other chair, sending it flying in one direction, while she crashed to the floor at his feet.

At the bottom of the stairs, just six feet away from where Benaiah now stood, Daadi sat up. He waved his hand dismissively at everyone peering down at him from the top of the stairs. "Go on, now. I'm fine. Don't worry about me."

Benaiah reached for Susanna to help her up. She took his hand, and rose with a grimace. Pain etched her face.

Understandably. This was the third time she'd fallen on the same hip. On the same day. If it wasn't already bruised, it was now.

"I'm fine, too," she insisted. But she limped across the room toward Daadi, still sitting on the cold concrete floor. She lowered herself to the bottom step. Neither moved.

Benaiah returned the chairs to the table, then walked over to the foot of the stairs. "Did you need something, Daadi?" He wondered if Daadi would admit to spying, or if he would kum up with an excuse about needing to look for a cot or some blankets or extra chairs.

Daadi's grin was lopsided. "Just being a dutiful chaperone, peeking in to see if you were actually talking."

Benaiah grunted. "Do you need help getting up?"

Daadi straightened his legs. Then bent them at the knee. But he didn't attempt to rise. "Nein."

Okay, then. Benaiah glanced at Susie. "How about you?"

She sighed. "Nein." She stood. "Can you get up, Daadi Micah?"

"Jah." But still he didn't try. "I think I should talk to Benaiah alone for a bit."

"Okay." Susanna looked at Benaiah. "Please turn off the lantern when you kum upstairs." She started the climb upward, her movements slow and halting.

He thought about insisting on helping her upstairs, but he didn't feel right leaving Daadi. What if he'd really hurt something and needed medical help?

Benaiah looked at Daadi. "You'd be warmer sitting in a chair than on the cold floor. Warmer still if we went upstairs to one of the rooms heated by the woodstove."

"Gut point." Daadi slowly shifted his position and lifted himself to the bottom step. He sat there a moment, then scooted up one step before pushing himself into a standing position. "Been a long time since I've fallen down a staircase. Pretty sure nothing is broken, but definitely bruised and battered. Probably knocked a few screws loose." Chuckling, he took a step toward the chairs. Then winced. "What a pair we are, Susie and I."

"We'll take gut care of both of you." Benaiah pulled out the chair Susie had been sitting in. "So, you were...chaperoning...for a bit before you fell." His face heated, and he averted his gaze. Daadi had probably witnessed Susie's bold move into his lap. If so, he'd seen them kissing…and had made the wise decision to interrupt them. But he probably hadn't intended to make such a dramatic interruption.

Would the next step be a stern lecture, like Daed had given him when he'd first gotten serious about Susanna? Like the one Peter was sure to give him if he found out?

"Jah." Daadi eased himself across the room, step by halting step. "I heard your pathetic excuse for a marriage proposal. Trying to talk her out of it, Sohn?"

"Nein. It wasn't a proposal, exactly." Although she had said jah before throwing herself at him. "I was just trying to present the facts. If I'm going to let her choose, then she needs to know enough to make an informed decision. Not one based on love alone."

"An informed decision…as you understand it?" Daadi continued across the room.

Benaiah threw his arms up in the air. "I don't understand you, Daadi. You know the situation as well as I do. I have nein money. If I use yours to buy the business from Peter, we'll have that, but nein home. If I use your money for a haus, I'll have nein job until Gott provides a new position, which…might take a while. Sure, I could do as many of the local men do, and go off to Indiana in the winter to work in the fabricated-home factory, and spend my summers on fishing boats on the Great Lakes or in logging camps in Michigan's Upper Peninsula. They see their loved ones for just a few weeks at a time. What kind of a marriage would that be?"

"Here's the challenge." Daadi stopped short, facing Benaiah, his hand on the back of the chair. "Are you willing to trust your heavenly Father, who so graciously made Himself known to you, or are you going to succumb to fear and to the lies of the evil one?"

"What?"

Daadi tottered another step before easing himself into the chair. "We are part coward and part daredevil. The coward is saying what you essentially told Susanna: 'It's better to be safe than sorry.' The daredevil says, 'Nothing ventured, nothing gained.' The thing is, if you're a coward, you'll never kum out ahead. You'll run from challenges every day for the rest of your life."

Wow. Daadi was calling him a coward? That hurt. But it did seem that his life was headed in that unappealing direction because of his fear.

"But if you try, you might just succeed. You'll buy the business and have a gut job. We'll find someplace to live in the meantime. The community isn't going to leave us homeless. Someone will take us in until you've saved enough money for a down payment."

"Daadi, I'm just not willing to risk—"

Daadi raised his hand. "Let's take this one step at a time. First thing, you take that precious girl of yours at her word. She said jah. Believe that. Then talk to Peter. Tell him what we have to offer, and see if he'll accept it. If he does, we'll go from there. If he doesn't, we'll pray and then decide on Plan B."

Benaiah nodded. "I prayed while I was sheltering under that sleigh in the blizzard."

"Gut. And…?"

Benaiah bowed his head. "Mostly, I wondered if the biblical Benaiah was as afraid of the lions in his life as I am." Except, there was that sense of peace he'd gotten, and the newfound determination to give Susie a choice. He needed to trust that God had answered his prayers—and was still answering them, even though he couldn't yet see the outcome.

"I've nein doubt he was, Sohn. But the biblical Benaiah trusted Gott enough to know He had his best interests in mind. There was nein guarantee that Benaiah would kum out of the pit alive after following a five-hundred-pound lion in there. But he had the courage to try, and that was part of what made him strong and courageous enough to eventually become King David's top bodyguard. While you won't ever become a bodyguard for a king, you can become known as a prayer warrior. As a strong man who isn't afraid of trusting Gott in spite of impossible odds."

Benaiah would rather not face impossible odds. And yet, like it or not, he was already facing them, raising his sisters and now being homeless with großeltern to support while unemployed. Since he'd already been given such a dire set of circumstances, what would he do with it? What could he do with it?

"A risk taker." Daadi pushed himself to his feet. "I'm going to brave the basement steps now. I'm choosing to take that step of faith rather than stay like a coward in the cold basement until my hip stops hurting."

"I'll be right behind you, Daadi. I won't let you fall." Benaiah extinguished the lantern and flicked on his flashlight.

"Jah, and Gott is going ahead of me. Think on that for a while. We'll continue this conversation at another time." Daadi reached the staircase and put his hand on the rail. He hesitated, pulled in a deep breath, and slowly lifted one foot. Planted it on the bottom step and hoisted himself up. Painstakingly, moving step by slow step, he ascended the stairs. And was welcomed into the embrace of his family.

It seemed a fitting picture for what it meant to follow Gott. Taking uncertain steps into the dark, steep, scary future. Risking it all on the belief that he was doing the will of der Herr.

One step at a time, do the next thing.

Gott, give me courage.

With shaking hands, Susanna resumed rolling out the dough while avoiding the curious glances of Benaiah's sisters. Had Daadi Micah seen her sitting in Benaiah's lap? Had he witnessed them making out? The kisses had grown increasingly passionate, going further than they'd ever gone while courting prior to the deaths of his parents. More intense. More...demanding.

Not that she minded, but it made her want more than he was giving. Made her want the gift that their wedding nacht would bring.

Hopefully, Benaiah would talk to the preachers sooner rather than later, so they could get married quickly. And maybe she could hint to Daed that an old farmhaus would make a wunderbaar Christmas/wedding present.

There was a creaking sound on the basement steps. She turned to see Daadi Micah's gnarled hand gripping the doorjamb.

"I'm right behind you, Daadi," Benaiah said. "You're fine."

Susanna dropped the rolling pin onto the dough, leaving a dent she would fix later. Ignoring the pain in her hip, she hastened over and held out her hands to Daadi Micah. He must've hurt himself worse than he'd indicated earlier. Would he require pain pills? A hot-water bottle? She'd send Becca to retrieve both from the bathroom. She glanced behind her, and Becca nodded her understanding before leaving on her errand. Benaiah's other sisters stood in wide-eyed silence. Mammi Wren's mouth gaped as she started to stand up from her chair.

Daadi Micah grasped Susanna's hands as he reached the main level. Then he released her and took a couple of faltering, wobbly steps.

"Let me help you to a chair, Daadi Micah." Susanna held out her arms.

He slipped his hand into the crook of her elbow and clung to her tightly. "Danki, sweet Susie. Take me to the living room so I'll be out of the way. Maybe Benaiah will be kind enough to bring me a cup of koffee and sit for a game or two of checkers."

Susanna's cheeks heated at the mention of checkers. Thankfully, there was nein way Daadi Micah knew about what had happened during her last checker game against Benaiah. She avoided Benaiah's eyes as she patted the older man's hand with her free one. "You wouldn't have been in the way. I'll make sure you get the first warm cookie out of the oven."

"And maybe a slice of fudge when it's set?"

"Definitely." She paused just inside the living room. "Where do you want to sit?"

"The rocking chair. The one beside the table with the gas lamp and your daed's Bible."

Susanna helped him into the chair, lit the lamp, and set a coaster nearby so it'd be ready for his koffee mug. Then she brought him the TV tray she'd knocked over that morgen, and set the checkerboard on top of it. "Do you need anything else?"

Daadi Micah held out one arm. "I'd love a hug."

It was pure joy to fulfill his request, because it meant he was officially welcoming her into the family. He wasn't holding her actions against her or scolding her for her brazen behavior with Benaiah. He didn't blame his injury on their obvious need of a chaperone. The implied forgiveness tapped a wellspring of love in her heart.

Susanna leaned forward to hug him, then kissed his weathered cheek. "Ich liebe dich, Daadi Micah."

"And ich liebe dich, Susie."

With a smile, Susanna straightened, then turned toward the kitchen. Benaiah stood in the doorway, holding a steaming mug of koffee in either hand. His blue eyes gave her a heated look.

He leaned near as she approached him. "Danki for taking such gut care of Daadi. For everything you do for my family and for me."

For him? Anything.

CHAPTER 18

*B*enaiah resisted the urge to turn and watch Susanna walk into the kitchen. Living in the same haus with her, albeit temporarily, was almost enough to make him want to pretend they were married. She ran the haus-hold, taking care of him and his family, giving warmth, food, and love. Ever so much love.

"You're a dummchen."

"What?" Benaiah startled, causing hot liquid to slosh out of the mugs. He set one koffee on the coaster near Daadi, the other on the TV tray, then wiped his wet hands on his pants before settling into another chair.

"I still can't believe that pathetic proposal in the basement." Daadi shook his head. "If I were Susie, I'd say nein just on the principle of the thing. I've half a mind to tell her so, too."

Except that if there was one thing Benaiah was certain of, it was that Susanna loved him. Always and forever.

He didn't deserve a girl like her. But he was beyond thankful he had her.

Daadi began arranging pieces on the checkerboard. "She deserves the type of proposal that makes a girl swoon."

Jah, she did. But Benaiah didn't know how to make that happen. He picked up his koffee and sipped the dark brew. It was stronger than the way Mammi made it, because at home, the koffee had to stretch. Finally, he nodded. "I know. But it wasn't meant to be a proposal. I was asking permission to court her again."

"Make it happen for her, Benaiah. When you defeat the lions you are fighting and get to the other side of this pit, make it happen."

He nodded again, because he didn't know what to say. How did one deliver a swoon-worthy proposal to an Amish girl?

He'd heard of several over-the-top Englisch proposals. There was the groom who'd picked up all those glass lilies and paid the balance due at the start of this very long day. He had paid the pilot of a small airplane to tow a banner that read "Marry me, Tiffany" across the sky. And another groom who'd picked up an order several months back, who'd gotten down on one knee, holding a huge, expensive diamond ring, in front of a flash mob at the mall in Kansas City and proposed after the singers performed a song about a woman who shared the name of his intended: Bobbie Sue. He'd even sung a few lines to Benaiah and Peter, who had stared at him, speechless.

The only song Benaiah knew that featured Susanna's name was a folk tune whose lyrics made nein sense. Hardly fitting for a proposal such as Daadi suggested.

There wasn't any point in thinking about that now. Benaiah still needed to fight the lions in his path to get to the prize.

And he wasn't even sure how to begin. Job first, then haus? Or haus, then job?

He had to-nacht and tomorrow to figure it out. Because, weather permitting, Monday morgen, he had to do *something*. He'd try to talk to Peter as soon as he returned home.

Outside, darkness had fallen, and the wind seemed to howl even louder than before. The windows rattled.

If Peter returned home.

Chances were, he'd be snowed in at Irene's until the blizzard ended and the roads had been cleared.

Susanna came back into the room with a plate of cookies. Her step lacked its usual bounce, probably due to her painful hip. "First ones out of the oven. Undecorated, but I promised them to you warm, Daadi Micah. How are you feeling?"

"I'm fine, Susie. Nothing time won't heal." He grinned at her, before his expression turned to one of concern. "But I notice you're limping even worse than before."

She smiled and shook her head. "I'm fine, too. Just a bit sore. I'm sure it's black and blue, but I'm not going to let it stop me."

"You're a gut woman, Susie. We're so blessed by your hospitality." Daadi took two of the treats, then glanced at Benaiah as if waiting for him to echo his praise. Either that or somehow deliver a proposal right there on the spot.

Benaiah felt like one of those bobblehead dolls he sometimes saw affixed to the dashboards of Englisch vehicles. "Jah. Danki, Susie."

Daadi scowled at him.

Susie held the plate out to Benaiah. "You're very welkum. But anyone would've opened their home in this situation."

Nein, not anyone. But she had, graciously, and without warning. And it gave him an excuse to imagine Susie as his frau. A daydream that would have to be nipped in the bud by nacht-fall, because, even though he wanted to, he wouldn't be following Susie to her bedroom.

But that reminded him.... "Do you need my help getting things ready for to-nacht? Cots, or...anything else?" He took two cookies from the plate.

"Nein, danki. Daadi Micah and Mammi Wren can sleep in the main-floor bedroom of the dawdi-haus, and you can sleep in the second-story bedroom. I figure the girls can divide themselves between my bedroom and the spare bedroom over here, and I'll take the cot in the mudroom. It's still set up from when Irene was here."

He shook his head. "I can't have you sleep in the mudroom. It's cold in there, and this is your home. I won't put you out like that."

"Daed had nein problem with my sleeping in there during Irene's visit came. It's fine."

Benaiah raised his eyebrows as anger worked through him. How could Peter treat his dochter so carelessly? Or was he even aware of how rude it was to expect her to sleep in the mudroom? "Your daed needs to have his head screwed on straight. Suz, there's an exterior door in that room. Anyone could sneak in. Besides, it connects the dawdi-haus and the main haus, so it'll have lots of traffic. Nein." Benaiah shook his head once more. "You stay in your own room. The girls can have the spare rooms upstairs, both in here and in the dawdi-haus. I'll sleep on the couch. That way, I'll be close to the fire."

Daadi nodded in agreement, even as he shot Benaiah a look filled with warning. "And plenty of chaperones, so Peter shouldn't object."

It almost seemed as though Daadi could read his mind.

Susie's face flamed red. She looked down at her slippered feet. "Jah…there should be nein objections."

Benaiah glanced over at the couch, where all the kissing had occurred during his last checkers game. A spring of mistletoe now hung above it. Just like Susie had asked his sister to put up. Right over the place where he would have sweet dreams of their kisses to keep him warm while he slept.

He couldn't keep from grinning, even though his face heated.

THE GINGERBREAD-HAUS CONSTRUCTION was well under way, so Susanna turned her attention to the meal that she would need to have ready to serve in a short while. Becca had expressed a longing for turkey and cranberry sandwiches, and while there was still plenty of sliced turkey available, there was nein cranberry sauce. Susanna did have a bag of whole cranberries, though, so she emptied it into a sauce-pan, then added several tablespoons of water and a cup of sugar. The warm, tangy sauce would taste delicious on the turkey.

But that seemed inadequate for a meal.

She opened the refrigerator to see what other Thanksgiving left-overs she had on hand. Irene had left all her foil containers full of food here, and Susanna's aent had donated most of her leftovers, too. Plenty to satisfy everyone to-nacht. Tomorrow, Susanna would need to cook.

Becca set aside the pan of fudge to cool. "I'm going to check on the sheets and see if I can get any of the beds ready for to-nacht," she announced, then disappeared into the mudroom.

Susanna frowned. Any sheets that were hanging in the mudroom would be stiff, as if freeze-dried. They wouldn't be pleasant for sleeping on.

Unfortunately, those sheets were all she had. With five bedrooms in a haus occupied by two, five sets of sheets had been more than adequate. Now, they weren't.

Susanna followed Becca into the mudroom.

Benaiah's sister fingered the corner of a sheet, folding it back and forth. "We could string a line in the living room. Or drape them over chairs near the woodstove. I've never had this problem before."

Susanna nodded. Gut thing Benaiah's sisters were standing at the counter as they did their assembling of gingerbread. She returned to the kitchen, arranged most of the chairs in a row near the stove, then went into the living room.

Daadi Micah and Benaiah had a checkers game going, and it looked as if Benaiah was winning.

Daadi Micah's face was a mask of pain. But he'd climbed the stairs by himself, so his hip couldn't be broken…right? Becca had given him a couple pain pills, and Susanna hoped he'd taken them instead of stubbornly refusing. The hot-water bottle was tucked beside him in the chair.

Maybe Benaiah needed to take his daadi to the hospital instead of worrying so much about her.

Susanna laid a coil of clothesline rope on the edge of a chair, then knotted one end. There were already hooks installed on opposite sides of the room from when Mammi had needed to hang the laundry inside several winters prior.

Benaiah stood. "Can I help, süße?"

Susanna shook her head as she slid the loop over one hook. "I've got this. Danki, though." She strung the line across one end of the living room.

Becca came in with a basketful of cold, damp sheets. "I draped some of them over the chairs you set out." She held out the bag of clothespins.

"Danki." Susanna fastened the other end of the line, and then she and Becca make quick work of hanging the sheets. When they returned to the kitchen, Susanna surveyed the chairs draped with sheets. "We'll turn these every so often to make sure they dry as evenly as possible."

Benaiah came back into the kitchen, carrying the two koffee mugs. He held one out to Lizzie. "Daadi would like a refill of the ser gut koffee. Please and danki." He scanned the room, then said, to nobody in particular, "I'm going out to get an early start on the evening chores. Darkness is falling already, and I'm thinking they can be done now." He hesitated, then met Susanna's eyes, a somber expression on his face. "May I speak to you in private before I go?"

Again? She looked around. "Where?" She couldn't take him to the bathroom or upstairs to the bedrooms. It wouldn't be appropriate.

"In the dawdi-haus, maybe?" He nodded in that direction.

She followed him through the mudroom to the door leading into the dawdi-haus kitchen, where Benaiah pulled her close. "I'm not going back on what I said in the basement. I was just thinking about something Daadi said to me earlier. He seemed to believe it was an actual marriage proposal. It wasn't."

Susanna's heart sank. Downgraded to courting rather than engaged? She looked at him with pleading eyes.

"I was just asking if you'd let me court you again. And I want you to know I'm not accepting your jah in the sense of, jah, you'll marry me. *Yet.* I want you to think about it. Pray about it. And when the time comes—if the time comes, and if you are still available—I'll ask you to marry me. For real."

She frowned. "What are you saying, Benaiah?"

"I want to court you, with the intent of marriage. I'm not asking you to marry me. Yet. I'm sorry if I didn't make that clear. But...." He chuckled. "I did kind of get interrupted."

Her face heated. She shouldn't have been so bold. And Benaiah's grossdaadi had caught her behaving in such a wanton manner. Hopefully, Daadi Micah wouldn't feel the need to inform Daed about her behavior. Daed would be ashamed of her, and there'd be nein question of whether she would have to move with him to Iowa or be permitted to stay here until Benaiah finally asked—for real—to marry her. Daed would force her to go. Period.

"Jah, about the interruption. I'm sor—"

Benaiah rested his forefinger firmly against her lips. "I'm not." He let his fingertip slide away, leaving tingles in its wake. "We'd better get back before a chaperone comes to interrupt us." He winked, then opened the door to the mudroom.

His twelve-year-old sister Ellie tumbled into the room.

THE BLIZZARD STILL raged on Sunday morgen. Unusual weather, for sure. Benaiah did the necessary barn chores and made sure there was still plenty of wood stacked on the porch before he went back inside. Susanna's cousin didn't kum to help. He'd likely heard through the Amish grapevine about the fire and knew where the Troyers were staying, thus trusting that Benaiah would take care of the work.

For breakfast, Susanna had prepared baked oatmeal with apples and cinnamon, as well as bacon, eggs, and toast. Only at her haus had Benaiah eaten such bounty at every meal. He wondered what his sisters thought about having a banquet for breakfast, but if they felt it odd, nobody said anything. Instead, they all wore smiles as they prayed silently.

While Benaiah ate, he studied the three gingerbread buildings—none of them looked like any haus he'd ever seen—lining one of the kitchen counters. They were all assembled, but the decorating hadn't begun. An unopened bag of mini marshmallows sat nearby—for snowmen, perhaps? On a baking sheet beside a stack of gingerbread men, some kind of chocolate goodie had been rolled into what looked like miniature logs, probably for a woodpile. A package of peppermint candy canes lay beside the mini marshmallows, and next to that a shoe box of colored sugars and decorative candies. Even unfinished, the gingerbread looked gut enough to eat. He couldn't imagine who each haus would be delivered to when the weather broke, but all the recipients were sure to be thrilled at the unexpected treats. Especially coming from a family that had lost everything but was somehow still hanging on to hope.

He didn't know which haus was Susanna's. Lizzie's was obvious because she'd done her usual half-hearted job. The building was put together about as well as a run-down shack.

Who had she said it was for? Benaiah shook his head and glanced at Lizzie, happily chattering with Becca and Susanna about how they should decorate each haus. He couldn't remember whose Becca's was intended for, either. Hadn't she said she didn't have anyone in mind? Was she telling the truth? He hadn't believed that either sister was being courted. Hardly appropriate table conversation, though, especially if they were to take offense at his asking.

After breakfast, Daadi handed Benaiah the Bible and asked him to read a specific excerpt to the family. The two men then went into the living room to play another round of checkers.

Even wearing the heavy robe he'd borrowed from Peter, Daadi shivered. A heated beanie was tucked beside his bruised hip once again. He'd barely walked today and moved only when he had to. A visit to the doctor would be in order when the weather cleared.

"I'm fine." Daadi must've noticed Benaiah studying him.

Jah, he might be fine, but his behavior suggested otherwise. Benaiah got up and checked the fire, then went out to the porch for another log. Viewed through the howling blizzard, the barn was a dim blur. It'd be foolish to attempt to go anywhere in this weather.

Back in the kitchen again, Susanna and his sisters had mixed up a batch of butter-cream icing and were decorating the buildings— adding windows, doors, wreaths, and rooftop embellishments. They sang Christmas carols as they worked. In the living room, Mammi sat near the fire, knitting something with black yarn. Socks?

The day passed at a crawl.

Benaiah's cell phone rang as he came into the empty kitchen after completing the evening chores, which he'd done early again today. He left his boots in a messy heap by the door and strode over to the hutch where his phone rested, next to Peter's. He picked it up and glanced at the number on the screen. He didn't recognize it. But both his number and Peter's were listed on the glass shop's website, which Peter had paid someone to design. It might be a business call.

But on a Sunday? Not likely. Business hours were clearly listed on the site.

He slid his finger over the screen to answer. "Hallo, Benaiah Troyer speaking."

"Ben, listen. It's Peter. I don't know if Susanna thought to check the phone in the shop...."

Benaiah glanced at the shop phone, lying silent on the hutch. Was Peter implying he'd called the shop phone? It hadn't rung at all, to his knowledge. He peeked into the living room, where Susanna, Daadi, and his sisters were gathered around a card table, laughing and chatting as they assembled a puzzle. Mammi dozed in a nearby chair, her knitting project dangling from her lap.

"...and I don't know what the weather is like there, but we're having a major blizzard. Roads are closed, buses aren't running...travel is not advised at all, except in case of emergency. From the forecast, it doesn't sound like it's going to clear up for a while, either."

"We're having a blizzard, too," Benaiah said.

"I am going to leave a message on Roger's phone, letting him know he'll need to do the chores for a few more days. Not sure he'll think to tell Susie I'll be delayed in returning, though, and I don't think it's wise to announce on the community answering machine that she's home alone—"

"Jah. Don't worry about the chores. I'll do them, Peter, because—"

"Nein, nein. I won't have you endanger your life by traveling miles in a blizzard—"

"We had a haus fire yesterday." Benaiah swallowed. "Lost our home. Susanna was kind enough to extend hospitality to my family during this time."

Peter was quiet. At least he'd showed some wisdom and care for his dochter's safety, not wanting the news to get out that she was home alone. A step up from forcing her to sleep in the mudroom, where anyone could've kum in and hurt her.

"I hope you don't mind," Benaiah added when the silence continued.

"Tough luck."

Tough luck? That was it?

"I guess I don't need to worry about her being alone, then," Peter finally said. "Your family is there, too?"

"Jah. Su—"

"Gut. Well, listen, I'll be home as soon as I can. Need to get things rolling so I can move us out of there and get us settled out here as soon as possible. Irene and I are thinking about getting married Thursday of next week instead of waiting till January. Already talked to the local bishop, and things have been set in motion. Ach, Irene's calling for me, so I need to go. See you sometime." A chuckle, and then the line went dead.

Hmm. Peter's reaction to the news of the loss of their home seemed a bit callous, unless it was just because he was trying to push Benaiah to propose with the threat of a speedy timeline for Susanna's moving away. But then, Peter had been under the impression that Benaiah was still courting her when he'd spoken in the glass shop about how love gave the other person a choice.

Ben frowned as he returned the cell phone to the hutch. He needed to have a serious talk with Peter, sooner rather than later. Perhaps by Monday, the weather would clear, and they'd get a better sense of when Peter would return to Jamesport.

With a sigh, Benaiah went back over to the door and lined his boots up the way they ought to be. He stared out the window into the darkness. The cold chill and lack of color seemed to fill his being, leaving him feeling weakened, saddened, and discouraged. Why couldn't he have received the potentially bad news while the kitchen was still full of the warmth and love and laughter that had migrated into the other room?

If Peter had his way, Susie would leave town in less than two weeks.

It wouldn't be enough time.

Lord Gott, help....

Trust Me. I am the Gott who closed the lions' mouths and protected Daniel. I am the Lord who gave Benaiah the strength to fight the lion. "Fear thou not; for I am with thee: be not dismayed; for I am thy God: I will strengthen thee; yea, I will help thee; yea, I will uphold thee with the right hand of my righteousness."

He'd read the verse from Isaiah 41 that very morgen.

Help me to believe, Lord. Help me to trust.

CHAPTER 19

*S*usanna opened her eyes to darkness. She lay in bed, silent and still. What had disturbed her?

The haus was quiet. Nothing moved. Nein floor boards creaked, nobody talked, nein....

Nein wind howled.

Another temporary lull? Or was the blizzard finally over?

Benaiah had said something about snow having been predicted all week. But that didn't necessarily mean it would all be blizzard, snow-storms, or even snow showers. It might be just flurries.

She crept out of bed, slid her feet into her slippers, and padded across the cold floor, hugging herself. She stopped at the window and stared out at the blackness.

The hush continued.

If the blizzard was over, then...then Benaiah would start looking for another place to live, and her opportunity to show him how well she could care for and love his family would be gone. Daed would kum home, and she'd probably have to start packing for the move to Iowa. Or start searching for a job and someplace to live around here.

A heaviness pressed upon her body. Her shoulders slumped. Would it be wrong to pray for the blizzard to start again so she would have more time with Benaiah and his sweet family?

With a long sigh, she slipped her robe on over her tank top and shorts—nein need to scandalize the Troyer family with her nacht-time attire, in case any of them was awake—and crept downstairs, avoiding the squeaky step.

In the kitchen, she heard the grating sound of the metal handles of the woodstove. There was a shower of sparks, and then glowing embers lit the room as Benaiah added a log.

Susanna stood in the doorway, watching him. Should she go back upstairs before he noticed her? Or….

He closed the stove door and stood. The beam of his flashlight skittered over her, paused, then returned, shining on her like a spotlight.

She imagined his gaze taking in her bathrobe…ach, nein. Her face heated. She'd forgotten to fasten it. She quickly pulled the two sides shut, then securely knotted the tie.

A low chuckle rumbled out of him, then the small light neared, stopping at the table where the dark lantern sat. He turned it on.

"The storm woke me," she explained. "I mean, the lack of storm. The quiet. I wanted to see if it was still snowing." She quickly crossed the room to the outside door and opened it.

A blast of frigid air hit her bare shins, hands, neck, and face, cooling the flame within. The dim light of the lantern filtered out onto the porch, showing snow flurries drifting serenely down. She shivered. Shut the door and stepped back.

Into Benaiah's arms.

They closed around her, hugging her against his chest. He bent his head to nuzzle her neck. "This weather is ridiculous," he murmured in her ear.

She shivered again. And not because of the cold this time.

"It's winter. And we live in northern Missouri. It's not all that surprising, ain't so?"

"Considering we average about seven inches, give or take, over the course of a typical winter, jah, it is." He flattened his hands against her stomach. "What do you have on under this robe?" His voice was husky.

Her face flamed again, hotter than before. "Um…." For a brief moment, she considered saying "Nix," but he'd probably take it literally—*nothing*—instead of how she would've intended it: *None of your business.* And that would be rude, albeit truthful. So, she said nothing.

His lips roamed across the pulse pounding in her neck, down to her shoulder. He pushed the collar of the robe aside to nibble the revealed skin. "I saw…I think…pink shorts and a black tank top."

Mostly correct. Except the shorts had a pattern of tiny koffee cups, and the shirt had a larger koffee cup front and center. And a slogan, though, at the moment, she'd be hard-pressed to quote it from memory. She probably wouldn't even get her name right, not with him nibbling her ear and kissing her neck and shoulders. And not with his muscular arms pressed against her curves.

Her stomach clenched. She turned into his embrace and ran her fingers through his hair.

"Can I see?" His fingers closed around the front hem of the robe, as if he had nein doubt what her answer would be.

She sucked in a breath. "Nein!"

"Aw, kum on, süße. Please?"

Something moved behind him. Susanna stiffened, then jerked away.

It was his sister Lizzie. She wore one of Susanna's hated long white nacht-gowns, with nein robe over it, since Susanna didn't have any extras of those.

Lizzie crossed her arms over her chest. "The quiet woke me. I came downstairs to see if it was true."

Susanna nodded. "Me, too."

"I was checking the fire." Benaiah raked his fingers through his hair, gave a casual glance around the room, then eyed his sister. "Who did you say you were giving your gingerbread haus to?"

"Daniel Zook." Lizzie's stance shifted into a more defensive position, as if she were preparing for an argument. "You aren't the only one in our family seeing someone. Becca has been taken home from singings a couple of times."

"By different buwe," Susanna countered. "At least, that's what she told me."

"Whatever." Lizzie looked away. "Do you mind if I make some hot chocolate?"

That sounded gut. Susanna crossed the room to the cupboard, took out the box of hot chocolate packets, and peeked inside. Exactly three left. Just enough, provided none of Benaiah's other sisters wandered in. "How long have you and Daniel been courting?" she asked Lizzie.

The girl shrugged. "Since summer. I dropped a pen at the market one day. He picked it up and asked me out."

"Works every time," Benaiah said with a grin. "Like Saturday morgen, when you dropped a knife." He winked at Susanna.

"Danki for reminding me that I'm a klutz." She got out three mugs.

"I thought you were flirting with me."

"By almost killing myself? Really?" Susanna turned to stare at him.

He chuckled. "Shows of vulnerability are powerful. In the old days, a woman dropped her handkerchief. You dropped a knife."

Susanna scowled. "I dropped my whole body. Twice. Nein, three times."

"Even better," Benaiah said. "It's the whole politically incorrect damsel-in-distress thing."

"And it works?" Lizzie pulled out a chair and sat.

"Daniel Zook asked you out, ain't so?" He grinned. "And Suz and I got back together."

Susanna filled the kettle and set it on the stove. "I blamed it on the mistletoe." And the scent of gingerbread.

BENAIAH PULLED OUT the chair next to Lizzie and sat. Visiting Daniel Zook would be on his list of things to do, sooner rather than later. He studied his sister. She was old enough to make her own decisions, but he wanted to be sure she was making a wise choice. And "wise" wasn't the first word that came to mind when he thought of Daniel Zook. Maybe after sitting down with him, he would be pleasantly surprised.

Would Benaiah meet Peter's expectations of an ehemann for Susanna? His gaze shifted to her.

She absently rubbed a hand over her right hip, as if it pained her, but she didn't hesitate or falter as she puttered around, waiting for the water to heat.

He could've seen how badly her hip was bruised if she'd let him pull her robe open.

Probably wise she hadn't. It likely would've tempted him beyond what he was able to handle. Daadi wouldn't have approved. Peter wouldn't have approved.

Speaking of Peter, did he know about Susanna's naughty side? Crawling into Benaiah's lap in the basement, dancing in the kitchen while wielding a knife, wearing immodest Englisch clothes beneath her robe?

He wasn't entirely sure about the last part, except that the brief glimpse he'd gotten hadn't been of a white nacht-gown like Lizzie wore.

He raised his eyes, and his gaze caught on the greenery hanging from the ceiling. He smiled. More of that mistletoe she'd hung in unexpected places in the haus and barn. Well, Peter knew about that. Encouraged it. After all, he was the one who always shot the mistletoe down and brought it to her.

Tradition, Susanna had called it.

Benaiah would have a conniption if one of his sisters did any of these things. But somehow, with her, it wasn't naughty. It was nice.

Or maybe it was naughty *and* nice.

The kettle whistled.

Susanna's long golden braid swung to the side as she turned from the counter to the stove. She retrieved the kettle, filled the three mugs with its steaming contents, then refilled it with water and set it back on the stove. "To moisturize the air." She tossed a grin over her shoulder.

The act of stirring the packets of hot chocolate into the mugs seemed to engage her whole body. She added a couple of miniature marshmallows to each serving, then turned once more, the material of her robe swirling around her knees. She carried the drinks to the table.

And he caught another—very brief—glimpse of pink.

IT WAS STILL blessedly quiet when Susanna awoke again several hours later. She rolled over, tucking her blankets more snugly around herself. Maybe just a few more minutes of sleep….

Long before she was ready, the scent of koffee and frying bacon assailed her nose. "Ach, nein!" She hadn't meant for Mammi Wren to go to all the work of fixing breakfast.

Susanna hurried out of bed and into her clothes, quickly and haphazardly stabbing the pins into place. She'd fix them later. She twisted her hair into a bun and dropped the kapp on top, jabbing it full of bobby pins as she hastened from the room.

Lizzie, Jackie, Ellie, and Molly were already seated at the table. Lizzie rested her chin on her hand, her face showing its usual frown. She rubbed her eyes. "Is the koffee ready yet?"

Mammi Wren had a wan appearance as she stood at the stove. Susanna hurried over to her. "Let me take things from here. Please sit and let me serve you. I didn't mean to oversleep." She shouldn't have stayed up those hours, talking and laughing with Benaiah and Lizzie.

On the stove, bacon simmered in a skillet. Nearby, on the counter, Eggs had already been broken into a mixing bowl, with milk poured on top, along with what appeared to be a dash of salt and pepper. The mixture hadn't been stirred.

While Mammi Wren hobbled over to the table and settled herself in a chair, Susanna got out another iron skillet, placed it on the stove, and got it heating. She added some butter, and once that had melted, she stirred the egg mixture before pouring it in. "Where are Daadi Micah, Benaiah, and Becca?"

"Micah's hip is worse today. Benaiah took his horse to fetch your daed's sleigh so he could take him to the hospital." Her voice held clear concern. "I took him at his word when he told me he was fine on Saturday nacht. Decided he must've had a bad case of weather-related arthritis in his hip yesterday, but couldn't quite figure out the fever. He assured me he was okay. But he hasn't slept well the last two nachts. Cried out a lot. And today, he didn't want to get out of bed. I talked him out and helped him get dressed but sent Becca to assist with his socks and shoes. If I get down on the floor, my arthritis won't let me get back up again."

A movement at the window caught Susanna's eye. Snow was falling once more—small white flakes that descended straight down, with nein wind to blow them. They would accumulate quickly on top of what had already fallen. "Should we call a driver instead of having Benaiah take him? It might be easier for Daadi Micah to get into a car or truck than to climb into the sleigh."

"Ben will likely lift him in. And...." Mammi Wren pointed to the two cell phones, lying side by side on the hutch. "Peter's phone is dead, and Ben's has only one bar left. He'll need to find someplace in town to charge them both."

"Isn't that even more reason to call a driver?" Susanna turned away from the window and flipped the bacon, then lifted it out of the skillet onto a platter lined with paper towels. "If something happens during the trip, they'll have nein way of calling for help."

"Ben has errands to run in town, too," Mammi said.

Susanna sagged as she dished the scrambled eggs into a bowl, which she then carried to the table. Errands? Such as finding a new place to live? Looking for a new job? He'd move out so quickly?

Maybe she should offer to go along with him. She could be the voice of reason. Keep him from jumping at the first unoccupied apartment or mobile home he saw. Besides, what would his family do with a cow and two horses at an apartment complex or in a trailer park?

But she wasn't sure she ought to leave Mammi Wren. She watched as the woman lifted her koffee mug to her mouth with trembling hands. And the pallor of her complexion was alarming.

Susanna glanced around. She didn't feel she could trust Lizzie, even though she had a job at a daycare center for Englisch kinner. In fact, she'd likely have to report to work soon. Benaiah would probably take her there on his way into town. Jackie had spent most of yesterday with her nose in a book she'd borrowed from their modestly stocked bookshelf, and likely wouldn't pay any closer attention today. Ellie and Molly were too young. Besides, they were still in school and would soon be grabbing their lunches and running out the door, although Benaiah would likely give them a ride, too.

Which left Becca. And she was capable. Unless....

"Is Becca going along to the hospital?"

"Susie, we've been wearing the same clothes since Saturday," said Mammi Wren. "Until word gets out and people begin stopping by with their cast-off clothing and such, we'll probably avoid going out in public."

"Ach! I should've thought of this sooner." Susanna went into the living room and opened a cabinet. She pulled out an armful of fabrics—green, maroon, navy blue, and purple—and carried it into the kitchen. "Here. I have plenty of clothes to wear for now, and the material has just been sitting there, unused. Daed bought it the last time he went on a business trip to Iowa."

Except she knew now that it wasn't a business trip. He'd been courting Irene, and he'd kept it from her. That still hurt.

"I'm sorry again I didn't think of this earlier. We could have spent Saturday sewing instead of decorating gingerbread." She glanced at the treats on the counter. Then again, the smiles and enjoyment were probably more important at the time.

Becca came into the room. "Daadi has his socks and shoes on, but he says he's not walking out here."

Mammi Wren rose from his seat. "I'll take his breakfast to him."

"I'll do it. You rest." Susanna dished out a scoop of eggs onto a plate, then added a couple slices of bacon. It was a lot less food than she usually fixed, but maybe it would be enough, just for today. "Go ahead and say your prayers and start eating. The girls will need to get to school soon, ain't so?"

She carried the plate back to the bedroom and found Daadi Micah seated on the edge of the bed where Becca had left him. His face was gray. He gripped his suspenders with white-knuckled fingers, as if he felt the need to hang on to something.

"What's going on?" Susanna sat next to him, and even the small disturbance of the mattress made him wince.

"Benaiah thinks I must've broken my hip. Not sure how it could be so, since I could walk on it Saturday. But I could barely move yesterday, and today it's even worse...maybe he's right." He nodded toward the plate of food. "I don't think I'd be able to enjoy your fine cooking properly right now. It likely won't stay where it's supposed to. I'm feeling a bit nauseous. But danki for thinking of me."

"Would you like some toast?" Susanna stood. "Tea?"

"Weak tea and a piece of dry toast would be gut, if it isn't too much trouble."

"I'll be right back." She hurried back to the kitchen, set the plate on the table, and started working on Daadi Micah's requests.

After she'd delivered the toast and tea to Daadi Micah, she returned to the kitchen and saw Benaiah eating his own breakfast while standing by the door. "Morgen. I need to take Lizzie to work and Ellie and Molly to school before taking Daadi to the hospital." His shoulders were slumped. Shadows filled his blue eyes.

Susanna could find nein words of consolation. While his sisters finished their breakfasts, she packed their lunches in Christmas-patterned paper gift bags, and handed off the meals as the girls went out the door. None of them had a coat. And Molly still had only flip-flops for shoes.

At least someone had cleared the porch and front steps of snow.

"I'll be back for Daadi." Benaiah looked at Becca. "Try to have him ready to go."

"He's ready now," Becca said. "But he doesn't have a coat, either."

"He can wear Daed's barn coat. There should be some gloves in one of the pockets." Susanna took the garment from its hook by the door and handed it to Becca.

"Danki." Becca hurried out of the room, and Susanna followed, intending to gather some blankets for them to use to keep warm in the sleigh. If only she had extra shoes to offer, or a storage box of things she'd outgrown. She'd given all those items away long ago, having nein younger sisters who would need them.

The chaotic morgen with lots of people needing to head in different directions would be her new normal if Benaiah ever proposed for real. Or if she was forced to move in with Irene and her kinner. Susanna straightened her shoulders and resolved to get organized going forward...on another morgen, when she wasn't trying to figure out how to hitch a ride to town. If she had to stay here today, at least she could get a jump on the sewing of some new clothes for Benaiah's sisters.

Benaiah leaned close. "Pray for us, Susie. If Daadi's hip is broken, I don't know what we'll do."

"Of course I will." Susanna was filled with a matching sense of despair. After all that Benaiah had shared about their situation, this seemed like the last straw.

But what should she pray?

The only thing she could think of was, *Gott, help! Help me to help them. Give me the ability to keep helping them.*

CHAPTER 20

Benaiah and Daadi returned to the Kings' haus without having run any errands. At least Benaiah had been able to charge his phone and Peter's at the hospital. Since he hadn't yet approached Peter about buying the business, it had seemed pointless to go to the bank after the long, drawn-out wait to see a doctor. And it was too cold to leave Daadi sitting in the sleigh while he went into a store and tried to find some shoes to fit all the members of his family. Not to mention, he had nein money to pay for such a purchase right now.

In the seat beside him, Daadi huddled under the borrowed coat and blankets, one hand clutching a pair of crutches. In his lap was a small white bag from the pharmacy containing a tiny overpriced bottle less than half full of pain pills.

"Whoa."

Peppermint Twist stopped in front of the porch, as near to the haus as Benaiah could get the sleigh. Benaiah set the brakes and clambered out as the kitchen door opened. Mammi, Susanna, Ellie, and Molly filed outside onto the porch and eyed the men expectantly.

"It's just a fracture. As in, a crack, not a complete break," Daadi said as Benaiah helped him out of the sleigh. "Nothing serious."

That wasn't the whole truth. Daadi had left out the part about how the doctor had wanted to hospitalize him for a couple days for bed rest and to treat his "walking pneumonia," but had finally agreed to send him home with crutches and a stern ultimatum to rest and let his hip heal. If he didn't, the doctor had said, the hairline fracture could worsen to the point of requiring surgery.

Benaiah would make sure to convey those details to the women later on.

He helped Daadi inside, both of them tracking snow through the haus, and got him settled in the living room. Becca helped Daadi out of his outerwear and shoes while Susanna swept a mop over the floor. Mammi prepared some koffee and brought a cup to Daadi.

"Sorry for causing you extra work, Suz," Benaiah apologized when he returned to the kitchen. "I'm going to take care of the horse and sleigh, then return a missed call that came in on the shop phone. The caller left a message and wants to place an order. I've a mind to fill it, because I still hope to buy the business."

If Gott smiled on him. But right now, His countenance seemed as dark and cloudy as the weather.

Even if he couldn't buy the business, the work would help to keep his mind occupied, plus it'd put a little money in his pocket.

"I'll go with you to the barn. I thought of something this morgen I want to check on." Susanna put the mop away and reached for her boots. "I found some things in the loft the other day, and I wondered if maybe that was where Daed stored the stuff he didn't know what to do with. For example, there's the furniture that used to be in the dawdi-haus...with your großeltern staying there now, a table might kum in handy. Especially since Daadi's on crutches."

Benaiah shrugged. "He wants to be around the family. The doctor said he's supposed to be bedridden, but I know better than to expect him to stay put, even if he risks doing more damage to his hip. Even so, I'm hoping to keep him as immobile as possible for a few days." He held out a hand to support Susanna as she balanced on one foot while shoving the other one into a boot. Meanwhile, he glanced at Mammi. "Did you hear me? Try to keep him still, or he might end up needing surgery."

Mammi nodded. "I noticed those pain pills are pretty strong. They'll probably put him to sleep."

"Rest would be gut for him." Benaiah doubted Daadi would take any of the pills without coercion. He'd grumbled that plain old ibuprofen would be gut enough when Benaiah had parked the sleigh in front of the pharmacy. "Plus, the doctor said he needed to take the painkillers because they *would* make him drowsy, and the body heals itself during sleep."

"I'll make sure he takes them, then." Mammi pursed her lips.

Susanna grabbed a lantern flashlight. "I'll open the barn doors for you." She went outside, Benaiah following her.

Once he'd unhitched Peppermint Twist and taken care of him, Benaiah went searching for Susanna. He couldn't find her in any of the rooms on the lower level of the barn, and the whole building was silent. Maybe she'd left.

Then came a thump and a squeal from somewhere above. He looked up. "Susie?"

"Up here." She grinned and waved at him from the second-highest loft. "Look out below." She shoved a big square box over the edge of the loft and sent it plummeting downward.

He stepped away and let the box land with a thud. "What is it?"

Susanna beamed. "Forgotten treasures. I'll be right back. I found more."

He set the box upright. It had been securely fastened with packing tape, and the label on top read "Susanna's too-small clothes." He smiled. This would be a blessing for some of his sisters. "Do you need help?" He took a step toward the ladder.

"Nein, danki. Just carry these things over to the porch and kum back."

"You aren't going to throw down the table you mentioned, are you?" He was only half joking.

She laughed and then tossed down a bulging white kitchen trash bag.

He glanced at the bag, recognizing the shape of the lumps protruding from inside. "You found shoes? Really?"

"I hope at least some of them fit your sisters. I can't believe I let Molly go to school in flip-flops. And if the shoes don't fit, they sure don't need to be up here serving as a nest for mice. They need to go to someone who can use them."

"Hopefully, this bag of shoes is unoccupied." He set the sack on top of the box. "Danki, Susie." His eyes burned with tears of gratefulness that Gott was providing for their needs so quickly.

Susanna waved a hand dismissively before vanishing once more into the darkness of the loft.

Benaiah hauled the two containers to the porch, set them just outside the door, then went back to the barn, almost expecting to find the table ready and waiting for him.

Instead, he found two more boxes. One had landed upside down, the other on its side. Both were closed securely with tape and bore the label "Clothes." He stacked them one atop the other, then bent to lift them, when a movement overhead caught his eye. He looked up. Susanna gripped the ladder with one hand and, holding a chair in the other hand, began to descend the rungs. Not safe. His breath caught.

Benaiah straightened, left the boxes on the floor, and started up the ladder. "Here, I'll take the chair. And once you're down, I can go up to get whatever else you had your eye on."

"Another chair and the table." She clambered down after him. "I'll carry the chairs over to the haus and clean them up, if you don't mind bringing those two boxes and the table."

"Sure." Benaiah still didn't think Daadi would use a kitchen set, but he climbed up to the loft to retrieve the table and chair, anyway. Susanna had moved both items near the top of the ladder. Benaiah glanced around. She hadn't been kidding—Peter had a whole treasure trove of stuff stored up here. Gut thing Susanna had discovered it, because if even one pair of shoes in that bag fit one of his sisters, it'd be a blessing. And if they all ended up being donated elsewhere, well, it would still be a blessing.

He carried the second chair down the ladder, then headed back up for the table, not entirely sure of how he would get it down without help. Might be best to wait for Peter to return home. He stood there and studied the piece for a moment. The table might be small, but it was still too heavy for one person to handle by himself on a ladder.

He supposed he could fasten a rope around the table and lower it that way. He remembered seeing a coil of rope atop an antique highboy dresser, and he walked over there to investigate. The rope wasn't too frayed. He picked it up and tugged it, testing its strength. It just might work. He tied the rope around the tabletop and, careful not to get too close to the edge of the loft, lowered it to the ground.

Daadi might enjoy having his morgen koffee in the dawdi-haus instead of having to maneuver his way through the cluttered mudroom to access the main kitchen. Then again, he preferred being with the rest of the family, right in the hub of the action.

Benaiah shrugged to himself as he untied the rope. Whether or not Daadi used the table, it was the thought that counted. Susanna was super sweet to think of him.

He rewound the rope and returned it to the loft, then hauled the table and the other two boxes over to the porch. One of the boxes toppled and bumped the wall of the haus.

Becca opened the door and peeked outside. "What's all this?" She stepped onto the porch and looked at him.

"Some treasures Susie found." Benaiah grinned. "I don't know exactly what's in each bag, but I believe it's mostly old clothes and shoes she hopes our family can use. They've been in storage in the barn loft, so I'm sure they'll need to be washed. And watch out for...extra occupants. Mice, bugs...you know."

"What a blessing." Becca reached for the bag of shoes. "Where's Susanna?"

"I don't know. I thought she was coming over here with some of the items she found." Benaiah glanced over his shoulder.

"You're chirping." Becca pointed to his pocket.

Benaiah took out his phone and glanced at the screen. "It's Peter."

He sent the call directly to voice mail, then helped Becca carry the bags and boxes of shoes and clothes inside.

After carrying the two chairs directly into the dawdi-haus via the mudroom, Susanna washed years' worth of dust and grime off them, being as quiet as possible, so as not to wake Benaiah's großeltern. The door to the bedroom was open a crack, and she could hear the gentle snoring of Daadi Micah. She peeked inside and smiled at the sight of the older couple sleeping side by side. Then she snuck outside to retrieve the table.

A horse and sleigh stopped in front of the haus. The back of the vehicle was piled full of bags.

"We've kum bearing gifts." Preacher Zeke tethered the horse, and then he and his sohn Caleb came up on the porch. "Where do you want this table? We'll help with whatever we can before we unload the sleigh."

"In the dawdi-haus, but please be quiet. Daadi Micah and Mammi Wren are napping. Danki." Susanna smiled. "When you're done, kum over to the main haus, and I'll have some koffee and cookies ready."

"Sounds gut," Preacher Zeke said. "Danki."

Becca stepped out the door and joined them on the porch. "Gingerbread cookies. I helped make them. And fudge, too." Her face colored.

Susanna blinked at her.

"Can't wait to taste them." Caleb gave Becca an odd look, then picked up one end of the table, while Preacher Zeke hoisted the other.

"'I helped make them'?" Becca muttered to herself once the men had gone. "I'm such a dummchen." She kicked at a spot of snow, then headed inside as Benaiah came out.

Benaiah watched the door shut behind his sister. "Caleb's a gut man, but I don't think he's interested."

Susanna shrugged. "He's taken Gizelle Miller home from singings occasionally, but I don't think they're serious. I know he's taken Becca home at least once, because I was with them. A mercy ride from Caleb."

Benaiah touched her arm. "I'm sorry, Suz."

She nodded. "I'd better get the koffee on."

Benaiah nodded. "I'll help unload whatever Preacher Zeke brought, and we'll be in."

The bags from Preacher Zeke were likely filled with more hand-me-down dresses, since Caleb was the only sohn of his still unmarried and living at home.

Becca was still muttering under her breath when Susanna entered the kitchen. "I can't believe I said something so stupid. But I'm going to offer him the gingerbread haus, anyway. Maybe he'll be my date for the singing after Sammy and Abigail's wedding next Thursday."

Susanna smiled. "Maybe so."

"I need all the help I can get." Becca began arranging gingerbread cookies on a plate.

"Mammi Wren says it's just a treat," Susanna reminded her.

"Jah, and I know that in my head. But I've had a crush on him forever, and he hardly notices me. I mean, he does, but not in the 'I'm special to him' way."

Susanna nodded. She'd never seen anyone catch Caleb's attention in that way.

But the conversation was over, because all three men filed into the haus.

"Susanna." Caleb stood before her after shedding his boots. "Several days ago, Ben told me you were looking for a job. My mamm's best friend, Judith—she's Mennonite—has decided to go on an overseas mission trip with her ehemann next year. She mentioned needing someone to manage the store while she's gone. She's praying about whom to ask, and I thought of you. Why don't you give her a call?"

Susanna thought for a moment. It sounded like the perfect opportunity. "It's worth asking, ain't so?"

"Sure. Call her now, if you want. You can use my phone." He took his cell phone out of his pocket, pressed several buttons, and handed it to her. "It's ready to go. Just press 'send.'"

"Danki." Susanna swallowed the lump in her throat and squeezed the phone against her ear. "I've never used one of these before." She covered her nerves with a giggle. How could she expect to handle working in a fancy store if she wasn't familiar with cell-phone technology?

Still holding the phone to her ear, she went into the other room. Her palms got clammy, and she wiped the moisture on her apron. She needed a job if she hoped to stay here instead of going with Daed.

"Thanks for calling Judith's Gift Shop, this is Judith...."

Lord, help. Please let her say jah.

Silence. Judith must have finished her greeting.

Susanna swallowed again. She probably should have practiced what she planned to say. "Um, hallo. This is Susanna King. Caleb Bontrager told me about your upcoming mission trip and said you might need someone to work in your shop while you're away."

BENAIAH COULDN'T BELIEVE all the bounty Gott had provided. Surely, in all the boxes Susanna had found in the loft, and in the bags Preacher Zeke had delivered, there would be clothes, coats, shoes, and other necessities to replace what had been lost in the fire.

And while he'd prayed for those needs to be met, that hadn't been the focus of his prayers. He'd prayed more for a job, for a home, for... well, for enough money and security to support himself, his family, and, if Gott smiled on him, a frau named Susanna.

Trust Me.

Gott had provided food, shelter, and now clothing for his family. He'd saved Benaiah's life when he'd been foolish enough to go out in the blizzard.

Benaiah would trust Him to provide a job and a home, and to make clear His will regarding Susanna.

Or at least he'd try.

It was just so hard trusting what he couldn't see.

"How are you doing, Ben?" Preacher Zeke gripped his shoulder, then gave it a pat. "You've been on my mind since...." He shook his head.

Would it be wrong to admit to the preacher his failures in trusting Gott? That he wasn't sure he would kum out alive after facing his lion in battle?

CHAPTER 21

*S*usanna pressed the phone tighter against her ear, but the silence that had followed her blurted-out inquiry after a job at Judith's Gift Shop stretched on. Maybe she should have tried harder not to kum across as needy. Or had she been too assertive? She didn't know how she'd sounded. Maybe just plain scared. If so, at least it was accurate.

Please, Gott, give me a job so I can stay around here when Daed marries. A job so I can help provide for Benaiah's family.

"Susanna King," Judith repeated. "I'm writing down your name, but, honestly, Gott has already spoken to me about who ought to fill in for me while I'm gone. I haven't talked to her yet, but I have been in discussions with her daed. However, I'll keep you in mind in case that doesn't work out. Would you be interested in a part-time, temporary job in the meantime? I'll need some extra help through the Christmas holiday and into the New Year. Maybe twenty hours a week or so."

"That would be great. Danki." A sense of peace washed gently over Susanna's soul. Gott had answered her prayer. Not exactly in the way she'd wanted, but every little bit of extra work would help.

"If you're able to, come on in tomorrow. I'm expecting a shipment of jams and jellies from an Amish lady, and I could use help pricing them and putting them on display. Could you be here around ten in the morning for a couple of hours?"

"I'll be there." Susanna grinned. "Danki, Mrs. Judith. See you in the morgen." She glanced at the phone, pressed the red button that said "end call," and returned to the kitchen.

Becca flitted around, arranging a variety of tea packets in a small square dish. Then she retrieved the canister of cocoa powder.

"I think koffee and tea ought to suffice." Susanna nodded toward the canister as she checked the perking koffee.

Becca stowed the cocoa powder. "Do you think I put enough cookies out?"

Susanna glanced at the plate in the middle of the table. It was piled high with a selection of homemade goodies. "Jah, I think that should be plenty." She tried to hide her smile as she turned to Becca. "Don't worry so much about it. If it's meant to be, it will happen."

Becca gave her a look that spoke volumes.

Susanna's face heated. She was a fine one to talk, after she'd stressed so much over winning Benaiah back. But it was nice being a part of his life again. Being single in a world of couples had hurt.

Still, it was better not to be in a relationship than to be in an abusive one.

Enough thinking. She couldn't force Caleb to be attracted to Becca. But maybe Mammi Wren was wrong, and the gingerbread haus would do the trick. It'd be interesting to see.

Soon the koffee was ready. The teakettle whistled as the water boiled. And the girls had set out some fudge with the cookies.

But the men weren't anywhere in sight. Susanna peeked out the window, expecting to see them standing by the sleigh, talking.

Instead, multiple sets of footprints marred the snow in paths across the yard. Smoke rose from the chimney of the glass shop. Benaiah must've built up the fire.

The men wouldn't be coming inside anytime soon.

BENAIAH FELT HE was being pulled in three different directions. Peter's phone burned through one pocket, urging him to return the missed call about the possible order that *could* jump-start Benaiah's solo career as a glass blower, provided Peter agreed to his offer. His own phone chimed with a reminder that he'd sent Peter's phone call to voice mail. And Preacher Zeke and Caleb had kum out to the shop to have a man-to-man chat with him about how he was doing.

As if there was a gut answer to that question.

He shoved another log into the fire, hoping to get the chill out of the air. It'd be more comfortable in the shop if it were warm in there.

But he knew the truth. He was stalling.

Preacher Zeke pulled up a chair as if settling in for a long, entertaining tale.

It wouldn't be very entertaining. Benaiah added another log to the fire, even though there wasn't room, shoving it in with the poker. Another stall tactic.

Preacher Zeke remained silent. Waiting him out.

Caleb put his hat back on his head and opened the door. "I'll go on back to the haus. Might be easier for you to talk without me here."

His friend's presence had nothing to do with it. Besides, Caleb already knew the cold, hard truth.

"You can stay."

Caleb shut the door once more, then settled down beside his daed.

"We're catching the bus tomorrow morgen for a funeral, weather and roads permitting," Preacher Zeke began. "One of my cousins and his wife died in a tragic fire, leaving behind four kinner and their grossdaadi. I invited them to kum here and stay with us, not that we really have room for five additional people in our home, but we would've made it work. They said nein; the oldest bu had a job, and they would make do. It worries me. Their situation reminds me of your family." He rubbed his hand over his beard and glanced at Benaiah. "I know you've tried to hide your financial difficulties from the community due to your pride, but I've seen how you've struggled. Yet nobody seems to know how to step in and help. We thought things would be easier when Lizzie found a job, but that doesn't seem to be the case."

"Lizzie keeps her money for personal needs and for her eventual marriage. She doesn't help support the family." Not even so much as a penny for groceries or rent. She'd accused Benaiah of being selfish to ask her for contributions. And, like the coward Daadi had accused him of being, Benaiah had let it go.

Preacher Zeke nodded. "Okay. I'll discuss that with her later."

"Danki," Benaiah said, but with trepidation. If confronted by a preacher, Lizzie would likely feel obligated to chip in, but not joyfully. Nein, she'd do so with great moaning and groaning. And yet, he would appreciate the extra income, especially with Daadi's recent medical bills. He glanced at his worn-out boots. "I'd gotten an eviction notice from our landlord. We had to be out by January first, anyway. I wasn't sure where we'd go, but thought we had a month to figure it out. Daadi and I were talking about buying Peter's business. I pretty much fulfill all the orders, anyway, while Peter takes care of the accounting and paperwork. Daadi figures he could handle most of that, except maybe the quarterly taxes."

"And if he can't, I'll help," Caleb offered, leaning against one of the worktables.

"Danki." Benaiah nodded. "But then, the haus burned, and… you're familiar with the rest of the story. I don't know how we can buy the business now, because we need a place to live. But Daadi says I need to face the lion, talk to Peter, and see what happens. In the meantime, we're living in Peter's haus, eating Peter's food, wearing Peter's clothes"—he plucked at the fabric of his borrowed pants—"and relying on the hospitality of Peter's dochter. I haven't gotten a feel for whether he's okay with the arrangement or not. Sometimes, I think he doesn't care what happens to Susanna, just so long as he gets his money for the property and can be with Irene in Iowa."

Preacher Zeke let out a sigh. "Peter hasn't seen past the hearts in his eyes since he reunited with his old flame." He frowned, tugged at his beard, and shook his head. "I've been worried about Susanna, too. She has the gift of service, like Martha in the Bible, when maybe she should be more of a Mary. But Irene has made it very clear to others in her district that Susanna isn't needed or wanted in her family unless it's for the extra help. Peter told me. And Susanna, like Martha, may not have learned to listen for the voice of der Herr instead of always trying to handle things on her own."

While it was true that Susanna was more like Martha than Mary, the preacher's final comment seemed a bit like a backhanded jab at Benaiah's own faith condition. He barked a brief laugh. "Guess we both have our lessons to learn."

Preacher Zeke was quiet for a moment before speaking again. "So, what is Gott telling you to do?"

Benaiah shook his head. "He's simply saying, 'Trust Me.'"

"Then trust Him. Take the first step toward your goal. Talk to Peter when he gets home, and see what he says."

Benaiah reached for his cell phone. "That reminds me. He called right as you were driving in. I sent his call to voice mail. Will you excuse me a second?" He stood and walked to the other end of the shop, entered the code to retrieve his message, and listened as Peter said that the roads were mostly clear, and he expected to be home Tuesday nacht.

Peter's tone was one of impatience. And that reminded Benaiah... Peter hadn't seemed to be listening when he'd told him about the haus fire or explained that he and his family were staying at Peter's haus for now. How would he react when he returned home to find so many extra people in his home? Maybe Benaiah should try to call Peter and warn him once more, lest he return to all sorts of unpleasant surprises.

Instead, he turned off his phone and shoved it back inside his pocket, forcing aside for now his concerns about facing off with that particular lion. "He'll be home tomorrow."

Preacher Zeke nodded. "We'll be praying for his trip, and for your discussion with him. I probably shouldn't say this...." He released a breath. "I'm in a position to see that Susanna stays here. But I wouldn't want to abuse my position, so I'm not going to do anything unless Gott leads me to do so." And with that confusing comment, he rose. "I'm sure the koffee is ready by now, so we'll stop over at the haus for a moment before heading home."

Caleb smiled at Benaiah. "I'll see you after we get back from the funeral. Should be Thursday evening after the wedding. Will you take Susanna to the singing?"

"Planning on it, jah." Benaiah wouldn't mention Becca's interest in Caleb. It was a moot point, anyway, if he'd be away at a funeral. "I need to return a call, and then I'll be right over." He picked up Peter's cell phone. He would accept the order. That would be his first step toward wrestling the lion that stared him in the face.

SUSANNA HAD JUST sat down with a cup of licorice spice tea when the door opened and Preacher Zeke and Caleb walked in. She bounced to her feet. "Would you like some koffee? Tea?"

"Koffee, please," they both said.

While they took off their outerwear and washed up, Susanna hurried to fill their mugs. "Danki for telling me about the job, Caleb. Mrs. Judith offered me a part-time, temporary job for the Christmas holidays. She has someone else already in mind for managing the store while she's away on her mission trip."

"Hmm. I didn't know. Sorry for getting your hopes up." Caleb rubbed his jaw and lowered himself into a seat at the table. He reached for a frosted heart-shaped cookie. "These look gut."

"They are. I helped Benaiah's little sisters make them when I went to help Mammi Wren with the pies the day before Thanksgiving." *The day everything changed.* Susanna tried to hide her frown behind a forced smile. *What a difference five days have made.*

"Have a gingerbread one, too." Becca slid the plate closer to him. "I hope you like those, because I made a gingerbread haus for you and your family." She turned to the counter, picked up her haus, and carried it to the table, where she set it down between Preacher Zeke and Caleb.

Preacher Zeke picked up his koffee and leaned back in his chair, a slight smirk on his face.

Caleb glanced at the gingerbread haus. "Wow, Becca. You went to a lot of work. Danki. My sisters will enjoy it, for sure. I didn't realize you were so artistic. Peppermint candy sticks for wall supports, an icing wreath, a snowman, fudge logs...look at this, Daed."

Preacher Zeke nodded. "Very creative. Danki for thinking of us."

Becca beamed.

The door opened again, and Benaiah came inside. "Susie, your daed says he'll probably be home tomorrow nacht."

She wasn't ready to go another round in the please-let-me-stay-here argument. At least she'd been forewarned and could brace herself.

"I also took an order for some glassware for a wedding reception. It's a rush job—they want it done by Friday—and they're willing to pay extra. I might have to work day and nacht to get it done, but I will. Especially since the caller was a wedding planner who hinted at more business in the near future." With a wide, confident smile, Benaiah pulled out a chair, sat down, and reached for a heart-shaped cookie.

It was so nice to see him happy and not as discouraged as he had been.

Susanna poured him a cup of koffee and carried it over to the table.

"Gut, gut. Glad to hear it." Preacher Zeke took a bite of his cookie. "Susanna, what are your plans with your daed remarrying? Are you moving to Iowa with him? Has he made arrangements for you to live with relatives? Or will you stay here—alone—until the haus sells? Maybe you don't know yet."

Susanna's face heated. She couldn't exactly blurt out her intention to remain in the area and marry Benaiah. But, other than that, she had nein real plans. Except to find a way to somehow stay here. "I haven't had much time to make any plans, since I just found out about Daed's own plans five days ago. I do have that temporary job lined up"—she turned to Benaiah with a grin that said she'd explain later—"and I'm hoping Daed will let me stay here until his property sells. If he doesn't, I'll ask some of my friends if I can live with them for a while."

"Have you prayed about what Gott would have you do?"

Other than brief gasps for help and fervent prayers for Gott to restore Benaiah's love for her, nein, not really. Nothing else really seemed to matter. And besides, she wasn't sure Gott would approve of her selfish plans to manage her own life instead of blindly and submissively following Daed to Iowa. But she couldn't admit that to the preacher, especially in front of the others. And she didn't want to lie. Not knowing what else to do, she shrugged.

Preacher Zeke's lips turned down. "You need to spend some serious time in prayer, Susanna. Gott will lead, if you acknowledge Him. Proverbs three, verses five and six, say, '*Trust in the* LORD *with all thine heart; and lean not unto thine own understanding. In all thy ways acknowledge him, and he shall direct thy paths.*'"

Ugh. Now she'd been properly chastised. And in front of Benaiah, Caleb, and Becca. She hung her head and scuffed her slippered feet. Avoiding the others' eyes, she sat at her place. If only she could find a reason to leave the room and do something else. But Mammi Wren and Daadi Micah were napping, Molly and Ellie were at school, Lizzie was at work, and Jackie was curled up in the living room, lost in a fictional world.

Becca sat next to Susanna, nervously twisting her hands in her apron. She gulped and looked up at Caleb, her face pink. "Do you know who you'll drive home from the wedding singing on Thursday?"

Benaiah's eyes widened.

Susanna jerked her head to stare at Becca. A girl didn't ask questions like that! It was too bold. And in front of the preacher? She would have to talk with Becca later.

"Uh, well…." Caleb's face flamed red. "We're going to a funeral out of town, and I'm not sure we'll be back in time for the wedding or the singing."

"Ach." Becca slumped, red-faced and fidgety.

Caleb cast a wide-eyed look at his daed and then at Benaiah before standing up. "Can I speak to you a moment, Becca? In private?" He headed toward the mudroom without waiting for a reply.

Becca rose and followed him slowly, as if she'd already realized it hadn't been a gut idea to put her heart out there.

Susanna picked up her tea and took a sip. Her stomach hurt. Whether from the preacher's scolding, mild though it'd been, or for Becca, because Caleb would likely break her heart, she didn't know.

Benaiah blew out a breath. "Danki again for everything you brought by, Preacher Zeke. I appreciate it, and I know my sisters and großeltern will, as well.

A squeal came from the living room where Jackie had been reading. And then Jackie shouted, "Christmas has kum early!"

Susanna rose as Becca dashed into the kitchen, tears streaming down her face, and ran through the living room. Her footsteps pounded up the stairs. Caleb followed her slowly out of the mudroom and stopped near the kitchen door, a muscle working in his jaw.

Preacher Zeke downed his koffee, glanced at his sohn, and rose. "Guess we should be getting on home."

"I need to go to work." Benaiah finished his koffee, as well. "You'll be okay, right, Suz?" He stood and headed for the door, fast on the heels of the other two men.

Leaving Susanna to handle the upset Becca and the squealing Jackie. Time to prove her worth if she planned to spend the next decade of her life with his family.

With a sigh, she went into the living room. Jackie's book had been discarded on a cushion of the couch, spine open, pages facing down. Jackie was on her knees in front of the pile of bags, carefully unknotting one of them.

"Look at all this, Susie. How did these bags get in here without my noticing? This is so great! Ooh, look at this orangey-rust-brown fabric. Isn't it pretty?" She stood, holding the dress against herself. "It looks like it'll fit, too."

Burnt orange wasn't exactly one of Susanna's favorite colors, but she nodded. "I'll be right back. I need to talk to Becca a moment."

"Okay. She's upstairs," Jackie said. "I think she's angry."

Becca usually remained calm when angry. She was probably more hurt than anything else, unless she was angry at Susanna for suggesting the gingerbread-haus scheme that had set her up for this disappointment.

Susanna hurried to the second floor and opened the door to the spare bedroom. Becca lay sprawled across the bed, her face buried in a pillow. "Go away." The words were muffled.

Susanna hesitated, not sure what to do. When Benaiah had broken up with her, she'd done the same thing, even used the same words, when Daed had followed her upstairs. Daed had quietly retreated and never mentioned her upset again.

In one way, that had been a blessing. But in another, she'd wanted—needed—someone to pull her close and love her. Tell her she would survive.

She entered the room, sat on the edge of the bed, and put her hand on Becca's back. The girl didn't flinch, so she started a gentle rubbing motion. "It's okay. You'll make it through this."

Becca sniffed, rolled over, and wiped her eyes. She reached for a tissue from the box on the bedside table. "He told me he was flattered but said he's not looking for a relationship, and asked if we could just keep it as friends. And…and…and when I asked him, 'Now or never?' he said, 'Never.'" The last word ended in a wail. "Doesn't he know how hard it was for me to ask?"

Wow. Becca had found some boldness Susanna hadn't expected. Susanna winced, not sure what to say. She bowed her head, but it felt wrong to pray about this situation when she was unwilling to submit to Gott regarding her own. What would Gott think if she prayed on Becca's behalf if she wasn't bold enough to pray for herself? But then, she had prayed for Benaiah's family, and He had responded in a clear, swift manner.

Maybe that was the key. She set her lips, lowered her head a little further, and shut her eyes. *Gott, please comfort Becca as only You can. This, on the heels of losing her home and all her belongings, must really sting.*

It seemed Caleb could've been a little more sympathetic, given her recent losses. Then again, it would've been cruel to lead her on when he clearly wasn't interested. Maybe Susanna should pray for Caleb, too. *Gott, please bring the woman You intend for Caleb into his life and help him to recognize her.*

That wasn't what she'd intended to say. She'd planned to ask Gott to open Caleb's eyes to see Becca, to really see her.

It seemed Gott had different plans.

If Susanna prayed for herself, would Gott tell her to go to Iowa?

She didn't want to have to give up Benaiah.

CHAPTER 22

$\mathcal{T}$he next day, Benaiah studied the specifics of the latest order, checked to make sure he had the necessary supplies, and called the wedding planner for clarification on a couple items. The bride-to-be collected all things dolphin and wanted as a cake topper a glass-blown figure of a dolphin jumping through a heart-shaped hoop. She had also requested a pair of blue-tinged wine glasses with stems that resembled dolphins diving through ocean waves. Benaiah had never made glass dolphins before. The wedding planner said she would e-mail him a few pictures of what the bride had in mind. Sure enough, Benaiah's phone chimed minutes later with an incoming text message. He studied the attached images and decided he could do those designs, easily.

But in a few days? He'd have to make it happen. He'd work nacht and day. Day and nacht.

Whatever it took.

The income from this order alone would equal what the shop normally made in two weeks' time. It would be enough for a down payment or a deposit plus the first month's rent on a new place. Or it would pay for new shoes for everyone, as well as cover Daadi's medical bills.

He couldn't keep from grinning as he sat at the computer to print out the designs, then recorded the details of the order in the log. Then he blew out a breath. How would Peter react to Benaiah's bold, spur-of-the-moment decision to fulfill the order without first consulting his boss?

Hopefully, Benaiah wasn't overstepping his place too much. With a whistle, he went to work.

Sometime later, he pushed aside an empty plate from the lunch Susanna had delivered to him hours ago. Eyed the six small dolphins that were ready to be attached to the wine glasses.

The frozen snow in the driveway crunched under the wheels of an Englisch van. Benaiah stopped working, stood, and walked to the window to better see who had arrived. Peter stepped out of the back door, then turned to retrieve his bag. He slipped a little on the ice as he made his way around to the other side to pay the driver.

While he worked, Benaiah had prepared and rehearsed the speech he would deliver to Peter. But Peter had returned before he'd built up enough bravery to deliver it.

Benaiah's stomach churned. Time to face the next lion: Peter, and the prospect of buying the business.

He pulled in a breath and moved toward the doorway. Should he ask Daadi to join in on this discussion? Probably, since Daadi's savings would fund the purchase.

He stepped outside the shop and hesitated as Susanna flew out of the haus and grabbed her daed by the arm. The van tires spit shards of ice as they spun for a moment before finding traction and driving off.

Jah, Benaiah could wait. And maybe take some time to pray. With Daadi. He went back into the shop to make sure the job was at a good stopping point, then left the fire burning as he trekked over to the haus.

Too bad the paper from the bank had been lost in the fire. But maybe Daadi would remember the exact amount. Besides, it might carry more weight coming from him.

Only the number in the ten-thousands place had been burned into Benaiah's brain.

"I NEED TO talk to you about something." Susanna steered Daed toward the side of the haus. She wanted to make sure he knew they had guests before he embarrassed himself or Benaiah's family by making a rude comment. And she wanted to let him know, without an audience looking on, that she'd found a job and planned to stay in Jamesport until the haus sold.

"Jah, gut to see you, too." Sarcasm colored Daed's voice. He set his suitcase on the bottom porch step and allowed Susanna to pull him away.

Susanna's face heated at her lack of manners. "Welkum home," she added belatedly. "Did you have a gut visit with Irene?"

Daed smiled, but the expression quickly faded. "So, what do you need to talk about? Your inviting the whole Troyer clan into our home without asking my permission? Just how long do they intend to stay?"

Was he teasing? She studied him, trying to get a feel for his mood, before responding, "Preacher Zeke showed up with the Troyer women Saturday, right around lunchtime. How could I say nein?" Not that she would've.

"You couldn't. They do know the haus will be listed for sale, ain't so? I've already spread the word among our people, and, if necessary, I'll enlist an Englisch realtor."

When had he found the time to get the word out to the community? Unless he'd done that weeks ago, without telling her. She sighed, feeling a deeper sense of betrayal. Everything was moving so fast, giving her nein time to react, let alone plan.

"More important, were you and Ben...uh, well, plenty of chaperones, ain't so?" Daed's eyes twinkled.

"The best chaperones ever," Susanna said.

"So, a fire? They lost everything?"

"Everything." She sighed once more. "But we found some boxes in the loft with my too-small clothes, and some others that must've been Mamm's, because I don't remember them. And I found a trash bag full of shoes. Plus, Preacher Zeke and Caleb came by with a load of outgrown clothing and shoes from their family. And earlier this morgen, Greta Yoder stopped over with canned food from her garden, and Zelda from the Hen Haus delivered a couple of jars of her dill pickle soup. She says it's best eaten cold."

Daed grunted and shook his head.

"It was nice of her to think of us." Susanna grinned, glad they had a stocked pantry and didn't need to serve that shudder-inducing concoction to Benaiah's family. "What I wanted to talk to you about is this: Benaiah has asked to court me again, with the idea of marrying me when he finds a job and a home, and...and I wondered if you'd consider giving us the farm as a wedding gift."

Daed's eyebrows shot up. "Does Benaiah think he doesn't need to play by my rules this time around?"

Susanna tilted her head. "What do you mean?"

Daed smirked. "I gave that bu my list of rules when I first caught him staring at you. Right around the time I offered to apprentice him."

Susanna rolled her eyes. "That was years ago." Still, the reminder that Benaiah had "courted" her since she was twelve warmed her heart. That Daed had known all along. "Anyway, about the farm."

"Took a while for him to work up the courage to ask you out." Daed shrugged. "About the farm...maybe."

It wouldn't do any gut to press him further. Daed wouldn't tell her anything he didn't want her to know. At least she'd asked.

"I've secured a temporary, part-time job, at least through Christmas, at Judith's Gift Shop. I started today." She was proud of being able to work and earn some money. Her first day on the job had been fun, even though the hours away from home that morgen had made more work for her in the afternoon as she kept an eye out for Daed's arrival.

Daed's eyes steeled. "You are going to Iowa next Wednesday—maybe as soon as Saturday, if we can get an auction scheduled before then—unless you're a married woman. I'm not about to shove you off on any of our relatives, having you live on your own, or organizing any other type of arrangement. You call Mrs. Judith and tell her danki, but nein more work.'"

Susanna could scarcely breathe. "But...but Daed, you really don't want me along when you marry."

"Oh, but you are going. End of discussion."

BENAIAH PICKED UP Peter's suitcase on his way into the haus and carried it back to Peter's bedroom, setting it on the floor just inside the door. He found Daadi in the living room, playing checkers with Jackie on the TV tray between them.

"Peter's home."

Daadi looked up. "I thought I heard a vehicle outside. I hope he's as okay with this temporary arrangement as your sweet Susie said he'd be."

"Guess we'll soon know." Benaiah flexed his hand. "I want you there when we talk about buying his business."

Daadi waved him off. "You're a man. You can handle it without me. Besides, not sure how sharp I'll be when it comes time to talk. Just took a pain pill. Those things make me sleepy and turn my brain to mush. I'll likely doze off before we finish this game." Daadi winked at Jackie.

"But it's your money."

"I'm giving it to you."

Benaiah sighed. "Where's Mammi?" Maybe she could talk some sense into Daadi and convince him to join them.

Daadi hesitated. "I think she and Becca are in the dawdi-haus, sewing some clothes for Lizzie and Becca from the fabric Susie gave them, since none of the hand-me-downs fit those two."

Somewhere in the haus, a door opened. Shoes clomped on the floor.

"Go on, Benaiah. Face this lion."

"But you're awake, Daadi. Please sit in."

Daadi shook his head. "You don't need me. I don't want to buy the business. You do. I'll be in here, praying."

"At least until you fall asleep." Jackie jumped one of his pieces.

"At least till then." Daadi chuckled. "Go with Gott, Sohn."

"Danki, Daadi. Appreciate the prayers. And your trust and support." With a sigh, Benaiah turned toward the kitchen.

Peter entered the kitchen via the mudroom. "Making yourself at home, bu?" The words were said with a smile.

"I need to talk to you." Benaiah wiped his damp palms on his pants. "Is now a gut time?"

"Figured you'd want to. Told Susanna to go back to sewing and not to disturb us. I could use a cup of koffee. Want one?" Peter turned toward the stove.

"Nein, but danki, anyway." Benaiah wasn't sure he'd be able to stomach it. "And danki for allowing Susie to take us in." Depending on how or when Peter had found out about the arrangement, Benaiah might need to add an apology to smooth things over. "I tried to tell you what was going on when we spoke over the phone, but you hung up so quickly."

Peter turned his shoulder and peered at Benaiah over the rim of his glasses. "Hmm." Then he went back to preparing his koffee.

Benaiah's stomach knotted.

Peter took a handful of cookies from the perpetually full cookie jar, arranged them on a plate, and finally approached the table. He sat in his chair. "Have a seat, bu."

Swiping his palms against his pants once again, Benaiah sat. "Jah. First, I'd like to buy your business. I do most of the work, anyway, except for the bookkeeping, and both Daadi and Caleb Bontrager have offered to help me with that. I'm about a thousand dollars shy of your asking price, but if you're willing to accept a cash offer at a reduced price, I'd appreciate it."

Peter leaned back in his chair and hitched his eyebrows. "That wasn't the first thing I expected you to ask."

"Everything else hinges on my having a job." Benaiah scratched at a green spot on the table—a drop of dried icing from the gingerbread decorations. He glanced toward the hutch, where Becca's haus sat next to Susanna's. Caleb hadn't taken it. Benaiah blinked, surprised to see it still there. He'd been so preoccupied with the latest order, he hadn't noticed how quiet his sister had been at mealtime. At least Susanna had managed to coax a smile out of her at breakfast that morgen. And he didn't necessarily need to talk to her, except maybe to point out the foolishness in asking a young man, in front of his daed, whom he planned to take home from a singing.

"Okay, Ben. I'll accept your cash offer."

Benaiah dared to breathe and just barely refrained from jumping to his feet and shouting "Hallelujah!" A job that would support his family. A load lifted off his shoulders. And the profits of the latest wedding order would go exclusively to him. "Danki. I'll go to town tomorrow and get the money from the bank." He'd call for a driver, since it would be easier for Daadi to get in and out of a car than a buggy.

"Anything else?" Humor colored Peter's tone.

"A couple things, actually. I'm sure you know I never stopped loving Susie."

"Jah...?" Peter's eyes sparked, and he rocked back in his chair, propping it on its back legs.

"Being with her these past several days...well, I don't want to let her go. I never did want to, actually. Just couldn't see how...." He shook his head. "I'd like permission to court her again."

"Granted." The chair thumped to the ground.

An even greater sense of joy and peace filled him. Gott was finally answering his prayers.

"I need a place to live before I approach the preachers about marrying her." Benaiah scratched at another missed drip of green icing. "I haven't been able to look for a place to rent yet. If I find a haus next week and talk to the preachers, we could be married at Christmas, before you move to Iowa."

"Hmm. Susie suggested I gift the farm to you as a wedding present."

Benaiah's face heated. Susanna had talked to her daed? He shook his head. "Nein. If we were to live in this place, I'd have to buy it from you." And he wasn't sure he could afford to purchase a haus this nice, especially when he'd struggled to make the payments on the dump they'd been renting. But would Susanna be happy going from this big farmhaus to a tiny three-bedroom rental shared with seven other people?

Peter grunted. "Be rather hard to court Susie when she's in Iowa, but I'm sure you can make it work."

"She's going to Iowa?" Still? Peter wouldn't reconsider?

"Next Wednesday at the latest. Irene and I will marry Thursday. Susie and I may go as early as this Saturday. I haven't decided."

"You initially said you'd marry in January." At the announcement about the moved-up wedding, he felt as if a rug had been jerked out from under his feet, sending him sprawling in a newfound sense of panic. He needed to finish the order in addition to finding a place to live so he could approach the preachers about marrying Susanna. Except, Preacher Zeke was out of town for a funeral. Maybe Preacher David or Preacher Samuel would be open to the idea of a rush wedding, under the circumstances.

Peter shrugged. "Why wait? We know what we're doing. The only issue is Susie. Irene doesn't really want her living with us—guess the reminder of my former frau is too painful. Except that Irene has a whole tribe of kinner to remind me of her first ehemann. It's not a big deal to me. I loved Susanna's mamm. I'll never forget her. And I know Irene loved her ehemann, and that's wunderbaar. She'll just have to accept that I have a dochter. That isn't going to change."

"Did Susie agree to go, then?"

Peter's chin jutted out. "She doesn't have a choice."

"A wise man once told me that love gives the other person a choice."

Peter grunted. "Different for daeds and their kinner."

Benaiah pushed his chair back. His stomach churned in a nauseating way. Somehow, some way, Susanna had to stay here. But Peter seemed adamant that she couldn't stay unless she was married, and between Benaiah's other responsibilities, he wouldn't have time in the coming week to arrange a rush wedding, plus finish the order and find a new haus.

"Danki for taking the time to talk with me." At least now he didn't need to ask Peter's belated permission to accept the order he'd taken on. As of tomorrow, the business would be his.

"I'll go with you to the bank tomorrow." Peter rose. "I need to have my money transferred to my new bank in Iowa. I think there's a way they can do it without my needing to withdraw everything. I also have some other business to take care of."

"I'm calling a driver." Benaiah met Peter's eyes, catching his frown of confusion. "Daadi broke his hip, and he needs to kum along tomorrow."

"It's not broken!" Daadi called from the living room. "Just a slight fracture."

Peter smiled and walked over to the doorway, peeking his head into the living room. "I'm sorry for all the losses you've suffered lately, including your mobility. Praying you'll heal quickly." He glanced at Benaiah. "I'm having an auction of all the furnishings and other items on Saturday morgen. Have a whole barn loft full of cast-offs, too, as I'm sure you discovered. We stored various belongings of my großeltern and my frau's großeltern, and when my parents moved into the dawdi-haus, we added the things they had nein need of, and...." He shook his head. "You get the picture."

"Why don't you wait on that? Or at least get some input from Susanna and Benaiah regarding what they might want to keep." Daadi glanced from Peter to Benaiah. "Ben is learning how to stretch his faith, and I want to see if there's any way Gott will bless us with this home."

Peter opened his mouth, but Daadi shook his head. "I heard what you said about the wedding gift, and the girl was sweet to ask it of you, but Benaiah has his pride."

"Pride is a sin," Peter pointed out.

This from the man who refused to let his dochter stay with relatives for the brief period of time before she married, insisting instead that she move to Iowa, where she wasn't wanted? Benaiah hitched an eyebrow. "Not all pride. Some is necessary. I wouldn't be worthy of Susanna if I wasn't willing to work to take care of her."

Peter shrugged. "We'll see what we can do. I'm going to make a list of the things I need to accomplish. Are you available to go up in the loft with me and see if there's anything you think you could use or might want for your eventual home, wherever that may be?"

"Jah. I'll grab a lantern." Benaiah turned away, thankful Peter would let him choose what furnishings he could use, as Daadi had suggested.

Gott, you are so gut. All the answered prayers…. Danki for helping me defeat the lions I've faced so far. Please give me courage for the biggest lion yet ahead of me.

A haus. Because he still had nein money for rent plus a security deposit, or for a down payment on a home of his own. Until Friday, when he would receive payment for the latest glass order.

And nein collateral. Would the business count for anything?

They would likely be laughed right out of the bank if Daadi suggested trying to get a loan while they were there tomorrow.

Trust Me.

CHAPTER 23

*S*usanna couldn't focus on sewing while Daed and Benaiah were having a conversation she wasn't privy to. A conversation that likely centered, at least in part, on her. Like when—or if—Benaiah requested permission to court her. If he asked, would Daed agree? Or stubbornly insist she move with him to Iowa? And if he did insist, what would it mean for her relationship with Benaiah? Would it be over before it had hardly begun?

She strode to the window and stared out at the dreary, gray sky as Mammi Wren chattered about Gott's grace and mercy while cutting out green fabric for a dress for Becca. Becca sat at the machine, working the foot pedal as she sewed a maroon dress. At least her attitude seemed better, even though her eyes were a little puffy from the tears she'd shed last nacht.

Susanna watched as Daed and Benaiah plodded carefully across the frozen lawn to the barn. What were they going to do out there?

She wavered, clutching her apron so tight that the seam bit into her fingers. Daed had asked her to leave them alone to talk, and she had. So why were they going someplace private right now?

She huffed out a breath and slid one step closer to the mudroom door. Her coat and boots waited in the kitchen, just on the other side of the narrow space. Would Daed object to her running out there and joining them? They might be discussing her future, and she wanted to pretend she had some say, even though that was far from reality. Daed would decide her fate until she married Benaiah, at which point he would take over making decisions for her.

Neither man was in the habit of listening to her. Or, if either one of them listened, he didn't *hear*. Well, oftentimes, anyway.

She took another step toward the mudroom as Mammi Wren talked on. Susanna didn't want to run out on Becca and Mammi Wren, but what other choice did she have? Daed's decisions regarding her future were based on what he wanted her to do. And Benaiah already made decisions for her without asking. Such as when he'd broken off their relationship because he believed she wouldn't want to be married to him when he had a family who needed his care.

As if she were that heartless.

She sighed.

The sudden silence startled her. She turned and looked at Mammi Wren, who was frozen in position, shears suspended above the pinned fabric. Becca had ceased sewing and stared at Susanna, too.

Susanna grimaced. "Sorry. Daed and Benaiah are talking, and I want to know what they're discussing."

"Leave them to their talk. They'll fill you in if it's anything you need to know," Mammi Wren advised.

But what if they thought she didn't need to know, and she really did? Case in point: Daed's decision to move to Iowa and take her with him. Would he change his mind if he knew Benaiah was courting her? And would she be allowed to work for Mrs. Judith through the holidays?

It didn't really matter. She *wasn't* going to Iowa. Not even if Daed insisted on it. She'd refuse.

Susanna slumped. As if she had a right to refuse.

Somehow, she had to figure out a way.

Lord Gott, if You hear me, if You care, please let me stay here. Help Daed to listen to me.

Susanna edged toward the mudroom door. Again. "I'm going to see what Jackie's up to." She would slip out to the barn to discover what it was Daed and Benaiah were talking about after she'd located Jackie.

"She's playing checkers with Daadi." Becca looked up. "I saw them when I went to get Mammi a cup of tea."

Ach. So much for that plan of escape.

Right now, being an only child was preferable to having a haus-ful of chaperones.

Or maybe she was thinking immaturely because what she wanted and what her elder had advised were two different things.

She firmed her shoulders, turned away from the window, and went to the table where Mammi Wren had resumed cutting fabric. "How can I help?"

"There's really nothing you can do at this point." Mammi Wren paused, mid-motion.

The door opened, and Benaiah peeked inside. "Süße, if you have a moment, we could use you in the barn."

BENAIAH DELIGHTED IN the spark of joy that lit Susanna's eyes, and the slight smile that curved her lips upward.

"Sure, I'll be there in a minute. I need to put on my coat and shoes." She was already heading for the mudroom as she spoke.

"Take your time. We'll be in the loft." Benaiah closed the door behind him.

Halfway across the yard, he hesitated when he heard a horse snort. He turned toward the road and eyed the buggy coming down the drive. A black bonnet and a shapeless black coat concealed the identity of the female visitor. He stepped aside and grabbed the bridle as the horse came to a stop beside him. Then he moved to assist the driver out of the buggy.

His heart fell as Susanna's cousin Amanda accepted his hand. But maybe she'd kum to visit Susie, or someone else in his family.

He forced a smile. "Gut afternoon, Amanda." He released her hand and stepped back. "Go on into the haus. My mammi and Becca are sewing."

"I came to see you." Amanda batted her eyelids. "I brought you something."

Clothes? Shoes? Maybe some food, even though Peter had a fully stocked pantry? Benaiah's smile became real as she reached into the backseat of the buggy. "Danki, Amanda. I appreciate...."

She produced a gingerbread haus that put Lizzie's, Becca's, and even Susanna's to shame. It was covered in store-bought candy: peppermints, Life Savers, M&Ms, and Tootsie Rolls, Nerds, gumdrops, Red Hots, and Gummi Bears. His mouth watered as his eyes took in the colorful array of treats.

"A gingerbread haus." A lump settled in Benaiah's stomach as he remembered all the talk of love potions disguised as gingerbread. *Ach, nein. Nein, nein, nein.*

With a shy smile, she stepped forward, holding the haus out to him.

His breath lodged in his throat. He should decline the gift. He'd already told Susanna he would, and he couldn't risk messing up their newly established courtship by accepting a gift from another woman. But after Caleb's rejection of Becca's haus, and her reaction, he didn't know how to refuse it. Would Amanda break down the way his sister had?

On the other hand, it was just a treat, as Mammi had reminded everyone.

They still had Susanna's haus. And Becca's, though she'd been making noises about feeding hers to the hogs. Noises that meant nothing, considering she hated wasting food. Or maybe she hoped Caleb would change his mind, return to claim the gingerbread, and ask to court her.

Benaiah heard the kitchen door open. Susanna came outside and descended the porch steps. Then she hesitated, her gaze on him and Amanda.

He swallowed. Looked back at Amanda. *How awkward.* He didn't have the foggiest idea what to do or say.

Amanda's smile faltered when he made nein move to take the haus off her hands. "Want me to put it inside for you?"

He shifted his stance so he could see both women at the same time. The adjustment took him half a foot farther away from Amanda. Susanna didn't move.

His innocent flirting with Amanda on Thanksgiving must've hurt Susanna. And his acceptance of the treat would injure her spirit even more. But if he rejected it in order to prove his love for Susanna, he would offend her family member at the same time. Might even anger Peter in the process.

"Ben, where are you?" Peter stepped out of the barn. His gaze lit on Amanda, still holding the shallow box containing the gingerbread haus. "Ach, Amanda. Didn't know you were here."

"Hiya, Onkel Peter. I brought this over for Ben. Thought it'd cheer him up after his horrible losses."

"Wow. Hope everyone likes gingerbread. We've got two of those already." Peter shrugged. "But that was nice of you to think of them. Curious that everyone seems to have had the same thought. Gingerbread, of all things." He shook his head. "Take it on up to the haus. Ben and I were right in the middle of something, but you're welkum to go on in and visit, if you'd like."

"Nein, nein, I've got to get home. Danki, though." Amanda turned toward the haus, but not before her shy smile became a smug-looking smirk—aimed at Susanna—as she sashayed her way up the stairs.

Susanna stiffened and bared her teeth in a grin that would've sent Benaiah running in the other direction if it'd been intended for him.

In fact, going the opposite way seemed like a wise choice. He looped the reins of Amanda's horse around a nearby sapling, and fled into the barn.

He'd salvage the candy, if he could, but the gingerbread would feed the hogs.

He wouldn't take any chances, love potion or not.

SUSANNA TRIED NOT to scowl as she opened the door for Amanda so she could carry her "treat" into the haus. How dare Benaiah look at it the way he did? Almost as if he lusted after it.

Susanna couldn't fault Daed for stepping in to accept it, because he likely didn't have a clue. But Benaiah? He knew. And yet he hadn't refused the gift, even though he'd assured Susanna he would. Although maybe he simply hadn't had a chance to do so before her daed stepped in. If she'd had more decorations on hand when she'd suggested the haus-making activity, her own might've turned out much nicer.

She repressed a sigh. A wail of dismay. An angry shout. All three.

Amanda set her gingerbread haus on the counter, then walked over to the hutch where Susanna and Becca's projects, pitiful by comparison, sat side by side. "Who are these two from?" She smirked again as she reached out and flicked at the corner of one roof. "Amateurs."

"Ach, Benaiah's sisters and I made those, just for fun. It isn't as if we were having a competition." Not until Amanda's showed up, anyway. "We already gifted one to somebody, just haven't found homes for the remaining two." Susanna waved her hand at them. "Well, we haven't really tried. Or had time since the blizzard."

She wouldn't announce that Becca's attempt to give hers away had been met with rejection. That was none of Amanda's business.

If Caleb could manage to decline Becca's gift, why couldn't Benaiah have done the same with Amanda? Taken her aside with a tactful "Danki, but nein danki." Or, even better, an "It's not you, it's me."

Pain knifed through Susanna. Self-deprecation at her lack of artistic abilities. Insecurity. She fought to keep from slumping. She glanced at her own gingerbread haus, which looked like a hovel compared to her cousin's elaborately designed cottage. She'd been proud of it before. Now, not so much. She'd just have to make sure Benaiah ate hers. Not Amanda's.

Just in case the love potion actually worked.

Amanda flipped her kapp strings over her shoulders. "It must be heartbreaking for you, having the Troyer family staying under your roof after Ben rejected you. But you'll be moving to Iowa soon. Maybe you'll meet someone there."

Susanna opened her mouth to say that Benaiah had asked to court her again, but she pressed her lips together, keeping those words unspoken. She didn't know if he'd asked Daed yet.

And besides, she really didn't want Amanda to know.

Yet.

It'd be fun to see the look on her cousin's face when Benaiah asked for Susanna at the wedding singing on Thursday. When Benaiah gave her a ride home afterward. Then everyone would know they were back together.

Susanna could hardly wait.

CHAPTER 24

As Benaiah helped Peter sort through furniture in the loft, he couldn't help raising his eyebrows at some of the items Peter had been storing. An electric guitar and an amplifier, in an Amish barn? Had Peter played in a rock band during his rumschpringe? The mental picture of an Amish man doing such a thing didn't fit, and sparked a whole slew of questions Benaiah would never ask.

A creak from down below caught his attention, and he moved to the edge of the loft. Susanna climbed the ladder, got off at the top, and glanced at him. "I didn't think she'd ever leave."

Benaiah grimaced at the sight of her tear-moistened eyes, belatedly realizing there had been another lion in the driveway he should have had the courage to face. "I'm sorry. I never meant to encourage her. Or to hurt you."

She offered him a weak smile. "The apology helps the hurt to start going away. Not enough for me to say it's okay, though. Because it isn't."

"The hogs will enjoy her gingerbread haus." Ach, it hurt to say that. Especially when he really wanted some of the candy decorations for himself. Not all of them, but maybe a handful of gumdrops. A couple of Tootsie Rolls. All the Nerds.

Susanna shrugged. "It almost seems wrong to feed that work of art to the hogs. Too bad we can't give it to someone else—ideally, someone who doesn't have the vaguest idea about the 'love potion' recipe going around. Like, um, Yost Miller, maybe."

Benaiah glanced at her. "Why Yost Miller?"

"Well, I feel bad that he hasn't courted anyone. But the girls seem not to be able to overlook that he's a beanpole, has a bad case of acne, and wears glasses. And he's extremely shy. But his personality is sweet. He's like a fantastic, can't-put-it-down book hidden underneath an unappealing cover."

Benaiah frowned, an ache of jealousy forming in his chest. "I'm not sure I like to hear you saying those things about another man." He raised one shoulder. "I don't care one way or another if you give it to him." He knew he shouldn't lie. But, really, Yost *could* have the haus, just so long as Benaiah got some of the candy.

Susanna giggled. "I saw the lust on your face as you eyed Amanda's creation."

"It was the gumdrops, not the haus," he said quickly. "It'd be nice to give a haus to Yost, I guess. If you're certain he doesn't know about the love potion."

Peter looked up from where he was working and frowned.

"How could he know?" Susanna asked. "He has nein sisters." She let out a quiet groan. "If only I'd never read about the love potion. Even better, if nobody had. I didn't expect Amanda to actually make you a gingerbread haus. Or for Becca to get hurt in her attempts to give her haus away."

Benaiah nodded. "Giving them away would be a gut method of disproving this crazy notion about a love potion. Why don't we give Becca's to Yost Miller, and Amanda's to Menno Swartz?" He glanced over his shoulder at Peter, who shoved something aside at the other end of the loft. Then he looked back at Susanna, raised his hand, and let his fingertip trail slowly down her cheek. "Love potion or not, you're the only girl for me. Remember that."

SUCH A SWEET thing to say. Susanna leaned into Benaiah's touch.

Too soon, he moved away. "I'm helping your daed for a while. Why don't you look around and see if there's anything you want to keep for our future home? Or that you think I might need in the meantime? Your daed's going to auction off whatever we haven't set aside."

"Including what's in the haus, Suz," Daed put in. "Mark what you want somehow, so I'll know not to sell it in the auction." He wiped his hand across his forehead, knocking his hat askew.

"You're auctioning off the furniture?" She hadn't meant to whine.

Daed didn't look at her. "The furniture, the farm equipment, the haus, the barn, the land, the animals, the buggies, everything. Jah. All gone. Auction will be Saturday."

Susanna frowned. "What about the shop?" Would Daed ruin Benaiah's dreams?

"Benaiah is buying it. He can store what he wants or needs in there."

"Daed!" Susanna resisted the urge to stomp her foot even though she was excited to know that Daed accepted Benaiah's offer.

Daed gave her his signature harsh look that always made her back down.

Except this time, she would stand her ground. "What about me? What about the Troyers?"

Daed grunted. "The Troyers can stay here until the new owners take possession. You, as I've already said, are going to Iowa after the auction Saturday."

"Not next Wednesday? But—"

"I changed my mind. We're leaving Saturday. You dare question me?" Daed straightened to his full height.

"Nein. Sorry." She slumped. Maybe she wasn't quite ready to stand up to him. But she needed to figure out a way to do so, because she couldn't—wouldn't—go to Iowa.

Benaiah rested his hand gently on her shoulder. Squeezed. "I need you to pick out what you want to keep and mark it. There's a package of colored stickers your daed bought. They're over on the hutch. It'll work out, süße. Don't worry so much."

And with those not-so-comforting words, he turned away.

Susanna huffed and spun around. Her sore hip rebelled, and she almost lost her balance but caught herself on a nearby chair.

Did Daed really expect her to play Suzy Homemaker and choose furnishings for a home that would soon become part of her past? If only she and Benaiah could plan to live in the haus where she'd grown up, instead of having to hope for a future haus that might never materialize.

Especially with her living in Iowa—out of sight, out of mind— and Amanda setting her kapp for Benaiah.

BENAIAH AND PETER worked late into the evening by the light of lanterns hanging at intervals throughout the barn and shop, as they moved all the pieces Susanna had tagged. The furniture cluttered the back of the shop, making it difficult to navigate. Not only that, but if a customer came in, the sight of such apparent disorganization might tarnish Benaiah's reputation.

He blew out a breath as he carried a wrought-iron bed frame into the shop. Not to mention he had an order due mere days from now, and time was speeding by faster than an angry, territorial rooster charging at an intruder.

At this rate, he'd have to work over-nacht, and possibly tomorrow nacht and the next, as well, to finish the dolphin cake topper and wine glasses for the wedding. But it'd be worth it for the money he would earn, plus the future business it promised.

"I'm going to head in for supper. The bell rang quite some time ago." Peter brushed his hands on his pants. "We'll work more on this project tomorrow."

Benaiah's stomach had started rumbling when Susanna had gone inside to prepare supper after marking the items in the loft that she wanted or thought they could use. She'd mentioned that she planned on making meat loaf, scalloped potatoes, and baked apples—three of Benaiah's favorite comfort foods. She'd also mentioned sweet corn, which he also enjoyed.

But he wasn't sure he should take the time to eat. He glanced at the cold wood furnace.

"Nein work to be done here, my bu," Peter crowed, clapping his hands together.

Except that there was. But Peter didn't know about the order Benaiah had accepted. And Benaiah didn't feel comfortable telling him about it, since he technically hadn't yet purchased the business. That would happen tomorrow.

On the other hand, his withholding the information could be considered a lie of omission—a sin. A knot settled in his belly.

He wiped his hands on his pants, trying to eliminate the sudden sweat that had coated his palms. "Uh, Peter? Actually, I was…proactive. An order came in this weekend, and I accepted it, trusting that you'd accept my offer to buy the business."

Peter raised his eyebrows. "That so?" But there seemed to be a glimmer of respect in his gaze. He glanced around at the cluttered shop. "After the auction, you ought to be able to move these things into the barn until you find someplace to live."

"Danki. I appreciate it." Benaiah removed his hat and slapped it against his hip, then put it back on. If only he could ask Peter to finance the haus for him, too. The big, sprawling farm-haus with the attached dawdi-haus would be the perfect home for him and his family. And he'd be able to marry Susanna ever so much sooner.

He opened his mouth. But the words didn't kum.

CHAPTER 25

*B*enaiah's stomach roiled for the entire trip into town on Wednesday morgen. Seated in the middle row of the van next to Daadi, he clutched the seat belt to keep it from pressing against his abdomen. Behind the steering wheel was a man Benaiah didn't recognize. His usual driver hadn't been available. Peter sat in the front passenger seat, chatting away with the Englisch man as if they'd known each other their entire lives.

And it seemed they had. Especially since they talked about the "good old days" when they played together in a band during Peter's rumschpringe.

Benaiah shook his head. If he hadn't seen the electric guitar in the loft, he never would've believed such a thing of Peter. And now this musically inclined, artsy-crafty man was giving up his career to live as a farmer in the district of his future frau.

The driver pulled up outside the bank and parked. Peter opened his door and got out of the van, a thick folder grasped in his hand. "We shouldn't be too long," he told the driver, "but if you have errands to run, don't let us keep you. I have my phone."

"I'll be fine. I have a book." The driver held up a thin black object that resembled a giant smartphone. "Actually, several books." He chuckled.

Peter nodded, then headed into the bank while Benaiah helped Daadi inch his way out of the van. Daadi rubbed his hip once he was on his feet. "Those painkillers make me too sleepy. I've a mind to stop taking them."

Sure enough, Daadi had dozed for most of the trip into town. But rest was necessary for healing, so Benaiah would encourage him to continue taking the pills. Especially if that meant he might be able to avoid a surgery they probably wouldn't be able to afford.

Inside the bank, Peter had disappeared, and Benaiah didn't know where to go. He usually took his horse and buggy through the drive-through to deposit his paychecks. He and Daadi slowly made their way through the lobby toward the tellers' counters.

"Hi! May I help you?" The teller's perky voice matched her appearance: sparkling blue eyes and light blonde hair held in place with a glittery barrette. Her diamond earrings shimmered in the light. An equally dazzling diamond shone on her left ring finger.

Benaiah wondered how her fiancé had proposed. Had it been one of those elaborate, memorable affairs, with an airplane or a flash mob? Heaviness descended over Benaiah. Daadi was right: Susanna was worthy of a swoon-worthy proposal. But as a plain Amish man, he didn't have the vaguest idea how to pull one off. Not even after days of thinking. He supposed he could craft her a glass Christmas rose, but when would he have time to make it?

It didn't really matter. He was in nein position to propose. Not until he had a haus.

Daadi's crutches thumped against the side of the wooden counter as he leaned in close. "I hope you can help me. I need to cash a CD."

With a smile, the teller gestured to the side, at a desk where a larger woman was seated across from an elderly couple. A row of chairs was arranged nearby. "Have a seat over there, and someone will be right with you."

"Danki." Daadi nodded, then looked toward the waiting area, located halfway between the entry and the teller stations, and gave a heavy sigh.

"You've got this," Benaiah assured him. He glanced around, wondering whether banks supplied complimentary wheelchairs for their patrons' use. He didn't see any chairs. Daadi probably would've refused one, even if it were offered.

"If I've got this, then you've 'got' your battle." Daadi spoke quietly yet with authority. "Talk to Peter. Tell him you want the haus, too. The land. Speak with a loan officer while we're here."

He should've figured Daadi would push the issue.

Benaiah settled in a chair next to Daadi in the waiting area, nausea building in the pit of his stomach, threatening to make him lose the two cups of koffee he'd consumed that morgen, along with his breakfast of bacon, eggs, and grits. He swallowed the rising bile and glanced around for a water fountain. Instead, he spied a small refrigerator stocked with water bottles.

Another female bank employee must've seen him staring at the fridge, because she opened the glass door, reached inside, and snatched two bottles seconds before crossing the room to deliver them to Benaiah and Daadi.

Daadi politely refused her offer, but Benaiah gratefully accepted it. He twisted the cap off the ice-cold bottle and gulped greedily. *Danki, Gott, for the water.* Before he could adequately express his thanks, the woman's heels were clicking down the corridor as she hastened to another part of the bank.

Peter emerged from an office on the opposite side of the building. Striding behind him was a man wearing a white shirt, a navy-blue tie, and matching dress pants. He was all smiles.

"I wish you all the best, Peter." The man turned from Peter and met Benaiah's eyes. His smile widened as he approached with outstretched hand. "And you must be the young man interested in buying his business. Step into my office, and we'll talk."

"Will you be able to transfer the funds from a CD?" Benaiah asked. He glanced toward the woman the teller had indicated earlier, still seated with the older couple.

The man nodded. "Indeed, I can. I'm Frank Daane, loan officer."

Why had Peter been speaking with a loan officer? Benaiah's nausea grew. Frank Daane would be the one to talk to about buying the land and the haus, too. But with Peter there, the conversation would be extra embarrassing, especially after Benaiah had told Peter of his determination to work to provide for Susanna.

He shook his head. Gott might be providing for their needs, but he couldn't press the issue by asking for more than Gott would give.

Ach, you of little faith.

Lord Gott…jah, I want it. I do. It would be so perfect for the family. But I'm scared.

"Ask, and it shall be given to you; seek, and ye shall find; knock, and it shall be opened unto you."

Could he believe it? Did he dare ask?

Daadi struggled to his feet. Hopefully, all this activity wasn't aggravating the damage to his hip. Benaiah moved alongside him and rested his hand against Daadi's back, helping him up. Lending support.

"Let me bring in another chair." Mr. Daane lifted a chair from the waiting area and carried it into his office. Peter followed him.

Daadi hobbled into the room, sank into the chair closest the door, and propped his crutches against the wall. Benaiah sat next to him. Peter took the third seat, the thick folder still clutched in his hand.

Mr. Daane shut the door and came around to sit behind his desk. "Now, how may I help you?"

Daadi leaned forward. "I'd like to cash in my CD and give it to my gross-sohn so he can purchase Peter King's glass shop. The CD is under my name. Micah Troyer."

Frank Daane nodded, then turned his chair to face his computer screen. He glanced at Benaiah. "And your name is…?"

"Benaiah Troyer." His voice came out hoarse. Raw. He uncapped the bottle of water and took another gulp.

"And…" Daadi prodded him.

The bile threatened again.

Lord, help me face this lion. Give me strength. Give me courage. Give me faith.

"And…." Benaiah swallowed. Hard. "I'd like to talk to you about the prospect of my buying the rest of Peter's property."

CHAPTER 26

*S*usanna fixed herself a sandwich for an early lunch. The rest of the family would eat when Daed, Benaiah, and Daadi Micah returned from town, but she needed to get to Judith's Gift Shop for her second day of work. She couldn't wait. Was it selfish to wish that Mrs. Judith would be so impressed with her, she would forget all about the other girl she wanted to hire for the period of time she'd be overseas?

Susanna needed to hurry so she could leave before Daed got home, since she was defying his order for her to quit. Her fingers fumbled in her haste as she hitched up Daed's horse and buggy and took off toward the road. At the end of her driveway, a white van approached the drive and turned in. Her breath hitched as the driver stopped and rolled down his window.

Daed leaned down in his seat up front so she could see him. "I sold the haus and said we'd be out after the auction on Saturday. Already bought our tickets. When you get home from whatever frolic it is that you're off to, you need to pack."

So soon? "Daed—"

"End of discussion." He looked away and motioned for the driver to continue.

The driver gave her a sympathetic glance but did as Daed directed.

Tears of anger burned Susanna's eyes. She brushed them away. Should she turn around, skip work, and argue with him? Or should she report to the shop and talk to every Amish customer with the intent of finding a temporary home? And a more-than-temporary, part-time job?

Where had Daed been all morgen, anyway? Seemed he still didn't think it important to tell her his plans. And who had bought the haus? Daed had told her he was going to list it. Or auction it. Except…wait. The auction wasn't until Saturday, so he must've listed it. And when Daed said he had done something, it didn't necessarily mean he actually *had*; sometimes, it meant only that he *intended* to.

But he'd said he'd sold the haus. Meaning it truly was *sold*.

Her heart folded in on itself. She brushed away more stinging tears. Even if she and Benaiah married, her home was gone forever. Soon a stranger would be cooking at the stove and washing clothes in the mudroom and snuggling on the couch by the fireplace.

It wouldn't do any gut to stay and talk to Daed right now. She wouldn't get her way. She never did. It'd be better to make her own arrangements, prove she was serious, and present him with the done deal. Maybe she'd even pack—but she would run away before he could force her onto a bus bound for Iowa.

BENAIAH GRABBED A sandwich and headed out to work in *his* shop. For the first time in almost a year, a heavy weight had been lifted from his shoulders, and he inhaled an unhampered breath.

His own business.

And if he met or exceeded the client's expectations with the dolphin wedding cake topper and wine glasses, he'd have a contract with a wedding planner that would generate plenty of business going forward.

After wrapping things up at the bank, Benaiah and Peter had met with the web designer who managed the business's Internet page. The designer had removed Peter's name and contact information from the site. Now only Benaiah's name and number were listed.

Benaiah Troyer. Owner.

It made his heart sing. And Daadi hadn't been able to stop smiling.

Especially when the loan officer—and Peter—had been more than willing to talk about what it would take for the property—the whole property—to become his. *His!*

He had a home. A business. A future.

And a hope to marry Susanna. Maybe in the spring. He would suggest that time frame once he'd figured out a swoon-worthy way of proposing.

After meeting with the web designer, Benaiah and Peter had parted ways, Benaiah accompanying Daadi on a dentist appointment he'd neglected to mention—or, if he'd mentioned it, that Benaiah had forgotten about. The driver had dropped them off, then had taken Peter to buy his bus tickets and then home again before returning to the dentist for Benaiah and Daadi.

Susanna was gone when they returned. Benaiah didn't know where. He looked for her, then asked Peter, who merely shrugged. "Maybe a work frolic."

Benaiah vaguely recalled hearing one of those mentioned last church Sunday. He didn't remember any of the details.

All he knew was, he couldn't wait for Susanna to get home so he could tell her the news.

And maybe, just maybe, an idea for a swoon-worthy proposal would surface by then, and he could ask for her hand. For real. Not just a hypothetical, casual mention.

He whistled as he built the wood fire and got to work, fueled as never before by the sheer exhilaration of having purchased the business for himself. When the dinner bell rang, the dolphins for the glassware were finished, and he'd started on the glasses themselves. But he couldn't quit mid-process without losing momentum. So, he continued working through the nacht.

Thursday morgen, with just the cake topper to finish, Benaiah staggered to the haus for some sleep that he needed more than food or koffee. He would snooze for a few hours, then start the topper in the afternoon. He estimated needing another ten hours or so to complete it, so he'd be able to finish the order to-nacht and have it ready for pickup in the morgen.

The haus looked and sounded empty. The younger girls must've gone to school, Lizzie to work; but where was everyone else? Too tired to try to figure it out, he stumbled through the kitchen.

A note on the table caught his attention. He rubbed his eyes and blinked until the words came into focus.

Benaiah,

Susanna is spending the nacht with a friend she saw in town. She called and said to tell you not to forget the wedding. See you there.

—Becca

He needed sleep first. Right now, he was too tired to remember his own name, let alone who was getting married. Or where. Or even if he was supposed to be in the ceremony.

Benaiah swayed dizzily and struggled to keep his eyes open. He folded the note and stuffed it in his pocket. After a quick shower, he collapsed on his temporary bed—the couch.

Thursday evening, after the wedding, Susanna stood in the back bedroom with the other single girls, to wait as, one by one, the young men came back to claim their special girl.

Had Benaiah kum to the wedding? She hadn't seen him, but there was a crush of Amish from surrounding districts and states, not to mention a lot of Englisch guests, since the groom, Sammy Miller, had made many Englisch friends in his work as a firefighter and an EMT.

Benaiah must've gotten the message she'd asked Becca to leave for him yesterday. He had to be there.

At the first knock, the giggles came to a complete stop, and all the girls peered at one another. Martha spritzed herself with body spray, handed the bottle to another girl, and opened the door. The giggles and whispers started again.

"Amanda." The man wasn't anyone Susanna knew.

"Martha."

"Tabitha."

"Becca." *Yost Miller!* Susanna grinned.

The requests kept coming. One by one, the room emptied of girls.

A smidgen of worry filled Susanna. Benaiah didn't usually wait this long. Hadn't he seen the note? Or had he forgotten? Becca had said he'd been out in the shop working on an order ever since he'd returned home the day before.

Soon there were only three maidals left: Susanna; the bishop's dochter, Bethany Weiss; and Lydia Hershberger, the bride's best friend, who was betrothed to somebody back home, in Ohio.

Silence stretched on. Long minutes passed.

Bethany pivoted abruptly and stalked to the window.

A hard ball formed in Susanna's stomach. She picked up the bottle of body mist. Sniffed it. Lightly sprayed herself, then returned the bottle to the dresser.

And then, another knock.

This one was quiet. Timid. As if the man wasn't sure of himself. Not Benaiah's knock. Although it might be, if he was just arriving now. He'd be embarrassed, coming so late.

The stubborn hope flared. Susanna opened the door.

Her hope died a violent, writhing, painful death.

The name he uttered was lost in the acute sense of disappointment roaring through her. She peered past him.

Nobody else loitered in the hall.

Benaiah wasn't there.

She squeezed her eyes shut and stepped aside, waiting for the chosen girl to let out a tiny sigh of relief and leave the room.

Seconds passed. The man repeated himself: "Bethany."

Susanna gathered her disappointment, tucked the hurt inside, blinked back the tears, and went over to the window. She touched Bethany's arm. "He asked for you." Her voice broke.

With nein other single men there, Susanna and Lydia also gathered around the man who'd asked for Bethany. They clustered close to avoid the shame of going unclaimed.

Where was Benaiah? He had better have a gut explanation.

CHAPTER 27

$\mathcal{B}$enaiah put the finishing touches on the dolphin cake topper, then set it aside to cool. The finished glassware exceeded his own expectations, and he was ashamed at the sinful pride that filled him. Even greater was his sense of exhaustion. He wouldn't take another rush job like this, if he could help it. After working countless consecutive hours, pausing for only a two-hour nap, he couldn't wait to sleep an entire nacht. As soon as he'd packaged the order in bubble wrap and cleaned up his tools, he was going to the haus for a giant meal, followed by a long winter's nap.

He fisted his hand and rubbed his lower back for a moment, then picked up his cell phone to text the wedding planner.

Order ready for pickup tomorrow.

A reply came almost immediately.

Wonderful. C u @ 8. I have another design 2 show u.

Another wedding cake topper?

Benaiah looked out the window into the darkness and saw the beams from a buggy's headlights.

He'd seen Peter, Daadi, Mammi, and his three youngest sisters when he'd awakened from his nap, whatever time that had been. After downing a bowl of cereal, he'd asked them not to disturb him in the shop, because he had another eight to ten hours more of work to do. They'd honored his wishes. Nobody had summoned him for supper.

He looked away. Probably one of his sisters, and he didn't want to interrupt them with their dates—unless the beau lingered too long.

228 Laura V. Hilton

Seemed he remembered something about Susanna having spent the nacht at a friend's haus, so it probably wasn't she.

The shop door opened. Susanna marched inside.

Marched.

"Didn't you get my message?" Her face flushed red.

He blinked at her. Why was she angry? "Message? What message? Oh, the note that said you'd be spending the nacht with a friend?"

"That was last nacht. I stayed with the bride and her wedding party. I'm talking about the wedding singing. You were supposed to take me home so Amanda would *know* that we're back together." She planted her fists on her hips.

Huh? He didn't remember anything about a wedding singing. "You were spending the nacht with a friend."

She rolled her eyes. "We've gone over that already. It was last nacht."

"It was?" He rubbed his eyes and leaned against the table.

"Yost Miller brought me and Becca home. I told him to wait while Becca went to get him her gingerbread haus."

He struggled to make sense of her words. "I thought Becca liked Caleb Bontrager. Why would she give her gingerbread haus to Yost? Or maybe she's just glad to get rid of it...."

Susanna's foot started tapping impatiently on the floor.

Okay. Clearly he'd missed something, somewhere. Something important. Something big that mattered deeply to her, even if he couldn't think what it could be. He scratched his head. An apology would be in gut form. He should've done more work earlier in the week so he could've been better rested by now.

"Suz, I'm so sorry. I had a rush order I was working on, and I lost track of time. I haven't really slept in two days, and I forgot...and...." Hopefully, his general penitence would smooth things over, and she would understand that he hadn't done whatever it was that he'd done on purpose.

The door opened again, and Peter strode in. "Susanna, you're home. Gut. I—"

"Jah, you told me." Susanna's shoulders slumped. "You sold the haus. We're leaving after the auction, and I'm supposed to pack."

Benaiah frowned. Wasn't she glad he'd purchased the haus? He'd thought she would be thrilled.

Peter nodded. "They're taking possession immediately."

"Why do I still have to go with you to Iowa?"

Peter expelled a heavy sigh of frustration. "You think I'm about to let you stay here and live with your beau?"

Susanna jerked, confusion clouding her expression. She looked at Peter, then at Benaiah, and finally back at Peter. "We'd have plenty of chaperones. You forget he has five sisters, and his großeltern."

A flash of happiness lit her eyes, then quickly faded behind a host of unasked questions he couldn't discern right now.

"I don't forget, Susie. It's still not right. I also don't like the idea of being accused of kicking you out. You and I are a family. We need to stay together, even if I am getting remarried. At least until it's time for you to marry." Peter cast a sideways glance at Benaiah.

What? He wasn't ready to propose right now. Nein way would getting down on one knee in his shop cause anyone to swoon. Daadi would say it was as pitiful as his basement request to court her again.

He frowned at Peter for being in such a rush.

Susanna pressed her lips together. She shut her eyes, as if she was praying. Outside, the headlights of Yost Miller's buggy swept around the circular drive as he headed homeward. Hopefully, he'd enjoy the gingerbread haus.

Susanna turned toward the door. Opened it. And stepped outside. "Nein. I won't go to Iowa."

Benaiah cleared his throat. "Susanna—"

She slammed the door shut.

SUSANNA STALKED ACROSS the driveway, tears blurring her eyes.

Yost clicked his tongue, and his horse stopped. He peered out of the buggy at her. "Everything okay?"

She forced a smile. "Fine, jah." Except it wasn't. Not only had she openly defied Daed, but she'd done it in front of Benaiah. Now, Daed would scold her—deservingly—and Benaiah would doubt her willingness to submit to his own authority as her ehemann.

But she wasn't ready to apologize. Anger roared about inside her head. Her fists were clenched so tightly, her fingernails created indentations in her palms.

"Ser gut your daed sold the property to the Troyers, ain't so?" Yost grinned at her.

She stretched her lips so wide that they felt stiff. As if they'd crack and fall off like shards of broken glass.

But reality crashed in on her like an avalanche of snow sliding off the barn roof and landing in a messy heap.

Daed had sold the property. To Benaiah. And here was the proof that neither Benaiah nor Daed had thought she needed to know. Just like when Daed had decided he was getting remarried and had told everyone else before her. She huffed, then clambered up into the buggy next to Yost. "Can you give me a ride?"

"Uh. Sure. Where to?"

She didn't know. And mutely shook her head as her eyes overflowed with tears.

Yost clicked at the horse once more, and the buggy moved toward the road. He glanced at her. "Your onkel's haus?"

Susanna shook her head. That was the first place Daed would look, and she wasn't ready to swallow her pride and ask him for forgiveness. Or to submissively bow to his will and move to Iowa to live with him, his new bride, and her innumerable kinner.

And Benaiah....

She wailed.

Yost looked at her.

Her friend Jen had recently moved from her family's haus into town to start a job at a restaurant. Susanna could stay with her at her new place.

Nobody would look for her there.

CHAPTER 28

*B*enaiah stood still a moment, torn with indecision. Should he race after Susanna and try to undo the damage? Maybe he should pray with her before they talked, because, so far, everything that'd kum out of his mouth had been wrong.

Or should he talk with Peter and try to reason with him? Probably not, since, considering his bumbling communication earlier that evening due to sleep deprivation, he would probably just make things worse.

Nein matter what, prayer seemed a gut first step. *Prayer and lots of koffee.*

He closed his eyes and bowed his head. *Lord Gott, help. I need direction. Guidance. Words. And wisdom in facing down this newest lion.*

When he opened his eyes, Peter was opening the door, preparing to leave.

"Peter, wait."

Peter paused, shut the door once more, and turned to Benaiah. "Jah?"

Benaiah swallowed. "I understand you want Susanna to go with you to Iowa. If I were in your shoes, I'd want to take my dochter along, too. But consider this: It's going to cause strife in your marriage if you don't honor your new frau's wishes not to have Susanna living there. And, as you once said to me, love gives the other person a choice. You aren't giving Susanna—or Irene—a choice. What you say goes."

"She's not married, Benaiah. I'm her father. She's in my care, and, chaperones or not, I can't let her live with you. It would ruin her reputation, and you know as well as I that you two would find opportunities to be alone."

Benaiah nodded in acknowledgment of Peter's point. Even in the few days he'd been staying there, they'd found time to be alone. And their passion had almost flared out of control. But….

"What would make you change your mind? Couldn't she stay with a friend? Or with relatives? You know our intent to marry."

Peter surveyed him with a frown. "When?"

"Well…I haven't actually proposed yet. I'm thinking spring for the wedding. But whenever Susie wants is fine by me. We could marry tomorrow. You know Missouri has a 'no-wait' policy."

Peter's nostrils flared, and his face flamed red. "I will *not* have my dochter married by a justice of the peace!"

"Love gives the other person a choice." Benaiah tried to keep his voice calm. *Lord Gott, help me. Make him understand.* "All I'm asking is for you to consider letting Susie stay."

If only Preacher Zeke hadn't gone out of town for a funeral. Otherwise, he would surely help. He'd said he would pull some strings to keep Susanna here, if he had to.

But, wait. Caleb had said they'd be back to-nacht, though he wasn't sure exactly what time. Benaiah made a mental note to himself. *Talk to Preacher Zeke.*

For a long moment, Peter held Benaiah's gaze as if participating in a standoff. But then he slumped. "I know Susanna has been helping your mammi as well as taking care of your family. And you will surely miss her if she goes to Iowa. But I want your word, as a man, that you will *not* anticipate your wedding vows."

Benaiah smiled and stepped forward, his hand extended. "I love her and respect her too much to dishonor her in any way. Danki, Peter." *Danki, Lord.*

Peter gripped his hand, shook it firmly, then released it and stepped away. "Be sure you don't."

Benaiah turned off the gaslights. For to-nacht, the shop was closed.

And now, to face Susanna. He'd asked her to go for a walk with him. Maybe then he would ask her to marry him, in the springtime, if she was agreeable to that idea. It wouldn't be a swoon-worthy proposal, but it would be coming from a plain, simple, and earnest Amish man.

Because that's what he was. A plain and simple man with a family to care for and a need to be practical.

He closed up the shop and headed for the haus.

"LET ME OFF here, please," Susanna said when they reached the town square. Judith's Gift Shop was in view, and it was only a short walk to Jen's small rental apartment.

Yost looked around as he pulled the buggy into a parking spot. "You sure? Most all the businesses are closed for the nacht. Even the ice cream shop, and they stay open late."

Except they closed altogether when it wasn't tourist season. But maybe Yost didn't know that, since he'd never taken a girl for ice cream, as far as Susanna knew.

"I'm sure." Susanna scrambled out of the buggy, then leaned in to add, "It's better this way. Now you can be perfectly truthful when you tell my daed you don't know where I am."

Yost paled. "He'll be furious."

Jah, he likely would be. But her disappearance would serve him and Benaiah right, ain't so?

Except, she felt like a two-year-old throwing a temper tantrum. She sighed and backed away from the buggy, ignoring her concerns.

Trying to, anyway.

Even so, something inside her insisted she was reacting and not listening. Not obeying. Not responding.

"Should I go?" Yost asked, but he didn't lift the reins or click his tongue. He sat there, watching her. "Nein, I can't go. I don't feel right leaving you here, Susanna. Because…well, you're upset, and maybe it'd be better if I took you to my mamm. She'd know what to do. And as for your family not knowing where you are…it seems rather…I don't know. Wrong. Your daed and Benaiah will be frantic."

Benaiah. Could she get a message to him without Daed overhearing?

"The first person they'll kum to is me, and I really don't want your daed to yell at me. His temper is the stuff of legends. Well, maybe not quite that bad." He got out of the buggy, tied his horse's reins to a post, and approached her.

He didn't need to worry about following her, because her feet had stubbornly planted themselves on the sidewalk and refused to move.

"Here." Yost kicked the slushy snow off the front step of a store, then grabbed a buggy blanket and spread it on top. "Sit down, and we can talk?"

She stared at the blanket but didn't move.

Yost fidgeted a moment, then slowly, hesitantly, reached out and grasped her elbow, handling it as if it were a fragile egg that might shatter if he pressed too hard. He gave a gentle tug toward the step. "Kum."

"Why are you doing this?" Susanna glanced at him. "Why do you care?"

"Because…because they love you. And if someone I loved were to leave like this, I'd hope that somebody would try to stop them. To go after them. To listen. And to pray with them."

He was right. She felt the same way. And he was gentle with her. Not intrusive. Not at all forceful, as Susanna might have been, were the situation reversed.

There was something to be said for not being pressured. For having someone to listen to her. For knowing he heard what she said, as well as what she didn't.

Susanna lowered herself onto the blanket and buried her face in her hands. And cried. *Gott, why? I don't want to do this thing Daed is asking of me. I don't want to leave practically everyone I know and love.*

She didn't know how long she sat there, crying and praying. Only that at some point, she became aware of Yost sitting beside her, his head bowed in prayer.

She wanted to be like Yost. A quiet, thoughtful, prayerful person who listened to the voice of Gott. Not someone who went chasing after everything she saw that needed to be fixed, done, or changed.

She wiped her face with her hands but kept her head bowed.

Lord, help me to hear You. Tell me what to do.

AFTER A QUICK, hot shower, Benaiah searched the haus and then the barn for Susanna. He doubted she'd gone wandering through the pastures, as they were a muddy mess thanks to the snowmelt. None of his family members had seen her recently. So, he searched the rooms again, in case he'd missed her.

Now he stood in her bedroom, surveying the neatly made bed and the display of gifts from her "secret admirer" spread atop her dresser, across the windowsill, and on the bedside table. He walked over to the window and picked up the glass rose he'd made for her. It was the last gift he'd given her—the one that had allowed her to catch him.

The gift he'd given her just before succumbing to the kiss under the mistletoe.

Lord, where is she hiding?

Susanna wasn't one to hide. She usually faced her battles head-on.

Except for the day he'd caught her dancing in the kitchen and then witnessed her crash to the floor in an undignified heap, just before she ran from the room to hide in the bathroom.

And ultimately took a bath.

He shook his head. He would never understand women, even though he lived with six of them. Seven, counting Susanna.

Lord, help me find her.

Frowning, he gazed out the window into the darkness. Yost had left about the time Susanna had run out of the shop. Was it possible…?

He pulled out his cell phone and scrolled through his list of contacts. Yost wasn't one of them. Of course, he wasn't a business owner, so he probably had nein reason to keep a phone.

Benaiah decided he would saddle up a horse—assuming Peter owned a saddle—and ride over to Yost's haus. Or perhaps it'd be better to take a buggy. That would make it easier for him to bring Susanna home.

Then again, the idea of the two of them riding together on the back of a horse, her arms wrapped around his waist, like Englisch girls riding behind their boyfriends on motorcycles…. Or would it be like the westerns he used to sneak into the barn and read, so his parents wouldn't know, where the heroine rode on the hero's lap, and he reached his arms around her….

Okay. The buggy it was.

He carefully returned the glass rose to the windowsill, then grabbed the lantern and left the room.

In the living room, Daadi glanced up from an issue of *The Budget*. "Nein sign of her?"

Benaiah shook his head. "I'm going to ride over to Yost Miller's and see if he gave her a ride somewhere. Have you seen Peter?"

Daadi shrugged. "He went out carrying his cell phone. Probably to call Irene. Maybe letting her know Susanna isn't coming, after all."

Of course. Because talking to his bride-to-be would be more important than searching for his own dochter.

To be fair, Peter probably didn't even know Susanna was gone.

Benaiah was the one with the burning desire to see her. To talk to her. To explain what had happened.

To get down on one knee.

CHAPTER 29

The trip home seemed a lot shorter than the trip into town had been. Susanna still didn't have her apology planned out when Yost pulled into Daed's driveway. Make that Benaiah's driveway.

Both hurts resurfaced. Nobody had told her about the sale, and Daed still expected her to go with him to Iowa.

Help me to listen. Help me to hear.

Benaiah came out of the barn, leading Peppermint Twist by his bridle. He stopped and stared at the approaching horse and buggy until it came to a stop beside him.

His gaze lit on Susanna, then shifted to Yost. "Had a stowaway, ain't so?"

Yost chuckled. "Appears so."

"Danki for returning her." Benaiah helped Susanna get out. She thanked Yost, and then he drove around the circle and headed for the road.

Benaiah turned to face her and gently took her hands in his.

Susanna moved a step nearer to him. His warm breath feathered over her. "I'm sorry I lost my temper. I'm really glad you bought the haus, but I was hurt because nobody seemed to think I needed to know."

Benaiah shook his head. "It's not like that. I didn't know you hadn't been told. And I don't know why your daed didn't tell you. Maybe he figured I had. And I would've told you if I had seen you right away, but you were gone when I got home from the bank."

So, she'd kind of imposed the hurt on herself in her hurry to escape Daed.

"I would've picked you up, like so." He released his horse and, with both hands, lifted her in the air before drawing her against himself. Her pulse raced. "And swung you around, like so." Still holding her, he stepped away from the horse, then whirled around in a circle, two, three, four, times. "And then I would've kissed you until one of us begged for mercy." He chuckled. "I'll demonstrate that later on, if you'd like."

She'd like it, all right. She grinned as he set her down.

"Seriously, Suz, if I had realized, you would have been the first—"

She put her gloved finger over his lips. "It's okay. I...I prayed. I think Yost prayed for me, too. I need to listen better and not jump to conclusions so often. Pray first and wait for Gott's leading before I automatically react." Things worked out better when done Gott's way rather than hers, anyway.

Benaiah smiled. "Do you want to go on a buggy ride? With me? I know a nice place we can stargaze."

"And kiss until one of us begs for mercy?" She grinned up at him, her stomach clenching.

He chuckled again. "I know it's cold, but I have more things to say, and I don't need—or want—an audience. But there are blankets in the buggy, and...." His gaze dropped to her lips. "I'm sure we'll be warm enough."

Ach, jah. Inside, she did a happy dance.

He leaned down and picked up the horse's lead rope. "Get into the buggy, and I'll hitch up Peppermint Twist."

Benaiah wasn't quite sure where he was taking Susanna, to be honest. The normal sparking places were likely slushy due to the melting snow, and he didn't want to risk getting the buggy stuck in the mud. That would hardly be romantic. Not to mention, it might cause Peter to second-guess his decision to let Susanna stay.

But Benaiah wanted somewhere more private than the farmhaus and more romantic than a barn.

He mentally reviewed the local sparking places. One of them had a dock leading out to a large pond. A canoe. That had potential.

Though he wasn't quite sure a canoe would work. In fact, he seemed to recall hearing that it leaked—according to Lizzie, anyway.

He would give it a try.

Benaiah reached for Susanna's hand, clasping it tightly in his. "Just so you know, I bought the business free and clear. Well, truthfully, Daadi did, but he gifted it to me. And we talked to someone at the bank about a loan for the property. Turns out I didn't need to finance it—well, not for the full amount, anyway. Your daed had a wedding CD he'd started as a kind of dowry for you, since, as he said, he *knew* I was the one. And that was why my earnings were so low. He put fifty percent of my paycheck right into that fund, planning to gift it to me when we got married. Instead, he gave it to me there at the bank, and we put it toward a hefty down payment on the haus." His grin widened. "It's so nice to see how Gott is answering our prayers and providing for my family."

He'd faced that lion and won once he trusted Gott. If he hadn't been brave enough to ask about a loan for the haus, Peter might not have thought to mention the CD until it was too late.

Susanna snuggled against him as he pulled the buggy off the road into the parking lot near the pond. It was located in a park, and all around were swing sets, seesaws, slides, picnic pavilions, and walking trails.

He parked, then helped Susanna out of the buggy before grabbing the blankets that were stored under the seat.

Susanna held the flashlight lantern as they walked past one picnic pavilion toward the play area. Benaiah carried the blankets to one of the upper lookouts on the play structure, where he spread them out, then sat down and patted the space next to him. "You'll see the stars better this way."

She giggled, then climbed up and lay next to him. She burrowed into his side and pulled another blanket up over them.

His blood heated. Maybe the view of the sky from here wasn't all that great.

And maybe the stars were overrated.

Ach, Susie. He turned to her, letting his hand trail over her face, her lips, her neck. He lowered his head toward hers.

LONG BEFORE SUSANNA was ready, Benaiah shifted away from her. His palm cupped her cheek for the briefest of moments, and then he pushed himself up onto his knees and motioned to a seat along the edge of the lookout. "Sit there. Please."

She opened her mouth to object, because she still wanted to cuddle, but he held up his hand. "Humor me."

With a shrug, Susanna stood and moved to the bench. A second later, he knelt in front of her.

He was proposing!

"I promised Daadi a swoon-worthy proposal, but I'm just a simple Amish man. I thought of making a dozen long-stemmed glass roses for you, but I ran out of time. But I hope that you'll let every gift I've ever given you, and every gift I will give you in the future, be a token of my undying love for you. And I vow to support you well—emotionally, physically, and spiritually."

Seeing his face every day would be a gift enough. She could imagine nothing better, and felt almost ready to swoon.

He reached for her hand. "Susanna Rose King, ich liebe dich. Would you do me the honor of becoming my frau?"

She stilled, pressing one hand pressed over her mouth. Then she erupted with a squeal. "Jah! Jah, a million times, jah."

"Your daed said you could stay here until we married, so I was thinking, maybe in the spring—"

She bounded off the bench and into his arms, pushing him backward into the soft folds of the blankets, and kissed him until he begged for mercy—and promised a Christmas wedding.

SUSANNA KING'S FAVORITE HOLIDAY RECIPES

SUSANNA'S CRANBERRY SALAD

Serves 16

Ingredients

+ 3 cups fresh or frozen cranberries (thawed, if frozen), chopped
+ 1 can (20 ounces) unsweetened crushed pineapple, drained
+ 2 cups miniature marshmallows
+ 1 medium apple, chopped
+ 2/3 cup granulated sugar
+ 1/8 teaspoon salt
+ 2 cups heavy whipping cream
+ 1/4 cup chopped walnuts

Directions

1. In a large bowl, mix the first six ingredients until blended. Cover and refrigerate overnight.
2. In a large bowl, beat cream until stiff peaks form. Just before serving, fold cream and walnuts into cranberry mixture.

SUSANNA'S CRANBERRY SAUCE

Ingredients
- 4 cups fresh or frozen cranberries (thawed, if frozen), chopped
- 1 cup granulated sugar
- 1 cup water or orange juice

Directions

Rinse cranberries in a colander and allow to drain. In a saucepan, mix water or orange juice and sugar, then bring to a boil until sugar is dissolved. Add cranberries and return to a boil. Lower to a simmer and cook about 10 minutes, until most of the cranberries have burst. Allow to cool before serving, and store in refrigerator.

SUSANNA'S "LOVE POTION" GINGERBREAD

Ingredients

- 6 cups all-purpose flour
- 1 tablespoon baking powder
- 1 tablespoon ground ginger
- 1 teaspoon ground nutmeg
- 1 teaspoon ground cloves
- 1 teaspoon ground cinnamon
- 1 cup shortening, melted slightly
- 1 cup molasses
- 1 cup brown sugar
- ½ cup water
- 1 egg
- 1 teaspoon vanilla extract

Directions

In a large bowl, sift together flour, baking powder, ginger, nutmeg, cloves, and cinnamon. Set aside.

In a mixing bowl, mix shortening, molasses, brown sugar, water, egg, and vanilla until smooth. Gradually stir in the dry ingredients until they are absorbed. Divide dough into three equal pieces, pat each one down until about 1½-inch thick, then wrap in plastic wrap and refrigerate for three hours.

Preheat oven to 350 degrees F. On lightly floured surface, roll the dough out to ¼-inch thickness. Cut into desired shapes and arrange cookies about 1 inch apart on an ungreased cookie sheet.

Bake for 10 to 12 minutes in preheated oven. Cool completely on wire racks before decorating as desired.

ABOUT THE AUTHOR

A member of the American Christian Fiction Writers, Laura V. Hilton is a professional book reviewer for the Christian market, with more than a thousand reviews published on the Web.

Laura's first series with Whitaker House, The Amish of Seymour, comprises *Patchwork Dreams*, *A Harvest of Hearts*, and *Promised to Another*. In 2012, *A Harvest of Hearts* received a Laurel Award, placing first in the Amish Genre Clash. Her second series, The Amish of Webster County, comprises *Healing Love*, *Surrendered Love*, and *Awakened Love*, followed by a stand-alone title, *A White Christmas in Webster County*. Laura's last series, The Amish of Jamesport, included *The Snow Globe*, *The Postcard*, and *The Birdhouse*. Prior to *The Christmas Admirer*, she published *The Amish Firefighter*, *The Amish Wanderer*, and *Love by the Numbers*.

Previously, Laura published two novels with Treble Heart Books, *Hot Chocolate* and *Shadows of the Past*, as well as several devotionals.

Laura and her husband, Steve, have five children, whom Laura homeschools. The family makes their home in Arkansas. To learn more about Laura, read her reviews, and find out about her upcoming releases, readers may visit her blog at lighthouse-academy.blogspot.com.

Welcome to Our House!

We Have a Special Gift for You ...

It is our privilege and pleasure to share in your love of Christian fiction by publishing books that enrich your life and encourage your faith.

To show our appreciation, we invite you to sign up to receive a specially selected **Reader Appreciation Gift**, with our compliments. Just go to the Web address at the bottom of this page.

God bless you as you seek a deeper walk with Him!

WE HAVE A GIFT FOR YOU. VISIT:

whpub.me/fictionthx

WHITAKER HOUSE